T0082838

What readers are saying about Rusty Bradshaw's books.

The Rehabilitation of Miss Little

Captivating!!

This story is very well written! Rusty does such a great job describing the scenario, he doesn't suck you in - he absorbs you! You feel like you are among the characters. And you have to keep reading to find out what drives the people to do what they are doing. I hope Rusty keeps writing! I look forward to reading another book by him!

Awesome book!

This book was highly recommended to me, so I bought it, I'm so glad I did! I'm not much of a reader, but this book was hard to put down, it kept my attention from start to finish. It's a great story, kind of sad of what she went through, but a good ending. I can hopefully look forward to more books from this author!

Moist on the Mountain

Awesome!

Another good book from the author! Love his writing. I got the book for me, finished it in a couple of days, I was so interested in the story, it was hard to put down.

Fun book to read

Keeps you interested and didn't want to put the book down until finished

Gorge Justice

Wow! Just wow!

This story was very well written and kept my interest all the way through! Excellent story. I look forward to Rusty's next work of art!

The Best 1 Yet

As I've said before, I'm not a reader, but after reading the first two books from Rusty Bradshaw, I thought I'd read the third. This book is his best yet, I finished it in three days! It made me cry, made me sad, get angry and happy. It's worth reading!!

Excellent reading...........

I couldn't put this book down once I started reading it. I was with the character the whole way and hoped that she would finally get justice. Rusty did an excellent job in writing this because you could feel yourself in the surroundings that he described and picture the beautiful scenery. You will not be disappointed in purchasing this book. It is unthinkable what the main character went throgh and it will keep you on the edge of your seat!

See more reviews at www.rustythewriter.org.

BATTLE
FOR
STEPHANIE

RUSTY BRADSHAW

iUniverse®

BATTLE FOR STEPHANIE

Copyright © 2023 Rusty Bradshaw.

All rights reserved. No part of this book may be used or reproduced by any means, graphic, electronic, or mechanical, including photocopying, recording, taping or by any information storage retrieval system without the written permission of the author except in the case of brief quotations embodied in critical articles and reviews.

This is a work of fiction. All of the characters, names, incidents, organizations, and dialogue in this novel are either the products of the author's imagination or are used fictitiously.

iUniverse books may be ordered through booksellers or by contacting:

iUniverse
1663 Liberty Drive
Bloomington, IN 47403
www.iuniverse.com
844-349-9409

Because of the dynamic nature of the Internet, any web addresses or links contained in this book may have changed since publication and may no longer be valid. The views expressed in this work are solely those of the author and do not necessarily reflect the views of the publisher, and the publisher hereby disclaims any responsibility for them.

Any people depicted in stock imagery provided by Getty Images are models, and such images are being used for illustrative purposes only. Certain stock imagery © Getty Images.

ISBN: 978-1-6632-5031-5 (sc)
ISBN: 978-1-6632-5032-2 (e)

Library of Congress Control Number: 2023901597

Print information available on the last page.

iUniverse rev. date: 01/28/2023

This book is dedicated to the late Bobby Lewis.
You are missed, Bobalew!

Chapter 1

Very little sun peeked through the curtains in the master bedroom window of the apartment tucked into the dead-end portion of Harrison Street as the early spring day got its start for Nathan Wallis.

It was like most mornings since Nathan and his family – wife, Cynthia, and their only child, Stephanie – moved into the apartment three-and-a-half months earlier. Cynthia was up before everyone and was getting the family started. After doing a little work on the home computer, she began to awaken eleven-year-old Stephanie. Once she was up and going, she went into the master bedroom to wake up her husband.

It had been a hectic time for the family in the last few weeks. Things were just beginning to turn around for them after nearly eighteen months of hard times. They had just returned from a trip to their former hometown to sign papers to sell their house there. It was only the second offer on the house after the first drug on for two months before finally falling through.

The proceeds from the house sale would allow the Wallises to pay off a number of past due bills, and give them enough left over to help them get back on their feet financially.

The couple had also been having their own difficulties with each other. Neither really knew what had started the problems, nor did they really know for sure what the problems were. But they had not talked much in previous months. Cynthia had been distant with her husband and had pushed him away repeatedly when he tried to get close, both emotionally and physically.

Because of her distance and the disdain she showed for him, Nathan was reluctant to try and talk to her about what was wrong. A man who tried to avoid confrontation whenever possible, he rather would let sleeping dogs lie and hope for the best.

But in the past week, the tension between the husband and wife seemed to be changing. They began to talk more, and when he hugged her, she did not push him away.

It was not, however, all good news.

The previous Saturday, on the return from signing the house sale paperwork, there had been an accident. Driving west on the freeway just as the sun was dipping below the horizon, Nathan was concentrating hard on the roadway. The setting sun was almost directly in front of his eyes and despite the sunglasses he wore, he had to squint to see details.

Suddenly, Nathan saw something out of the corner of his eye to the left that appeared to be entering his lane within only a few car lengths ahead of their SUV. Instinctively he started to swerve to the right to avoid hitting whatever it was and at the same time taking his foot off the gas pedal.

"Watch out," Cynthia shouted, almost simultaneously with the grating sound of metal crashing against metal. Nathan wasn't sure if she was warning him of the pickup truck in the adjacent lane or whatever he had seen coming into his lane. Whichever was not important now because a second after hitting the pickup with a glancing blow, they slammed into an object straight ahead.

The side impact damaged the front fender, but the head-on impact folded the hood and pushed the grill into the engine compartment, immediately killing the engine and bringing the vehicle to a screeching halt. That was followed by a lesser impact from directly behind.

The husband and wife looked behind them. In the seat behind the driver was Stephanie, still buckled in her seat belt swiveling her head back and forth. In the first instant her parents saw her, there was a look of fright on her face. But that was quickly replaced with curiosity.

Stephanie first wanted to know if her parents were safe. When they both stared at her with the look of concern on their faces, she knew they were okay. She then began looking around to see if she could determine what happened.

Stephanie's curiosity seemed head and shoulders above other children her age.

"What happened?" Cynthia asked.

Nathan took a moment before answering. He studied the surroundings of their vehicle. Just ahead on the left shoulder of the two-lane westbound portion of the freeway he saw a blue Dodge Ram pickup truck parked with its emergency flashers on. A man, presumably the driver, was walking toward the SUV.

Nathan reached to the dashboard and clicked on his vehicle's emergency flashers. When he looked into the rearview mirror, he saw white lights blinking, not red. That meant the rear collision had broken the plastic coverings on the flasher lights. But his flashers were mixed with amber flashes from the vehicle that rear-ended them.

Nathan heard knuckles lightly tapping on glass. He turned to face a large man wearing a ball cap and flannel shirt. He had a rough-skinned face, a man who clearly worked hard and most of it outdoors in the state's harsh weather, both winter and summer.

Instead of powering down his window, Nathan opened the door and got out. The man was about three inches taller than him and had the build of a man who did heavy lifting, either through his work or in a workout routine.

"Are you alright?" the man asked with concern. "How about your wife?"

Nathan looked back inside his SUV then back at the stranger.

"We're all okay," he answered. "So is our daughter."

The man looked again at the SUV and for the first time noticed Stephanie looking out the side window.

"Okay," the man said. "Let me go check on these people behind you and I'll be right back."

Nathan moved to the front of the SUV to inspect the damage. The crumpled grill of the Ford Explorer was pushed backward and the hood was folded in half. Peering through the opening caused by the fold, he could see the grill mashed up against the engine block, which drooped on the right side, indicating an engine mount was damaged or destroyed.

"This one won't run again," Nathan heard from the other side of the SUV. The Ram driver peeked around the front of the vehicle.

"Everyone in the other car is okay," he said. "They called 9-1-1. They should be here soon."

Nathan knew that was a relative measurement. With manpower shortages due to state budget cuts, highway patrol and sheriff's deputies were stretched thin.

Later, as state troopers finished going over the scene and the tow truck driver prepared to load the Wallises' Explorer, the only vehicle involved that was undrivable, Nathan went over what had happened.

Except for some bumps and bruises, there were no physical injuries in the crash. A dead buck deer was found alongside the Ford Focus behind the Wallises' Explorer. Troopers found deer hair embedded in the Explorer's grill. They also found evidence that the animal, after being struck, flipped over the Explorer and grazed the passenger side front fender of the Focus.

Because it was a clear case of an animal strike and there was no way Nathan could have avoided it, there were no citations issued.

He took stock of his family. Cynthia seemed shaken, but was aware of the situation and sequence of events as the troopers outlined them. Stephanie was curious – not surprising for a young child surrounded by excitement. She continually questioned her father about the details of the accident, and he dutifully tried to answer each one in a calm and reassuring tone.

The next challenge was how the family would get home. They were still a little more than one hour away from the apartment they rented in a small town along the river.

Their Explorer, with their belongings still inside, was to be taken to an auto body shop on the outskirts of the metropolitan city just 10 minutes away from the accident scene. One of the state troopers offered to take the family home after they retrieved a few small things from their vehicle before it departed.

The following day, a Sunday, after arranging for a rental car for Cynthia to use while he was gone, Nathan got a second rental and traveled back to the city. The Explorer was the only vehicle the family had, so another one had to be secured. That was the reason for the trip into the larger city, since there were more car dealers to choose from. Nathan's plan was to use the small amount of cash available to them and a possible trade-in of the damaged Explorer to trade for a used car to get them by until they could come up with a better plan for transportation.

Being a one-vehicle family had been difficult, but they had not been in the best financial position two years ago when Nathan's small Chevy pickup truck had quit running. Since then, they had done what they could to make it with one vehicle. That meant adjusting schedules with Nathan's job as a restaurant manager and Cynthia's job at a modest certified public accounting firm.

Some money from the house sale was already earmarked for a new family car to give each parent transportation. But now they had to rethink that plan. There would not be enough house sale profit to purchase two brand new vehicles. They would have to settle for two used vehicles, not a situation either wanted. Nathan and Cynthia decided if he could get a reliable used car cheap enough, they could still get a new vehicle.

The first part of the plan was accomplished when Nathan, after going to several dealerships, found a Volkswagon Rabbit with about twenty-five thousand miles on it.

So, that Monday morning when Cynthia went into the bedroom and gave her husband a warm hug and kissed his shoulder, Nathan woke with a good feeling that his family had gotten back on the right track, despite the trauma of the accident two days before.

The morning seemed to continue on a high note when Cynthia told her husband she had been looking over their income tax material and discovered it they filed separately they might come out better than if they filed jointly, as they always had done.

"If I file mine with the expenses I have with my job, I should get money back and you should come out even by using all the moving expenses," she explained.

"Do it," Nathan told her without hesitation. "If we'll make out better that way, go ahead and do it."

Because she had the financial background, Cynthia had always done the financial work for the family. Nathan trusted her judgment without question.

But even this morning, with its more upbeat beginnings, there was a small crisis to take care of. The car Nathan had purchased the day before would not start. A turn of the key brought only a light click. Since he had already turned in one rental, they would be stuck with the rental Cynthia was driving if the Rabbit wouldn't run.

No problem. After all the disasters the Wallises had to deal with in the last eighteen months, this was very minor indeed. Nathan and Cynthia pushed the stick shift compact car into a small alcove formed at the end of the parking area and Nathan jump started it rolling down the hill on which Harrison Street was located. Problem solved. He planned to have it checked out later to find the issue with starting it.

Once everyone was ready for the day, Stephanie got in the "new" car with Nathan and Cynthia got in the rental. She was out of the driveway first and down the hill she went. Nathan followed not far behind.

As Nathan pulled out onto Marine Drive, he noticed that Cynthia was now behind him.

"How did she get behind me?" he asked aloud, not really expecting an answer from his daughter. "I wonder what she wants. Did she forget something?"

The second question appeared to require an answer, however, as Nathan looked into the back seat. But Stephanie just shrugged.

Nathan pulled into a grocery store parking lot and Cynthia followed, parking two spaces away from his car. Both got out of their vehicles and started to walk toward each other.

"What's up? Did we forget something?" Nathan asked.

"Don't forget to tell Stephanie to stay after school for computer club. I'll pick her up when they're done," Cynthia said, as they stopped walking several feet away from each other.

"OK," Nathan answered, then walked back to his car.

As he returned to Marine Drive, Stephanie had a question.

"Why can't I just skip computer club today?"

"No, go to the club. Your mother is expecting to pick you up there," her father instructed, wondering why his daughter was trying to get out of computer club. She enjoyed learning how to use the computer, and was becoming quite competent.

It was going to be a busy day. After dropping Stephanie at school in time to participate in the breakfast program, Nathan continued on to work, making the usual stop at the post office to check the box where the family was receiving its mail. Cynthia's office was only two blocks from the restaurant he managed and he looked forward to seeing her when she came in for lunch, as was her habit during the work day when her schedule allowed.

When he walked into the restaurant, Nathan saw a bustling crowd. Half were just finishing their breakfasts and the rest were placing their orders.

The restaurant opened at seven o'clock in the morning and did a brisk business with people trying to get their first coffee of the day, or following the old creed that breakfast is the most important meal of the day, before they headed off to their jobs. Nathan even saw the coffee klatch of seven older men in their usual booth near the front window. He waved to them, and they returned the gesture as he headed to check with the assistant manager.

One of the schedule quirks Nathan worked out at the restaurant was that the assistant manager opened on weekdays, so Nathan could get Stephanie to school, and Nathan opened on the weekends, giving the assistant manager those days off.

"How did it go this morning, Rob?" Nathan asked the assistant.

"Everything went smooth as usual," Rob answered. "It was about as busy as usual."

He smiled at his assistant. They had worked well together, and Rob was pleased with the arrangement of opening during the week. That gave him the opportunity to go home just before the lunch rush and help get things ready at home for when his wife came home from her job at a hardware store.

With the lack of big industry in the community, most households were two-income families, mostly in service-type jobs.

"I appreciate the work you are doing," Nathan told Rob. "It really lifts a weight off my shoulders knowing there is someone I can really count on to gets things going in the mornings."

Rob blushed a little.

"It works well for me, so I've got to thank you for being so flexible," Rob said.

"No problem," Nathan said, then headed for the small office off the kitchen to dive into the paperwork involved in managing a restaurant. There were supplies to order, schedules to make and a variety of other things to attend to.

Cynthia had an appointment at 10 o'clock. It was a new client she was trying to persuade to sign up for the agency she worked for. As she was preparing, the phone rang at nine-thirty. It was an open office and several other employees were at their desks nearby preparing for their own clients and prospective clients.

Cynthia did not want her colleagues to know the subject of the phone call. So she did not respond to the caller by name; her side of the conversation was a series of "uh huhs." She finally said, "How about at the Red Lion Inn at 11," She then hung up.

"Got another hot lead?" she heard Valarie, the agency manger, ask from behind her.

"Yeah," Cynthia answered without turning around. She shuffled some papers on her desk, grabbed her briefcase and stood and headed for the door.

"Good luck," Valarie offered, a little taken aback because this was not normally how Cynthia interacted. Usually, she would tell her boss who she was going to see and the prospects of success. A rush out the door without more than a few words was just not done.

Cynthia, not looking back in her direction, threw her a half-hearted wave as she exited the office.

When Nathan and Cynthia had lunch together, which was infrequent because of her varied schedule, it was at the restaurant he managed. The time was always set for one o'clock, just as the lunch rush was dialing down. That way they could eat their lunch and visit with no, or at least few, interruptions.

After sittling at his desk in the small restaurant office just before one o'clock, Nathan was trying to decide whether or not to call his wife to see what to order her for lunch. As that thought filtered through his brain, his cell phone buzzed on the desk.

"Hi, it's me," he heard Cynthia say on the other end. "I just wanted to call and let you know I was running a little late. I scheduled another meeting with a potential client."

"No problem," Nathan told her. "Do you want me to order something for you?"

"No, I should be there in a few minutes," she answered.

When she had not shown up by one-thirty he grabbed an order of French fries for himself and settled in to work on scheduling employees for the next month. Cynthia not showing up for lunch when they had agreed to meet was nothing new. It happened from time to time when she got calls from people looking for information on the agency's services or discussing details with existing clients. Sometimes she got so wrapped up in her work she forgot to call and let him know.

It was a bit annoying, but Nathan got used to it.

Following an uneventful afternoon, the first hint of something odd came when Cynthia did not drop Stephanie at the restaurant after picking her up at school. It was the normal modus operandi for Nathan to meet her at the school bus stop just two blocks from the café and take her there until it was time to go home. It was more awkward for Cynthia to have Stephanie at work with her than at Nathan's. When at the restaurant she usually enjoyed a small milk shake and began work on her homework.

But today was different with the plan for Cynthia to pick Stephanie up at the school, then take her to the restaurant.

When Cynthia and Stephanie did not show up by four o'clock, Nathan was a bit concerned. But he quickly put it out of his mind. There was a small possibility Cynthia had said something about not bringing Stephanie to the restaurant and he had forgotten. The fact was he had been forgetting small details lately. Not at the restaurant but at home. He had passed it off as a muddled mind with the difficulties he and Cynthia had been having.

But now that things seemed to be improving, he expected the forgetfulness would be gone. But it seemed here it was again.

With that in mind, he decided to call Cynthia's school to make sure Cynthia had picked up their daughter after the Computer Club. The call to the school revealed that Cynthia had picked up their daughter. Another odd factor was that he was told Stephanie had not stayed for the Computer Club.

"Her mother picked her up before school was out," the woman on the line told him.

But Nathan thought little of it. Perhaps Cynthia's plans for the day had changed and she had a free afternoon and had taken their daughter shopping. He didn't give it another thought.

Such was the level of trust he had in his wife.

After the evening manager came in and gotten briefed about a few things that needed done before the next day, Nathan decided to call it a day at four-thirty.

The first item of business when he got home was to remove the dealer license plate frame on the car. He did not believe in being a rolling advertisement for car dealers.

A quick trip inside the apartment to get a screwdriver, a few minutes with the car and the job was done. Now it was time to wait for the rest of the family to come home.

Nathan went back into the apartment and switched on the power strip to get the personal computer started. He thought he might play a quick game of digital football before the family came home for dinner. After flipping the switch, he headed for the bathroom with the sound of the printer starting up ringing in his ears.

On the way back into the large kitchen, he could see that the computer screen was still dark. But there was no worry – the rotating screen saver program had a star field as one of the tiles and it looked black from a distance. But when he sat down at the computer desk, the screen really was blank. He glanced down to the monitor power switch, but something just below the monitor caught his eye. There was something missing – the hard drive tower for the computer.

Puzzlement went through his mind. Why would the computer's hard drive be missing? Had Cynthia been working at home and something gone wrong? Had she had to take it in to a shop for repairs?

That didn't make a lot of sense. Why would she do that without telling him?

It was then that another thought crept into Nathan's mind. When they settled into the new apartment, they got a dog. But when everyone was away from the apartment during the day, they had purchased a large indoor kennel for the dog. But ever since he had come into the apartment, Nathan was so preoccupied with the car task and starting a football game he had not heard a single noise from the dog. He glanced around the dining room table and saw for the first time that the door to the keeper was open. He got up, moved to the front of the keeper and looked inside. The dog was missing.

Where would Cynthia and Stephanie have gone that they would take the dog?

Once again, something registered in Nathan's mind that he had seen but not really taken conscious notice of – there were things missing from the bathroom. A second look confirmed that toothbrushes, toothpaste, deodorant and other "overnight" items were missing.

An idea began forming in his head. But it was so repulsive, so unthinkable that Nathan didn't dare give it too much thought.

He stood and tried to comprehend it all. Suddenly, like a sledgehammer blow to the head, the repulsive thought came crashing into his brain – Cynthia had taken their daughter and left him. It was to be just the first of many such sledgehammer blows to the head.

11

Chapter 2

It was not a fairy tale romance.

Nathan and Cynthia met in high school in a small town in Illinois when he transferred in from another school within the state. For each there was an attraction the minute they laid eyes on each other. But that is where the fairy tale quality of the romance ended.

They dated throughout that first year, the sophomore year for both. By the time they were juniors, their relationship had become so routine that neither was satisfied. They drifted apart and began seeing other people. The same held true through the first half of their senior year.

But the attraction they held for each other was too strong. During Christmas break they began exclusively dating again. They reclaimed the magic that had been there at the beginning. It remained so strong that when they planned their futures after high school, they decided to attend the same college.

Both were interested in pursuing careers in business, and in college took many of the same courses together in pursuit of degrees in business administration. Nathan and Cynthia had talked of starting their own business together and they were eying something in information technology, a fast-growing industry.

The couple's personal backgrounds were almost complete opposites.

Nathan was the product of a broken home, his parents having divorced when he was about eight years old. He was raised by his mother, Mary Anne, who never married again but had several boyfriends. However, she never got serious with any of them and none got very involved in Nathan's life, nor the lives of his three siblings.

A single mother's time is hectic, having to work multiple jobs to make ends meet and try to find the time to spend with her children and their varied activities.

His father moved to Utah, remarried a woman who had two daughters about Nathan's age and embedded himself into his new life. So much so that before he graduated from high school, Nathan saw his father only twice since the divorce from his mother. The first meeting was when ten-year-old Nathan, his mother and siblings made a trip to Utah for a reunion with members of his mother's side of the family. The second meeting was when his father came to Nathan's older sister's high school graduation when Nathan was in seventh grade.

In his younger years, Nathan had an absentee idolization of his father. Most of what he did was designed to make his father proud of him. He could devote all his time to this endeavor because he knew his mother was proud of him, because she told him every day.

Even when his father, George, did not agree to come back for Nathan's final home basketball game, the annual Parents' Night where senior players' parents were introduced with them, or his high school graduation, Nathan's main goal in life was to win his father's love and acceptance.

That is why when it was time to choose a college and his father called to offer him an opportunity to live in his home and attend the university in the community where he lived, Nathan jumped right on it, and convinced Cynthia that Utah Tech was where they should go to college.

Cynthia was the youngest of two children in a financially privileged family. Not millionaires by any stretch, but Kenneth and Jennifer McAdams wanted for very little, and they lavished the same on their children.

Bartholomew "Bart" McAdams was two years older than his sister, Cynthia. While he lived in a family of luxury, he rarely took advantage of his parents' financial position. He preferred to make his way on his own.

His sister seemed to have the same attitude. A hard worker in school, she was driven to reach the business goals she set for herself.

The difference between the siblings was that while Bart was just as determined to reach his goals, they were different than his parents wanted for him. He was just as determined to distance himself from the financial advantages they wanted to provide, preferring instead to provide for himself financially. In contrast, Cynthia took no jobs while she was in high school, relying on her parents for her financial needs so she could focus on her school work.

Cynthia's philosophy was that if her high school and college grades were top of the mark, that would carry her through any business she chose to pursue.

When Nathan and Cynthia got settled into their new environment at the university, had their classes scheduled and checked out the campus and the immediate vicinity, they turned their attention to finding activities that would enhance their educational experience.

Cynthia joined a business group in hopes of getting some real-world experience in business, and she got involved with the university's student government as the historian. She hoped to later become a student representative.

Nathan took a part-time job in the university's sports information office. In that position he was able to be part of the Trailblazers' athletic scene, although he was not athletically talented enough to participate at the college level.

He was in a different element than he was used to. In his final years in primary school he lived in a town about one-third the population of the one in which the university was located. That meant more people, more diversity and more women.

Nathan was not movie star handsome, but there was something of an attractiveness to him. He was five feet ten inches tall and weighed about one hundred-ninety pounds. His skin was light colored, but tanned to a light brown with just a little bit of sunshine exposure, almost making him look as if he spent his days on a sandy beach. His sandy brown hair tended to blend in when he was tanned. He got his father's strong, square jaw line and there were dimples in his cheeks, especially when he smiled.

The look was enough to draw the attention of more females than he was used to. At first, he found their attention flattering. But he was not interested in pursuing anything but friendship with any of them because of his commitment to Cynthia.

Through his life, Nathan had conjured up a vision of a tall, slender, blonde, very attractive, very sensuous woman as the person he would spend his life with. She would have blue eyes, a quick smile, a curvaceous figure and her hair would be long, at least to the middle of her back. He would meet just such a woman in the future, shortly after Cynthia's departure.

While Cynthia fit some of these characteristics, she did not fit them all. At first glance, only the long hair fit the bill. Cynthia was short, about five feet four inches, and while she was not obese, she was not as slender as Nathan's vision. That long hair was jet black, not blonde. Cynthia was what was called full-figured. Large breasts had never been an attraction for Nathan, and Cynthia's were neither large nor small. She had average good looks.

Despite this seeming non-match, there was something about this woman that attracted him. It was something he could not explain, especially since she did not measure up to that long-held vision.

Nathan was a man of deep feeling. When he loved, he loved hard. Conversely, when he was hurt, it was also hard.

Prior to transferring to the high school where he met Cynthia, Nathan had fallen hard for a girl, Cheryl, a year older than himself during his freshman year. Even at that young age, she fit all Nathan's characteristics of his perfect mate vision. The dated regularly from the start of that year until the following spring. It was then the girl broke off the relationship suddenly. It was a shock to him, and he felt very betrayed.

It was that more than any feeling of routineness that led to he and Cynthia ending their relationship in their junior year. He was cautious about making a firm commitment to her for fear of being abandoned again. But when they reconnected the following year, he was certain he could trust their love would not allow Cynthia to hurt him as he had been before.

It felt good to talk to Cynthia and she was a good listener. In fact, she was doing now for Nathan what Cheryl, his freshman girlfriend, had done for him. They both listened to him as he related his feelings and desires, and they both helped him through very tough times. It wasn't until much later that Nathan really realized just how much Cynthia and Cheryl shared some similarities in their relationships with him.

Between Nathan and Cynthia in Utah, there were long talks through the night, many times along a back road with little traffic near the university and back to the campus. Through these talks, Nathan laid his emotions bare to Cynthia. It felt good, it felt right. Cynthia was a woman he believed he could trust.

During the Christmas break of that first year at the university, Nathan and Cynthia traveled back to their hometown to spend some time with their families. Nathan had taken a quick liking to her parents. They were friendly people. They always made him feel right at home.

The same could not be said of Sally Anne Crawford, the girlfriend of Cynthia's older brother, Bart. His parents did not think much of their son's choice. Nathan heard them talking disparagingly about her when she and Bart were not around. They found her to be beneath Bart's station in life, and they found her too possessive of him.

Cynthia took a middle of the road stance about Sally Anne. She tended to agree with her parents when they talked about her behind her back. But Cynthia treated her well when she and her brother were in her company.

For his part, Nathan liked Bart and Sally Anne. But he did not know either of them well enough to know whether or not the McAdams' assessment of Sally Anne was correct.

In the coming months there would be more visits to the McAdams' home, and more snide conversations about Sally Anne. It appeared Bart was becoming more serious with his relationship with Sally Anne. As that seriousness increased, the McAdamses even talked about how they could end the relationship.

Unbeknownst to his parents and sister, Bart became aware of their outlook on his girlfriend. There was no way he could have heard them talking about her, because they were very careful to make sure they were not overheard by anyone but Cynthia and Nathan.

But Bart could read the body language in his parents when Sally Anne was around, and the intonations in their voices when they spoke to her. He could tell they did not approve of the relationship.

But he was certain in his choice and was prepared to be with her for the rest of his life, no matter what the consequences may be.

Though Nathan and Cynthia were very committed to each other, and it was assumed they would eventually marry, the subject was never discussed openly between them. That changed on one early spring visit to her parents' home.

They were in the home alone one night when Kenneth and Jennifer were at a city function. Nathan was laying on the living room floor while Cynthia was perched on his butt as she gave him a back rub. The touch of her hands alternated between hard pushing of massage to light rubbing. It was so soothing he was on the verge of falling asleep until Cynthia spoke.

"Did Cheryl ever do this for you?" she asked.

Nathan jolted awake at the mention of Cheryl's name. Of course, he had told Cynthia about the old relationship. He was very detailed in his description. It was a frequent topic on their walks on the back road near the campus.

"A couple of times," he answered.

"Was she better than me at it?" Cynthia quired.

Nathan turned his shoulder upward so he could look back at Cynthia, then laid back flat.

"You are better, of course," he said, not sure she believed him.

Cynthia continued the massage for a moment in silence before she spoke again.

"Did you want to marry her?" she asked.

This time Nathan turned his entire body so he was facing upward. Cynthia lifted her body enough to let him get settled on his back then she lowered herself back down on him.

"Well, I was only a freshman in high school and she was a sophomore," he said. "I don't think we ever talked about that."

"But I have seen pictures of her," Cynthia said. "She was gorgeous. How could you not want to marry her eventually?"

Cynthia was a very confident person – with one exception. She was not excited about her own appearance, thinking she was fat and not very attractive. It was something Nathan had chided her about on numerous occasions. He called her beautiful and sexy. He had a good idea where this conversation might be going.

"There is a lot more than looks to consider when you decide to commit to someone," Nathan explained. "That is especially true with marriage."

Cynthia paused again, trying to gather her thoughts, so Nathan believed. But she was really trying to build up her courage to go on to the subject she really wanted to address.

"What is it you are looking for in a woman to marry?" Cynthia asked.

It was then Nathan's turn to pause while he gathered his thoughts. It was not a subject he had spent much time on since Cheryl broke up with him. Not even since he started dating Cynthia. It was a few moments before he answered, which made Cynthia a little uneasy.

"Someone very much like you," he finally answered.

She gave him a playful slap to the belly.

"You're just saying that because I rubbed your back," she said, not entirely joking.

Nathan reached up and put his hands on each of her hips and pushed up gently. She read the signal and moved to a cross-legged sitting position beside him. Nathan sat up, curling his legs underneath his butt and supported himself with his right hand on the floor. His look turned deadly serious, Cynthia noticed.

"No, I'm not," he said. "You have a lot of qualities I would look for in someone to marry."

"Like what?" she asked.

He reached over with his left hand and caressed her cheek.

"You are beautiful and sexy," Nathan said. Cynthia turned her face away from him and he recognized the look and gesture.

"You are. I've said it before and I'll say it again," Nathan said.

He gently pulled her face back to look at him.

"You are also very caring and you accept me for who I am," he went on. "You are sensitive, but also hard when you need to be. You are also confident and independent."

She was blushing lightly and looked at the floor.

"So, you want an independent woman?" she asked.

"Of course I do," he said, nodding vigorously. "I don't want a wife who can't do things for herself. Not that I wouldn't do it all," he added quickly. "But I want a woman who can fend for herself if necessary."

Cynthia took it all in. She was silent for a minute or two, then launched gently, a bit reluctantly, into the matter she really wanted to talk about.

"So, you said 'someone very much like me,'" she said. "Does that mean you are still looking for someone?"

Nathan suddenly realized that while they had discussed their futures, including starting a business together, they had never talked about doing so as man and wife.

It wasn't that he had not thought about it, which, in fact, he had. But in all their talks on that back road and in other situations, neither one had brought up the subject of marriage. It occurred to him that Cynthia, like he, had also thought about the two eventually getting married.

"Well, I have thought about us being married," he said. "And I very much like that idea."

He could tell by the look on her face that his answer did not satisfy her curiosity.

"I would like to marry you," he said. "But it's something we have never talked about. So, I don't know how you feel about it."

Cynthia leaned back and put both hands on the floor. At this point in their relationship, they had not had sex. Sure, there was kissing and petting, but they had not taken it to the next level. She alluded to that.

There had been indications from Cynthia that she wanted to take that plunge. But Nathan knew that for him if a relationship went to the point of sex, he would feel an obligation to make that marital commitment. It was not that he did not want to make that jump with Cynthia, but he did not want to base a relationship on sex. So, he had not acted upon her subtle advances.

He explained all this to her now.

"I understand," she said. And Nathan could see that she meant it.

"I would love to make love to you," she said. "But I can see where you are coming from."

She paused for a moment again to make sure of what she was about to say.

"I would love to be your wife," she said. "But there are things we need to do before we get to that point."

They agreed that finishing college and getting real jobs had to be a priority before they took the marital vows.

"And we need to talk more about how we look at things," Nathan said. "Like raising children, if we even want children, how we would do our finances, where we want to be after college and so much more."

Cynthia agreed whole heartedly. Now their conversations would take a more open path.

Chapter 3

Monday night in the Harrison Street apartment was the first of many sleepless nights to come for Nathan.

The blow of realizing that his wife of nearly thirteen years had left him without warning was hard enough on him. But now his mind was filled with a mixture of thoughts and emotions. The first and foremost concern for this broken man was where was his family and were they safe?

Cynthia had left no note. In addition to hints he noticed earlier, Nathan found other things as he looked around the apartment. Some clothing was missing, for both Cynthia and Stephanie. It wasn't much that was missing, and that brought on other thoughts.

Nathan began to doubt his feeling that Cynthia had taken their daughter and left him. He was beginning to believe that Cynthia felt she needed a night alone and would be back. After all, she hadn't taken many clothes, or any of the items she valued. But where had she gone? There weren't many people they knew in the area who would take her in and not let Nathan know.

The first thing he did after the realization hit him that Cynthia had left was to call her parents' home. There was no answer at the house. Not quite six o'clock in the evening, he knew there might still be someone at Cynthia's father's office. Nathan quickly dialed the number.

"Kenneth went out of town for a few days, but he didn't say where or how long he would be gone," the man who answered the phone said.

Having worked at the office from time to time while visiting or on vacation, Nathan recognized Jared's voice on the other end of the line. While Jared was something of an emotionless man and hard to read, Nathan picked up on some hesitation in his voice.

"He's holding something back," Nathan thought to himself. But he fought back his impulse to push Jared for the truth.

It was then that Nathan began to think that Cynthia had arranged something with her parents to come and get her. But why had they only taken Cynthia, Stephanie, the dog and the barest of essentials? If she were leaving the marriage, wouldn't they have taken everything else? If this had been prearranged, it was possible Kenneth and Jennifer had been in town that morning. That would have given them all day to clear out the apartment.

After the call to Kenneth's office, Nathan then called two of Cynthia's friends in the town where they previously lived. First came Sue. Cynthia and Sue had gone to lunch together when the Wallises were in town the previous week to sign the final papers to sell their former home.

"Hello, Sue," Nathan began hesitantly. "This is Nathan. I think Cynthia has taken Stephanie and left. Did she say anything to you when the two of you had lunch last Friday that might explain any of this?"

"No," she answered. "We didn't talk about anything except catching up on each other's lives since you guys left."

There was that slightest hesitation again.

"I don't know what's going on, Sue," Nathan said, feeling the tears coming.

"I don't know what to tell you," she said. "We didn't talk about any problems between you."

Next was Liz. This woman lived just thirty miles from their former home. But she and Cynthia had established a friendship when Liz had lived in their former town. Liz had offered her services to the Wallises when she borrowed a pickup truck and brought their freezer to their new home. Nathan had never been fully comfortable with this woman. But her support and assistance through this move indicated to him that despite her faults, Liz could be a good friend.

"Liz, this is Nathan," he said, still fighting back the tears. "I came home from work today and Cynthia and Stephanie are missing. Has she talked to you recently about anything that might be wrong?"

"Well," Liz answered, "I don't know what could be wrong."

No hesitation this time. In fact, the answer came too quickly, Nathan thought.

He was to find later that these two women were not good sources of information or honesty. While that suspicion was growing within him now, it was not the uppermost thing on his mind. He was frantic about his family. While he was fairly sure that Cynthia had simply taken Stephanie and left him, there were other thoughts coming into his head now.

He called Stephanie's favorite teacher at her home. She said Stephanie was taken out of school about a quarter after one that afternoon. The teacher explained that she was told that Stephanie would not be back to school for a couple of days.

Frantic with worry over his family's safety, Nathan tried to sleep but found no success. He lay on his back on the bed and his heart pounded against his chest as hard and fast as a jackhammer. He began to sweat as if he were in a steam room. With his arms across his chest, he felt dizzy and the feeling began to fade from his arms. Thinking it was just the position of his arms, he moved them to his side, flat on the bed. But the numbness only increased.

He tried watching television or reading several times during the night and early morning. But neither held his interest at all, and neither did much to put him to sleep. The concerns he felt for his family, combined with the awful possibility that his wife had left him and taken their only child just chased sleep and relaxation completely out of his mind.

When six in the morning finally arrived, Nathan made another call to Kenneth's office. He knew that his father-in-law usually got in at six, and with him out of town, it was a good bet someone would be there. He was right, but the news he got was not good.

The man who answered the phone repeated what had been said the day before – that Kenneth had gone out of town and did not say when he would be back. But the man did offer one additional bit of information that hadn't been offered the day before – that Kenneth had gone to the town where his daughter lived.

An early morning tour of the motels in town was the first order of the day for Nathan. He drove through the parking lots of each in turn to see if the McAdams' car was there. But he found no such vehicle. Nor did he see the rental they had gotten for Cynthia when he went looking for another family car.

For three hours, he went from the restaurant to the apartment to aimless driving around town, still looking for the McAdams' car or Cynthia's rental car. During one stop at home, he got a call from the county mental health office. The woman on the other end of the line identified herself as Jane.

"I'm calling in response to a call from your wife," she said. "She said you would be despondent. I would like to have you come into the office so we can talk about this."

Nathan was a little confused at first. If Cynthia were leaving him, why would she take the time to call someone and ask them to call because he would be despondent? If things were so bad that she felt she had to leave him, why would she care about his welfare? That confusion would stay with him for a long time.

"I'm okay. I just want to know where my family is and why they left." He answered Jane in calm, even tones. It wasn't entirely true. Some very disturbing thoughts had been running through his head concerning his own safety. But he wasn't ready to share that with anyone just yet.

"Are you sure?" Jane asked.

"I'll feel better when I know what is happening," he responded.

"I'm afraid I can't help you with that," Jane answered matter-of-factly. "But if you need to talk, call me."

After taking her number, he told her that he would call, if necessary, then hung up the phone.

But several hours of chasing between the restaurant, Cynthia's office and home, and continued aimless driving hung heavy on Nathan's mind.

The situation became worse when, during one of his stops at the restaurant, a county sheriff's deputy came in and asked for Nathan.

When he identified himself to the officer, he handed Nathan some papers.

"This is a restraining order against you," the deputy said sternly. "You are not to have any contact with your wife or daughter."

The deputy then turned and exited the restaurant, leaving Nathan standing there open-mouthed.

Several of the staff stopped what they were doing during the deputy's announcement. They were all dumbfounded. They had the impression Nathan and Cynthia had a solid relationship and there were no issues in the marriage. The fact that Nathan was kind and fair to them simply reenforced their impression of that.

It only took a few minutes for the shock Nathan felt at being hit with a restraining order to dissipate. He quickly read the documents then left the restaurant. He knew what he had to do. But in the middle of the afternoon, those disturbing thoughts returned. Much of the day had been spent in tears and worry. Nathan felt the time had come to seek out help. He called the mental health office and asked for Jane. An appointment was set up for later that afternoon.

Called a screening appointment, the meeting was an uneasy one for Nathan. All his life he had felt that the best way to take care of his problems was to face them and take care of them himself. Going to a "professional" was a hard thing to do for him. It took a lot for him to even go see a medical doctor, let alone a mental health professional. He remembered a period in college that reinforced that.

However, even in his present state of mind, Nathan could also tell the meeting was an uneasy one for Jane. That struck Nathan as odd. Wouldn't this woman be used to dealing with distraught people on a regular basis? Why would this encounter give her cause to be hesitant? And hesitance was not the only emotion Jane betrayed to her new client.

When Nathan spoke of his wife and her disappearance, Jane betrayed a hint of defensiveness. She spoke very little about Cynthia, and tried to contain the conversation to just Nathan and his feelings.

But all Nathan could think of was his family, and why had they left him. Sobs racked his body with nearly every word he spoke, and the tears flowed freely. Jane appeared frustrated and somewhat confused at his tearful appearance. It was as if she were seeing a scene that was very unexpected.

The appointment did nothing for Nathan's state of mind. In fact, having gotten no answers as to the whereabouts of his family and the state of their safety, it only increased the worry and frustration. He seemed deeper in the depression he had sunk into beginning with the previous evening. It was another long, sleepless night.

At six o'clock Wednesday morning, the telephone rang in the Harrison Street apartment. Before the echo of the first ring could die away, Nathan picked up the phone and said hello, betraying his sense of frustration, depression and even hope. He was simultaneously delighted and disappointed to hear his father-in-law's voice.

"Hello," Kenneth McAdams said slowly and deliberately. "I'm at my office. I'm calling to let you know where Cynthia and Stephanie are, and what's going on."

Chapter 4

"I need professional help. Am I going crazy?"

A whirlwind of feelings for many different events in his life brought Nathan to ask himself this question while attending college. These feelings confused him. Not just because there were so many pressures weighing upon him, but because some of them were very personal.

Cynthia was one of those pressures. The feelings he had for her were the most intense he had experienced for a woman in his life. But there was something about her that caused some hesitation in him to explore their relationship past the point of exclusive dating. It was a certain sense of innocence, an innocence he did not want to destroy.

What Nathan was most worried about where Cynthia was concerned was escalating their relationship and then having to face the consequences if it went sour. He was concerned about his own emotional well-being if that were to happen. The memory of Cheryl leaving him was still very fresh in his mind.

But it was not just his own well-being that Nathan was concerned about.

He had always considered himself a gentleman in his dealings with women. His thinking in that regard could have been termed old fashioned. In fact, he believed it to be himself. To Nathan, women were something special and needed to be treated that way. He liked opening doors for them, letting them go first, carrying their things for them and treating them special in many other ways.

Trouble was, women were becoming "liberated," and many of them were offended when they were treated special. On a number of occasions, he tried to get ahead of women heading for doors so he could open the door for them. But most times, they would grab the door before he could, or while he was opening it, and go on through without a word. One time he went through a door ahead of two women and let the door close behind him.

"Not much of a gentleman, are you?" one of the women said, perturbed, "Can't even hold a door for a woman."

Trying to figure out these contradictions also added to his consternation.

Cynthia, though, was different. She enjoyed the special treatment. That was one of the reasons Nathan found himself attracted to her in a way that he had not expected.

But in this new environment, Nathan found there were other women on his mind. There was the director of the Big Brother program, there was the college newspaper staff member, there was even a young cousin and there was a woman whose name was a mystery to him. They all occupied his thoughts, along with Cynthia.

In another vein, there was also his father.

Since moving into his home and beginning school, Nathan could see problems developing. For starters, his father hardly knew the man Nathan had become. In some ways, George treated his son as if he were still a youngster and needed discipline and guidance, which was far from the case. Nathan was now nearly nineteen years old and charting his own path in life.

A complicating factor in the relationship between father and son was the step mother.

Barbara Wallis married George shortly after his split with Nathan's mother. Nathan had never met her until he moved into his father's house. Nathan quickly saw that Barbara was not only the jealous kind, but very controlling.

She resented the fact there was someone else in the house taking some of her husband's time and attention. It was also clear that she ruled the roost like an old banty hen, clucking out orders like a barnyard drill sergeant. Nathan was forbidden from operating the washer and dryer and the kitchen appliances. And one night when he came home to an empty house while George and Barbara were bowling, he ate some Cheetos from an open bag. When he had his fill, he forgot to put them away and had left them in his room. The next night when he came home late from an outing, Barbara was sitting on the couch. She gave him a dirty look and threw the Cheetos bag at him, scattering the contents.

Barbara was also a neat freak. Her husband worked an early shift at a bakery in town and after he left the house at four o'clock in the morning for work, Barbara promptly began running the vacuum cleaner. This happened every single day. Even with his door shut, Nathan could hear the racket. He could hear the vacuum as it went from room to room, getting closer to his own. Then suddenly the door would burst open and in would come the vacuum followed by its operator.

The first time this happened, Nathan protested.

"What the hell," he shouted over the loud drone of the machine. "I was asleep. This is my room."

Without looking at him or missing a spot as she vacuumed, Barbara replied testily, "This is my house and this is how things get done. Don't like it? Get out."

From then on, he did his best to be in the shower as soon as the vacuum began each morning. Eventually, he spent fewer nights at the house, staying at George's parents' home across town or finding other places to catch a few hours sleep — sometimes at friends' homes, sometimes sleeping in his car.

George's invitation to Nathan to live in his home while he attended school did not include Cynthia. She lived in the university dormitory. A couple of times he was in her room late talking when her roommate was out of town and ended up sleeping in the room. But the university had strict rules about males being overnight guests in females' rooms. That didn't happen very often, and when it did Nathan had to sneak out in the morning.

It was all that which made Nathan ponder whether he needed professional help.

Cynthia picked up on that anxiety. She spent some time talking to him about getting counseling. She even suggested he see the college counselor. It was a persistent train of thought from her, so much so that he finally agreed to give it a try.

Nathan believed he already had a counselor in Cynthia. He shared with her all the things on his mind – the new settings of the college campus and the more intense studies, the other women he was thinking about, the trouble at home. She had listened and offered advise during their many walks.

Psychologists and counselors did not have a special place in Nathan's mind or heart. Even at nineteen, and having absolutely no previous contact with either, he had formed some very distinct impressions about the "mind benders," as he had come to call them.

He came to look on members of the psychological profession as people interested in testing theories on the workings of the human mind at the expense of those who sought their help. Clients were used simply as guinea pigs for the "mind benders."

Yes, it was a narrow-minded line of thinking, especially from someone who had no first-hand experience with psychologists or counselors. But it was a theory that someday would gain new validity in his mind.

He met with Ben Cardoza, one of the college counselors, and gave a brief summary of why he believed he needed assistance. They arranged a schedule of visits. Ben told him to think, in the two days before the next session, about what exactly was confusing him about his feelings for the different pressures on his mind.

Because she had been so insistent on his counseling, Cynthia was eager to know what had happened.

"There isn't much to tell," he told her. "We just talked briefly about why I was there and set up the next sessions."

The disappointment on her face was evident.

"You didn't talk to him about the women you've been thinking about and the problems at your dad's?" she asked.

"Not really in any detail," he responded, a little suspicious about why she was so eager to know. "It was just a first meeting."

His answer did not satisfy her, but Cynthia let the subject die for the time being.

***

"Would you have stayed in Vietnam?"

Ben's question took Nathan by surprise. He had been talking about his devotion to and love for Cheryl, describing their private, intimate, late-night moments.

At first, Nathan thought the therapist was making a comment about the pilot's wings on his jacket. He had purchased them at an air show and wore them on the gray jacket with fur lining, a cheap version of a pilot's jacket. He looked down at the wings on the left breast of the coat and back at Ben.

"I wasn't in the military," he said, touching the wings. "These are just decoration."

"I was not asking about that," Ben said. "It was a metaphor. What I wanted to know is would you have stayed in the relationship with Cheryl if you had known it was not working."

Nathan fidgeted with the jacket's zipper near his throat.

"No, I wouldn't want to stay in something that was not working," he answered. "But until she left, I didn't see anything that indicated our relationship was not working."

In the months they had been together, Nathan and Cheryl had enjoyed a relationship that, for the most part, was idealistic and somewhat fitting of a fairy tale.

They had some similar interests, but they also had different ways of looking at life in general. Nathan looked at most things with an idealist's point of view. At that age he was very naïve and believed that if people lived their lives by always doing the right thing, they would find nothing but good things in store for them. He also believed that living such a life would earn one respect.

In terms of male-female relationships, Nathan believed if he treated a woman with respect and love, he would get the same in return.

Cheryl's outlook on life in general was somewhat different – more of a realistic perspective. She knew there were no fairy tales to live. Cheryl knew the notion of a good, hard work ethic were not always the secret to success. Most times success came through connections and doing what was expected.

In terms of relationships, Cheryl's approach was "live for the moment." A long-term commitment to a man was something that was not yet on her radar, if it would ever be at all.

"So, knowing all that about Cheryl, you would still have stayed in the relationship?" Ben asked.

Nathan thought about it for a moment. He could understand what Ben was getting at. But he was not the kind of man, this early in his development as a man, to just walk away from a commitment without trying to find ways to fix it. He relayed all that to the counselor.

"But some things, even relationships, cannot be fixed," Ben said.

Nathan again gave that a moment's thought. Again, he understood what Ben was getting at. But Nathan could not shake his determination to live up to the commitments he made in life. Even though Cheryl had ended their relationship, he still felt an obligation to her. And now that he had made a commitment of sorts to Cynthia, he was still thinking about other women, and that made him feel guilty.

Ben intruded onto his thoughts with another question.

"So, how committed are you to your relationship with Cynthia?" he asked.

Nathan was jolted back to the counseling room, and he answered without hesitation.

"Very committed, I would like to marry her and have children, some day," he said.

"Some would consider you too young to make such a commitment to a woman," Ben said.

"What does my age have to do with it?" Nathan asked.

"You are still young and, Cheryl not withstanding, still inexperienced in regard to relationships," Ben said. "Wouldn't you want to explore a little, see if there is someone else out there who would be a better fit for you?"

"It's not like I don't think about it," Nathan said, and immediately regretted it.

"How do you mean?" Ben asked.

"I have thought about other women and what it might be like with them," he said. Nathan knew it was a lame answer, but Ben compounded it with his next response.

"You do know thinking about it and following through on it are two different things," he said.

Nathan was a little peeved. Of course he knew the difference. But what was he supposed to do, tell Cynthia to wait while he checked out other women? That went way against his grain.

"I can't do that to Cynthia," Nathan said.

Ben could read the anger in his tone and expression. He decided it was time to take a break in his talks with Nathan. But he had one last thing to say.

"I think we need to end our discussion here. But I want to give you something to think about before we talk again," Ben said. "There is a saying, 'If you love something, let it go. If it comes back, it is yours. If it doesn't, it never was.'"

In a few days Nathan was back for his next session with the counselor, but he was not alone.

Cynthia wanted to attend Nathan's sessions. She talked with him about it daily since the last time he saw Ben. Nathan was not comfortable with her proposal.

"I don't think that would be a good idea," he had told her just the day before his session was scheduled.

"Why not?" she asked.

"It's really not done that way," he answered. "These are supposed to be private between the client and counselor."

Cynthia's justifications for attending his counseling sessions were varied. First, she said she wanted to learn more about him and she believed he would open up more to the counselor and, therefore, reveal more than he had to her so far.

Nathan argued that they talked all the time and he had been nothing but open and truthful with her in those talks.

Cynthia next claimed she could provide some insight to Ben that Nathan may not divulge. But he countered that he was being forthright with the counselor.

However, she was so insistent that she attend the sessions, he relented – mostly just to end the disagreement before it escalated into a confrontation. Though he had agreed to allow her to attend, he placed a caveat on it. Ben had to agree to her attendance.

Nathan had hoped Ben would refuse the request. But because Nathan seemed agreeable to it, he allowed Cynthia to sit in. He did caution her that he was allowing it so she could be an observer, not a participant.

"So, when we met last, you were talking about some of the pressures you feel and what you can do to ease them," Ben said to start the session.

Nathan nodded. No details were being discussed yet, but he was already feeling awkward with Cynthia in the room.

It wasn't that they would talk about things he did not want her to know. In their walks, he had already talked about his failed relationship with Cheryl, how he felt about it and his outlook on emotional commitment. He had also talked with Cynthia about his thoughts about other women he had met after settling on the college campus.

What made it awkward for him was the fact that he was, after only one session with Ben, just getting used to talking to someone else other than Cynthia about his innermost feelings and emotions. Having them both in the room made him uncertain just who to address his thoughts to. He was more comfortable talking to Cynthia, but that was not the point of the counseling.

"Have you thought about the saying I left you with last time?" Ben asked.

Nathan looked around the counselor's office while formulating his response. The room was not much bigger than a small bedroom in a home, which, in fact, it used to be. The counseling center was in a converted home on campus. The room had bookshelves covering two walls and they were full of textbooks and casual reading material. Ben's small desk was about the size of a card table. The remainder of the room contained a love seat and two folding chairs.

"Yes, I have," Nathan said.

"And what do you think it means?" Ben asked.

"Well, I think it's self-explanatory," Nathan said.

"Yes, but I'm wondering what it meant to you personally in regards to your past relationship," Ben prompted.

Cynthia sat forward in her chair. Nathan noticed, as did the counselor. Ben gave her a sideways glance to send the silent message, *"Remember, you are allowed here as an observer only, no contributing to the discussion."*

Cynthia remained poised at the edge of her seat. Ben turned his full attention back to Nathan.

"Well, I'm sure that it means I should move on from Cheryl because she did not come back to me so she was never really that interested," Nathan said.

Before continuing, the counselor glanced at Cynthia and saw she had not settled back into her seat, but she had the beginnings of a smile on her face.

"And are you going to move on?" Ben asked.

Nathan's answer was an immediate yes.

"Now, in terms of relationships, do you want to move on with any of the women you have told me that have been on your mind?" the counselor asked.

"I can't see me having a relationship with any of those women," Nathan answered.

He and Ben both noticed that Cynthia had settled back into a comfortable seated position in her chair. But her attention was still riveted on the conversation the two men were having.

"Why do you say that?" Ben asked.

As he spoke, Nathan counted off the points on the fingers of his left hand.

"One of them is married, another wouldn't have anything to do with me, one is related and the last one, I don't even know her name," Nathan said.

"But you could get to know her," Ben said.

Nathan hesitated a moment. The conversation was taking a turn he was not sure he wanted to follow, especially with Cynthia in the room. He was beginning to regret having allowed her to sit in on his sessions. But he decided to press on.

"I'm not very good at approaching women," Nathan said. "I don't know how to handle rejection, if it comes."

"But you have had relationships before," Ben said. "How did you approach them?"

"They always approached me first," Nathan said.

"You have friends, right?" Ben asked. "How did those get started?"

"Mostly the same way," Nathan said.

Ben nodded and stayed silent for a few seconds.

"Do you consider yourself shy?" Ben asked.

Nathan put his chin in his hand and rested his elbow on his knee.

"I suppose a little," he said after several seconds of pondering the question.

"There's nothing wrong with being shy," Ben said, emphasizing the word "wrong."

Nathan's cheeks took on a pinkish hue. He had always looked upon his shyness as a weakness, especially when it came to achieving his goals, whether it be in relationships or life in general.

"But it can hold you back in some ways," he said.

"But only if you allow it to," Ben said.

Nathan was silent for a few minutes. He felt he had said all there was to say. He was ready to call it a day with counseling. In fact, he was ready to end the sessions altogether. He did not believe it was making any difference in the pressures he felt upon his shoulders.

"We have a little time left in this session," Ben said to break the silence. "Is there anything else you would like to talk about?"

Nathan was ready to say no when he heard Cynthia's voice from her chair.

"You should talk about your father," she said.

Nathan and Ben turned to look at her in surprise.

"Again, Cynthia, we agreed that you were here just to observe," Ben said.

Nathan was a bit perturbed. He had laid out his angst about his father to her in their walks. But he assumed those conversations would remain between the two of them. He was disappointed that she would bring it up in front of someone else, even in the vague way she had.

"But there are some serious issues that he needs to work out about his father," she said.

"It is for Nathan to decide whether he wants to talk to me about it," Ben told her.

Nathan started to get up from his chair but Cynthia's voice stopped him and he settled back down.

"But if we could get his father to come to his sessions, they could talk it out," Cynthia said.

This time Nathan shot out of his seat like a missile.

"No, that's not going to happen," he said. "If I do talk to Dad about anything it won't be here."

He looked at Ben.

"No offense, but I don't think this is the place for that," he added.

Ben nodded his agreement.

"I think we've done enough for today," Ben said standing and motioning toward the door. "Just give me a call when you are ready for your next session."

Nathan nodded and followed Cynthia out the door. But he knew right then and there that there would be no more counseling sessions.

Chapter 5

"Cynthia is here with us," Nathan heard Kenneth say through the phone. "And she wants a divorce."

While Nathan had already gathered that Cynthia had left him, he assumed she just wanted to get away for a while. With all the family had gone through in the last year who could blame her for wanting some time to herself. It was something Nathan had thought about himself. But up until the word divorce left Kenneth's mouth, Nathan was certain the family would be reunited eventually.

Or maybe it was just wishful thinking.

"But why?" was all that Nathan could muster at the moment.

"I don't know," his father-in-law said. "She's not making a lot of sense right now."

That is what Nathan had been thinking sense it dawned on him his wife had left. But the initial shock of the word divorce had worn off and his need for information kicked in.

"What do you mean she's not making much sense right now?" he asked.

There was a pause on the other end of the line. Nathan could hear movement and then the sound of a door closing. Kenneth was obviously on his cell phone and had gone outdoors. Nathan waited as he heard the metallic click of a lighter. Then his father-in-law took a long drag on a cigarette.

"She is saying things about you that I am finding it hard to believe," Kenneth finally said.

Nathan waited for him to go on, and when he did not, he prompted him.

"Like what things?" he asked.

Again, there was a pause while Kenneth sucked in his cigarette smoke. It was a sign he was nervous. In fact, his smoking was the first sign. A life-long smoker, Kenneth had quit cold turkey two years ago after a small cancerous tumor was removed from his right lung.

"Like you have been unfaithful multiple times, including with a man; that you've siphoned money out of your joint checking account; and other things," Kenneth said after taking another drag.

"What else?" Nathan asked.

"I don't really want to go into it," Kenneth replied. "I'm not sure I believe any of it, and I don't want to upset you any more than you are."

Nathan was a little stunned. The two things Kenneth mentioned were emphatically untrue. No matter what troubles he and Cynthia had, nothing would make him turn to another woman. The accusation of him being sexually intimate with a man was especially rankling.

Nathan was not what the politically correct called a homophobe. He was not afraid of gay people, nor did he hate them. But he did not agree that people of the same gender should engage in sex. It was not a religious thing; for Nathan it was a biological thing. If nothing else, the epidemic of AIDS should have made that plain, in his view.

"Do you really think I'm capable of any of those things?" he asked Kenneth.

His father-in-law took two more long drags on his cigarette before answering. For Nathan, it was a signal of Kenneth's increasing unease with the situation.

"I don't believe the man I got to know, in the short visits we've had, could do these things," he finally said. "But the two of you have been through a lot in the last couple of years. People change under those circumstances."

Nathan let an exasperated sigh leave his lips.

"I have never been unfaithful to your daughter – ever, with anyone," he said. "And it would be pretty hard for me to siphon money out of our account since Cynthia took care of all our finances."

Nathan was starting to get angry, both because of the accusations Cynthia had made and his father-in-law's reluctance to fully support him in his assertion that he had never done those things. But he needed to keep control of that anger and not show it. He knew that would only paint him in a bad light.

"I know it's my word against hers, and she's your daughter and you're going to believe her over me," Nathan said slowly and as evenly as he could muster. "But I swear to you that what she said I did is not true."

He paused to collect his thoughts, and he heard Kenneth light another cigarette.

"Thank you for calling and letting me know where they are and that they are safe," Nathan said.

"You deserved to know," Kenneth responded.

"What's going to happen now?" Nathan asked. "Has she filed divorce papers already?"

"No," Kenneth said. "We're trying to make sense of what she is saying. One minute she talks divorce and the next she's wanting to keep the family together. And then there's the other stuff."

Nathan breathed a little easier. If Cynthia was talking about keeping the family together, at least there was a chance of it happening. How much of a chance he had no idea.

"Look, Nathan, I know this is hard on you, especially not knowing what's going on," Kenneth said. "But I will keep you posted as much as I can."

Nathan hoped that would be true. But there was something about Kenneth's promise that bothered him.

"As much as you can? What does that mean?" he asked.

Kenneth drew in another lungful of smoke, held it for a couple seconds then blew it out.

"She is my daughter, Nathan. As much as I like you, I have to do what they want," he said. "I'll call when I can." He then ended the call.

Kenneth's reference to "they" hung in Nathan's mind. Was he referring to Cynthia and Stephanie, or Cynthia and her mother.

Nathan got another call within minutes of hanging up with his father-in-law. It was Trudy Watkins, a friend he had made through the restaurant. More than 20 years older than him, Trudy came regularly to the restaurant Nathan managed. She was drawn to him, but not in a romantic or sexual way.

She had lost her husband within the year and was still dealing with the trauma of it. They had been together 10 years and were so much in love. They were together nearly constantly and had many things in common.

When she first saw Nathan at the restaurant shortly after he was hired, she felt he was a sensitive soul. She had a waitress introduce her to him and they chatted for a few minutes. That short conversation convinced her she was right about him. She started making it a point to come to the restaurant after the morning rush when Nathan was not as busy and she found an excuse to talk to him again. She continued the routine nearly on a daily basis.

In their conversations, Trudy told Nathan about her marriage and how much she missed her husband. She also shared that she felt there was no reason for her to go on living. But Nathan gave her many reasons why she should not feel that way, chiefly that her husband would not want her to end her life.

The more they talked, the more she realized she had so much more to live for. It was then their conversations turned more toward Nathan and his life. He had been open and honest with her. They both enjoyed their talks and each gained self-confidence through them.

"We need to go to lunch," she said when he answered her call.

They set a time and place, which was not the restaurant where he worked. Trudy wanted a neutral place so they would not be interrupted.

"I am treating you to lunch because I know you have not eaten in a couple of days," she said after they had placed their orders.

While it was true, and Nathan had lost fifteen pounds in those days, he could not understand how she would know. His quizzical look prompted Trudy to explain.

"I was at the restaurant this morning," she said. "Since you weren't there, I asked one of the waitresses where you were. She told me about Cynthia's and Stephanie's disappearance."

Nathan nodded. He remembered in one of their early talks at the restaurant how Trudy shared that for nearly a week after her husband's death she was so distraught that she had no appetite, despite her family and friends urging her to eat. He acknowledged she was correct about his lack of nutritional intake and told her of his weight loss.

"It's not just the lack of eating, it's the stress you've got over you that takes those pounds off," she said.

Nathan poked at the fish he had ordered and was just delivered to their table.

"But you have to eat," Trudy said. "You have to keep your strength up. And you need to lower your stress level. You need all your strength and a clear head to find your family."

"I already know where they are," he said as he swallowed a mouthful of halibut.

He shared his conversation with Kenneth.

"So, what happens now?" she asked.

"I don't know," he answered with a forkful of mixed vegetables poised to go into his mouth. Trudy's encouragement was giving him back his appetite.

At that moment an older man, between his and Trudy's age, stopped at the side of their table. Nathan recognized him as Jason Campphere, a supervisor in the county courthouse that was also a regular at the restaurant Nathan managed.

"Nathan, how are you?" he asked in a halting voice.

"Not the best at the moment," he answered.

"Have you been served yet?" he asked.

"Well, yeah," Nathan said, holding out his left hand in a gesturing motion toward his food.

"No, I mean the restraining order," Jason said.

"Oh, yeah, I got that yesterday," Nathan said.

"Are you going to appeal?" Jason asked.

"Of course," Nathan answered, a little perturbed that Camphere would think he would not.

"Well, you might get on it," Jason said. "The longer you wait to get the ball rolling the more chance the judge will assume you're going to let it stay in place."

Jason Camphere's advice about the restraining order appeal stirred Nathan to action.

Still reeling from the fact that his wife would so suddenly leave him without any hint of problems, and that she would go to such lengths, he now felt the urgency to at least correct the order situation.

Trudy stood with him at the information window. Nathan had wanted to go to the courthouse alone, but she insisted on going with him.

"In your state of mind, there might be questions you should ask that you won't think of," she argued.

"I understand there is a restraining order filed against me," Nathan told the clerk, a youngish brunette, showing her the documents the deputy had given him. "How do I appeal this?"

She asked his name and searched the records.

"An order was granted yesterday, but I see here that it hasn't been entered into the system yet," the clerk responded after a few minutes.

"Can you tell me any details about it, like specifically why it was filed?" he asked.

"It says here that it was taken out by a Cynthia Wallis," the clerk explained. "Is she related to you?"

"Yes, she's my wife," Nathan said.

The clerk's face took on a slightly sad expression, but Nathan could also tell from a light audible sigh that escaped her lips that she had seen this scenario all too often.

"The restrictions are that you are to have no contact of any kind with your wife and a minor child named Stephanie," she said.

Nathan's body went limp and he felt dizzy. Trudy reached out to steady him. The clerk's sad expression became more evident.

That was all in the paperwork Nathan was given, but the reality of it again shocked him.

"Does it give a reason for the order?" Trudy asked as Nathan tried to regain his senses.

The clerk hesitated. She could see by Nathan's reaction that the restraining order was a complete surprise, and it had affected him deeply. She had seen this play out all too often. Women would take out restraining orders against men and claim the same reason, only to have the orders eventually dropped because their claims had no merit.

"It says here that she was in fear of her life," the clerk said.

Nathan's felt his legs completely give out and he dropped to his knees and rested his head against the counter that jutted out from the clerk's window.

"What the hell?" he muttered.

Trudy kneeled down at his side, urging him to stand. He looked at her and she saw the utter devastation in his eyes. Nathan finally stood, but could still feel his knees trembling.

"I have never, ever done anything that would make her afraid for her life from me," he said in a shaky voice. "I've never hit her or threatened her or anything like that."

"I'm sure...." The clerk began, but quickly checked herself. "That may be true, sir, but I'm just telling you what's on the order." Her look of sympathy seemed sincere.

"Can this be appealed?" Trudy asked.

"Well, you can ask for a hearing," the clerk explained.

Nathan's frustration level began to rise. But he knew he had to keep it in check so he didn't fly off the handle and make it appear Cynthia had grounds in her claim of fearing for her life.

"How do I get that started as soon as possible?" he asked.

The clerk's facial expressions began to show her own frustration with the situation.

"Here are the forms you need to fill out," she said, handing Nathan some papers. "Turn them back in here when you are finished."

Trudy put her hand on his shoulder and gently signaled for him to step away from the window. As he turned to comply, he rotated his head back to the clerk.

"Thank you for all your help," he said with all the genuineness he could muster. "You have been very helpful."

Nathan and Trudy went to his restaurant. Nathan filled out the paperwork for a hearing then they went back to the courthouse to file the papers. After a short wait, Nathan was informed one had been scheduled for the following week.

"Now that you have a hearing, you should go home and get some rest," Trudy suggested. "I know you haven't gotten much of that either."

Nathan agreed and thanked her for her support.

"If you need anything else, don't hesitate to call me," she said.

Rest was not something that came easy to Nathan. His mind was filled with the dizzying events of the last few days. He also kept racking his brain trying to understand what he had done to make Cynthia so certain he was a danger to her, and to Stephanie, that she felt the need to file a restraining order.

While they had had their differences over the years, and a few arguments got heated, there was never any violence or threat of such.

The thoughts running through his head gave him a headache like he had never experienced before. Not one to rely on medications, he took the extraordinary step of taking some aspirin to dull the pain. It took some time for it to take effect, with the last few days events and his search for explanations continuing to swim through his mind.

But when it finally did take effect, he dropped into one of the deepest sleeps he had encountered in some time.

Chapter 6

Cynthia's push to get Nathan to talk about his father and their relationship during the college counseling sessions had a number of motivating factors.

Her upbringing was such that she believed all family members got along. The rift between her brother and her parents was a dent in that philosophy, and it was one she could not seem to fix. She had tried everything she could to get them to get along better. And she had seen some indications that what she was doing was working.

But Bart wasn't interested in mending the fences with his parents – and part of it was because of Cynthia herself. Not because of her efforts to get them to be civil to each other, but because she herself engaged in the bad treatment of his girlfriend. She was good at keeping her thoughts to herself when Bart was in her presence, but when he was not she enthusiastically contributed when it was just she and her parents, or her friends.

In fact, it was the latter that provided the avenue for Bart to discover his sister's true feelings about his girlfriend. Bart did not make an issue out of it, because he dearly wanted to preserve a relationship with his sister. However, he let her know he was aware of things she said to others about Sally Anne.

So, in one respect, Cynthia believed that repairing the relationship between Nathan and his father would make up for that.

Cynthia also saw herself as a relationship fixer. She had some success bringing people together, or back together, while in high school. That is what convinced her she could fix relationships.

Cynthia was also eager to get Nathan and his father to have a better relationship because of the way she perceived her future husband's family.

Since she grew up with her family intact, Cynthia had no experience, and could not understand, couples who professed their love enough to marry to ever break that bond. And it was more than that. Nathan's mother's lifestyle after divorcing her husband was, to Cynthia's way of thinking, slutish. In regards to his father, she believed he was a weak man, not strong enough to keep his family together.

In a real sense, Cynthia looked down her nose at Nathan's family. She considered them redneck trailer trash.

She had known little of his family's traits when they first met and started dating, nor when they got back together again. But as her relationship with Nathan grew closer, she spent more time with his family. She was not happy with what she saw, but it appeared to her that Nathan did not share in those traits, so she allowed their love to grow.

When they agreed to go to college in the Utah town where Nathan's father lived, Cynthia saw it as an opportunity to put her fixer skills to work. While her main goal was to bring Nathan and his father closer together, she fantasized about curing all the ills of his family.

She knew that would be a tall order, but she was determined.

Cynthia never shared those goals with Nathan – short-term or long-term. But he had an inkling of what she was trying to do. He was just as determined to not actively participate in her efforts. But he would not discourage it, and would welcome positive results if they were achieved.

However, Nathan was not confident they would. He knew his family. He also knew human nature. People only changed their behavior if they believed it needed changing and if they truly wanted to. Where his parents were concerned, they were happy with who they were.

***

George Wallis was not a complicated man.

Born into a large family, he had six siblings, being a middle child. His mother and father divorced shortly after the seventh child was born and both remarried quickly. There were no half siblings coming out of those unions.

He barely finished high school and went straight into the U.S. Navy. A squat man of five feet nine inches, he was solidly built. He had a blunt nature and was a bit of a control freak. That fit the qualities for a Navy drill sergeant, and he thrived in that role.

He was still in the Navy when he met Mary Anne Barnarini, a petite woman with dull green eyes and short brown hair. She was three years younger than George and working as a waitress just out of high school when they met. Being so young, Mary Anne was not yet wise to the ways of the world and was taken in by George's commanding personality. She also thought of being with a Navy man as something glorious.

Carolyn was their first born, followed four years later by Nathan, then Bryan and Tessa, the last two separated by about fourteen months.

George was a taskmaster with his children, and was emotionless as well. In his mind, they were part of a family group, no more. They were also an extension of his Navy recruits, getting the same treatment as them, although in a somewhat toned-down way. Nathan did not enjoy the part of his childhood when his father was in the picture. But in his later years he had a different perspective. He believed his father's approach with his children made them understand the value of a good work ethic. That was borne out by seeing his siblings' success in the world of work.

But the lack of emotion toward his children was something that stuck in Nathan's craw since his parents' divorce. Their father rarely had contact with his blood children, and when there was contact it was the children, one hundred percent of the time, who initiated the contact.

And then there was his devotion and love for his step-children after he remarried. Nathan and his siblings grew to resent that.

But Nathan continued to try and please his father and would have welcomed a closer relationship with him. But to no avail.

When Nathan and Cynthia went to college in the same community where he lived, George had been retired from the Navy for a few years and he was still pretty distant with his son, even though he lived under the father's roof. There were even times when Nathan saw his father try to change his son's personality to more closely match his own.

By the time Nathan went to college, his father's step-children were grown and on their own, both having married young. But though they were out of George's house, the step-father took every opportunity to spend as much time with his second wife's children as possible. That further inflamed Nathan's resentment.

There came a point when he could not keep his feelings in check, so he decided the living arrangement was not in his or his father's best interest. After a short stint living with his grandparents across town, he found a small studio apartment and got a second job in a restaurant to fund it. That was his living arrangement for the remainder of his college years.

Once the move was made, the contact between he and his father diminished to nearly nothing. George did not even attend the college graduation ceremony in which both Nathan and Cynthia received their degrees. Very shortly thereafter, George moved to Idaho.

Years later, after Stephanie's birth, the new parents took their daughter to George's home so he could see his first grandchild.

"That's nice," was George's only comment about the child before launching into a rant about problems at his job as a machinist.

That convinced Nathan that his father was not interested in his life, or that of his daughter.

After they completed college, Nathan and Cynthia married and moved to Illinois, in a town not far from her parents and his mother. It was a deliberate choice on Nathan's part to create as much distance between he and his father as possible.

Cynthia was disappointed she could not bring them closer together. But it was something she had no intention of giving up on.

In their new state, they settled into their new home and jobs. Cynthia went to work in a bank as a teller and Nathan began work as a chef in a high-end restaurant.

It was not the career path either wanted. They wanted to start their own business. But they had not decided just what kind of business they wanted for themselves. Cynthia's job at the bank, which she secured first and prompted the move, would give her an opportunity to learn about basic finances. She had hoped that after a year or two she could move up to a loan officer's position. Nathan had not really wanted to work in a restaurant, but it was the job he got. He decided it would be a good way to learn business management.

They set a goal of five years before having children. They missed it by two years.

Having a child so quickly after starting their journey of life presented certain challenges. While Cynthia was able to get three months' maternity leave from the bank, when that period was over, they had to either put Stephanie in day care, which neither wanted to do, or find ways to make it work.

What they came up with was a job switch for Nathan. He left the high-end restaurant because the morning shift and afternoon shift overlapped and neither was able to allow him to stay home with his daughter while Cynthia worked her nine in the morning to five in the afternoon work schedule.

Instead, Nathan worked in a warehouse for Stephanie's first three years of life. He managed the shipping department.

But it wasn't too large a sacrifice because the warehouse was a different kind of business and allowed him to diversify his hands-on education.

In the meantime, after returning to the bank Cynthia advanced quickly and attained the loan officer position six months ahead of her self-imposed schedule. The rise in salary was also to the young family's advantage.

When Stephanie was five years old, Cynthia got an offer to transfer to a branch of her bank in Nebraska. They offered her an assistant manager's position. The salary increase was significant and it was hard to say no.

The move took them away from their parents. While Nathan dealt with that fine, Cynthia did not. Nathan's siblings were spread out. Carolyn lived in Illinois in a town thirty miles from where Cynthia's parents lived and fifty from her mother. Bryan lived in Colorado and Tessa lived in New York City. Cynthia's brother, Bart, had married Sally Anne, and they lived in Minnesota. But the young Wallis family was making a move based on Cynthia's employment and he had to find one after they moved. He was able to do that, this time hired by a sporting goods store. He was also an assistant manager, and because of his experience at the warehouse he was put in charge of shipping in addition to his other duties.

It was not the ideal job for him. But in the first few months he learned a lot about that particular type of business and began to form an idea in his mind about what kind of business he wanted for he and his wife.

Sports apparel was becoming very popular. But professional teams, and even college teams, were charging outlandish prices for their merchandise. In addition, local public schools and youth teams were finding costs for their uniforms rising at alarming rates. Nathan believed he could create a business that provided those items at lower prices.

The largest obstacles to that endeavor were the pushback he would get from other suppliers, who would not want to give up their huge profits, and the pro and college teams for much the same reasons.

Another obstacle was Cynthia. She was not that interested in sports and may not want to be involved in such a business.

But those were things Nathan believed he could work around. In the meantime, he wanted to soak up all the knowledge he could.

But Nathan's dream of a sports apparel business had to be put on hold when Stephanie was seven years old as her mother got another transfer opportunity to manage a bank. Once again, the family made the move because of the increase in salary for Cynthia.

And as luck would have it, there was an opening at a sporting goods store in the same city.

This move kept them in the same state.

For two years the Wallises continued on their upward journey in life. But after two years the bottom fell out.

For eighty years the country's economy was like riding a roller coaster.

It started with the Great Depression, starting in August 1929 and not improving until March 1933 following the election of Franklin Roosevelt as president and the anticipation of his announced social programs. While the Great Depression officially ended in 1933, the country continued to suffer from financial difficulties through much of the 1930s.

The country's recovery took a detour from May 1937 to June 1938 with a recession before World War II brought back limited prosperity. In the last months of the war the country went through another recession, which was followed by ten more such periods, stretching through every decade into the 21st century.

Everything in the country's economy is measured by the Gross Domestic Product. When the GDP growth rate turns negative, the economy enters a recession. The most important part of the economy is consumer spending. The other three components are business expenditures, government spending and net exports.

All that played into the Wallises lives when the country suffered its next recession. This one was the worst one since the Great Depression. The Wallises and working-class families like them were hit hard.

Nathan and Cynthia were forced again to relocate when the bank Cynthia managed had to make cuts in staff. To save money, bank leadership decided to incorporate shared branch managers. They chose a longer tenured employee from a branch in a city twenty miles away to manage her bank. They terminated Cynthia's employment.

Because sales at the sporting goods store where Nathan worked dropped dramatically, he was also let go.

In their search for new jobs, they were fortunate enough to find employment, but at least still in the same state. Cynthia was hired by the small CPA firm and Nathan got the job at the restaurant. But because their period of unemployment took much of their savings to just survive, they were forced to rent a home rather than buy a new house in their new town.

The latest move for the Wallis family was the hardest. With their savings nearly drained from the expenses for the move, they were living paycheck to paycheck. Cynthia had suggested they ask her parents for financial help. Nathan refused, but turned a blind eye when Cynthia did it on her own.

But as they settled into their new jobs and routine, things began to improve for them financially. They were able to keep their bills paid and have enough left over for some luxuries. Not many, but they could eat out from time to time and took some days trips when they both had time off from work.

Kenneth and Jennifer visited them almost monthly on weekends, even more than they had when the lived closer. Nathan enjoyed their company – Kenneth's at least – and didn't question the visits, although they seemed a bit much and sometimes interfered with their plans.

During the visits, Jennifer seemed to be getting more and more attached to Stephanie. Without Nathan asking about it, Cynthia explained, when they were alone, that her mother just wanted to bond with the only grandchild she would ever have. Bart and Sally Anne, seeing dysfunction in so many other families, decided not to have children. Nathan accepted the explanation, though he had begun to grow annoyed about some of Jennifer's actions that seemed possessive of both her daughter and granddaughter.

During one visit prior to their latest move, one in which Nathan's mother was also present, the group was preparing to go out to dinner. Nathan had told Stephanie to clean her room before they left. Sitting on her maternal grandmother's lap, Stephanie made no move to comply.

Cleaning the room was not a monumental task. It required Stephanie simply to pick up and put away several toys left lying on the floor and putting some dirty clothes in the hamper by the washer.

Nathan, in increasingly firmer tones, repeated the request that his daughter clean her room. With each new request, Jennifer held Stephanie tighter, and whispered in her ear. Nathan later learned from his mother that Jennifer had whispered to her granddaughter that she didn't need to clean her room.

Another time, Cynthia had some minor laser surgery to a ligament near her knee that would keep her off her feet for at least a week. Nathan made preparations with his employer to have a flexible schedule to allow him to be home to take care of his wife off and on throughout the days.

But Jennifer would have none of that. She convinced Cynthia that it would be best if she went home with her for two weeks for her recovery.

"And, of course, Stephanie would come with you," she said. "Nathan won't be able to handle work and taking care of a child alone,"

Nathan was not happy about the arrangement, and was even less so when the two-week absence stretched into a month.

When Cynthia and Stephanie returned, Nathan said nothing about his irritation. But Cynthia could tell that her husband was hurt that her agreement to go with her mother gave the impression she did not trust Nathan to take care of her. She could also see that made him a little angry.

But she did nothing to sooth either his hurt feelings or his anger.

Chapter 7

Nathan sat in the courtroom waiting for the judge to enter for his hearing on the restraining order his wife had taken out against him prior to leaving town with their only child. He had gotten a transcript of the hearing in which that order was granted and got a free consultation with an attorney to go over it.

"The problem, Mr. Wallis, is that judges tend to be very liberal in granting these orders," Ray Jones started the conversation. "She said she was in fear of her life, and those, essentially, are the trigger words for just about every judge in these matters."

"So, she doesn't have to provide any proof of that?" Nathan asked.

The attorney knew from previous experience that in most cases – but not an overwhelming majority – the women asking for the restraining order experienced some domestic violence in varying degrees. But he also knew that in some cases there was no threat of death or even physical harm, and those women manipulated the system to get out of relationships they simply had grown tired of.

And in some cases, the restraining orders were a way of humiliating their partner.

But Jones also understood the reasoning behind granting orders in cases where women said they were in fear of their lives. There were a small number of cases in which restraining orders were not granted and the woman was later beaten up – or worse – by the man from whom they were seeking protection.

"The vast majority of judges believe that the safer option is to err on the side of caution," Jones told Nathan.

He fingered the copy of the hearing transcript in front of him, which the attorney had briefly read after Nathan had explained the situation.

"But there is no record of me doing anything physically violent to her, or my daughter," Nathan said, almost pleading.

But Jones explained there really was no way to prove that. He related a couple of examples of women who, for whatever reason, denied any such violence, or found other explanations for bruises and other injuries in documented cases.

"There are even women who take these guys back even when the violence is documented," Jones said. "That is one reason judges are quick to grant orders in cases where the women claim they are in fear of their lives."

Nathan felt a bit deflated, but was still not willing to just give in to having the restrictions of the judge's order placed upon him.

"But she did not say that at first," he said. "She offered several other excuses for wanting the order."

Nathan flipped through the pages to find examples.

"The judge even told her a few times exactly what she should say, but she kept throwing out this other stuff until he finally said he wouldn't grant the order until she said she was in fear of her life," he continued while looking through the pages.

He stopped in one section and was about to read aloud what was there. But Jones interrupted.

"It really doesn't matter what she said before. Once she said she was in fear of her life, the judge followed his guidelines and granted the order," Jones said.

"But he flat out told her what she had to say," Nathan said, exasperated.

"It doesn't matter. She said those words," Jones said.

Nathan sagged in his chair. He sat that way for almost a full minute before speaking again.

"So, there is nothing I can do to get the order lifted," he said, not even framing it as a question.

"I'm not saying that," Jones said. "You can go through with the appeal hearing. Maybe you'll be able to persuade the judge that the order is unwarranted. But what I am saying is it will be an uphill battle – a steep one."

"So what good is the appeals process?" Nathan asked. It was meant to be a rhetorical question.

"An appeal process has to be in place to be fair," Jones said.

Nathan stood up, the anger starting to rise in him. He grabbed the transcript copies from the table.

"Where's the fairness if the deck is stacked against me from the beginning," he said, and turned toward the door of the conference room.

"I wouldn't say the deck is stacked…." Nathan heard Jones begin as the door shut behind him.

Nathan's opinion of attorneys, not the best even before the meeting, took a nose dive.

In the day he had before the appeal hearing, Nathan called the police departments in communities in which he and Cynthia had lived and asked them if there were any reports of domestic violence against him in the time they lived there. He also called several of his friends to get them to offer their observations on whether they saw any indications of domestic violence between himself and his wife.

Each of the friends he contacted said they saw no such indications, and sent him emails testifying to that. All but two of the police departments, after a day of searching records, responded that no reports had been filed. They, too, emailed him those results.

Two departments told him right up front that they did not have the time or resources to do the research his request required before the hearing.

All this information he provided to Judge Carl Dixson. It was fortunate for Nathan that he was not the judge who granted the restraining order.

The judge took the time to read every email Nathan had printed out and presented at the hearing. As he read, the tension in the small meeting room in which the hearing was conducted was thick enough that cutting through it would have been difficult even with a razor-sharp knife. Other than Nathan and the judge, only a stenographer was in the room.

Dixson finally laid the documents aside and looked at Nathan.

"The information you provided is very compelling, and it's clear you worked hard to gather it in the short time you had before this hearing," the judge said.

Nathan's spirits rose, and Dixson could see it as Nathan's face registered relief and hope.

"But as compelling as it is, I still have some concerns," Dixson said, He was trying not to give him false hope. "Sometimes in domestic violence situations women don't report abuse for fear the spouse will retaliate."

Nathan began to protest, but the judge held up his hand, palm out, to stop him.

"I'm not saying that is the case here, just that it is possible," Dixson said.

Nathan relaxed, but only a little.

"Plus, the testimony given by your friends don't carry a lot of weight because as they are your friends, there could be bias there," he explained.

Nathan's confidence took another hit. His shoulders slumped and he dropped his head in resignation.

But the Judge was not finished.

"But there is one thing I am willing to do in this case," he said. "I can see that this has taken a toll on you, and you don't exhibit the characteristics of a typical abuser."

Nathan's posture did not change.

"I have never abused my wife or my daughter," he mumbled. "Ever."

Dixson let that statement hang in the air a few seconds before he went on.

"What I will do is call your wife and see if she still feels in fear of her life," Dixson said.

When he saw no reaction from Nathan, he went on.

"If she does, I will keep the order in place," he said. "If she does not, I will lift the order."

Nathan still remained slumped in his chair with his eyes pointed toward his feet. Dixson saw the tears tracking down his cheeks.

"Is that acceptable to you?" he asked.

"I suppose," Nathan said. "I don't think I have much choice."

Dixson gathered up the copies of the paperwork Nathan had given him and stood to leave the room.

"That is true, Mr. Wallis," the judge said. "Give me a few minutes."

The stenographer followed him out the door and Nathan was left alone. His dejection and feelings of defeat made it feel like he was alone in more ways than just in a room waiting for a judge's decision.

After what seemed like hours, but in truth was only fifteen minutes, Judge Dixson and the stenographer re-entered the meeting room and took their seats. Nathan slowly raised his head and searched their faces for some clue as to what would come. But their expressions were as blank as the tabletop.

The judge shuffled through the paperwork he brought back with him, then looked straight into Nathan's tear-watered eyes.

"Mr. Wallis, I spoke with your wife for a few minutes," he said. "She seemed very lucid and confident in her manner."

Nathan's heart skipped a beat. To him, the judge's words sounded ominous.

"I explained that we were conducting an appeal hearing and that you had presented information that could indicate there had been no abuse or domestic violence in your relationship," the judge said.

He paused for a moment to let Nathan take that all in.

"I also explained to her that because of that information I was leaning toward lifting the order," Dixson said. But this time he did not give Nathan any time to absorb that.

"I then asked her if she was still in fear of her life," he explained. "Before she answered, I also told her that if she said no and the order was lifted, that action could work against any future restraining order requests."

Nathan sat up straight in his seat. He had no clue which direction this would go, but knowing Cynthia as he did, he was afraid her determination once she had made up her mind about something would bring the same answer she had given at the original hearing. He was gearing himself up for bad news.

"She told me that she was not in fear of her life," Dixson said.

Nathan sat staring straight at the judge, not fully comprehending what he had just said. The blank stare, like a deer in the headlights of an oncoming vehicle, remained on his face until Judge Dixson spoke again.

"I'm going to lift the restraining order," he said, then signed a piece of paper in front of him and passed it over to Nathan.

He read the wording of the document three times before it sank in. He looked up at the judge, the relief pouring out of his face like Niagara Falls. Dixson reached across the table and handed Nathan a pen, then pointed to a signature line with Nathan's name underneath. With a last look at the judge for confirmation, which came with a nod of his head, Nathan scribbled his signature and handed the document back to Dixson, who in turn gave it to the stenographer who left the room with it.

"It will take 24 hours for it to be recorded and distributed, but you will then be free to visit your family, if they agree to it," Dixson said.

Nathan was at a loss for words, but he did manage a "Thank you," that in retrospect was weaker than he thought was deserved.

"For what it's worth, and now that we are off the record, in speaking to your wife I read between the lines and I believe she never really was in fear of her life from you," Dixson said.

He could see the vindication fill Nathan.

With the restraining order lifted, Nathan could now go see his wife and daughter. But he was not sure what her state of mind was, or whether she would agree to him visiting. He did not want to make matters worse by going to see them if that is not what she wanted.

At the same time, he missed his family and wanted the three to be reunited. Cynthia was not only his wife, she had become his world through the years. He also did not want to lose any connection with his daughter. Being a father had been a dream for Nathan for years, even before he and Cynthia married and brought Stephanie into the world. Nathan's goals as a father were to be a much better one than his own father had been.

But he struggled with the conflict of just what to do now that the restraining order was lifted. Nathan did not want to make a mistake now that it seemed the door was open just a crack to bring the family back together.

Before he could work out a decision about how to move forward, his phone rang. It was his father-in-law.

"How are Cynthia and Stephanie?" he asked after the exchange of hellos.

"They are fine, physically," Kenneth said.

That did not set Nathan's mind at ease. The way his father-in-law phrased it indicated there were some problems.

"What do you mean, physically?" Nathan asked.

Kenneth paused before answering.

He had always liked Nathan, and the feeling was mutual. The two got along well. Kenneth respected the fact that Nathan treated his daughter with trust and respect, and worked hard to provide for her and his granddaughter. He would have liked to see them want for nothing, as they would have under his care. But Kenneth appreciated the efforts Nathan put forth in the marriage.

Kenneth also knew that Nathan loved and adored his daughter very much. It was clear to see whenever the couple visited them. Nathan doted on her, but at the same time was firm when it was necessary. Cynthia's father knew his daughter was a bit spoiled because of the way she was raised. He also knew that he and Jennifer would not always be around to provide for her in life. He was pleased she had married someone who would do his best to provide for her in every way.

For those reasons, he wanted to be honest with his son-in-law.

But Jennifer was more sentimental when it came to their daughter and how she should be cared for. Much of the influence in giving her everything she wanted when she was young came from her mother. And during her marriage Jennifer had been quick to send her daughter any amount of money her daughter asked for to take care of debts she and Nathan had that they could not keep up with. And that had been a lot in the last eighteen months.

Jennifer asked her husband not to share with Nathan all that had transpired since they had helped Cynthia leave Nathan. But despite his wife's over protectiveness of their daughter, Kenneth believed he needed to find a middle ground in what he said to Nathan.

"Stephanie is confused, she does not understand why her mother took her and left you," Kenneth said. "And Cynthia has been having her own difficulties."

Nathan could understand Stephanie's confusion. While he and Cynthia had their difficulties since their daughter was born, it was rarely displayed in front of her. He knew that from Stephanie's perspective, she had two very loving and caring parents, not just toward her but also toward each other.

But having gone through a broken home himself, he recalled that his mother had no emotional troubles when she decided to leave his father. Mary Anne was very determined in making that decision, and she went about it very methodically and in control of her emotions.

"What kind of difficulties?" Nathan asked.

"Just some trouble coming to grips with the decision she has made," Kenneth said.

Nathan heard him light a cigarette and take a long drag. Since Kenneth was smoking again – and Nathan could tell it was not just one every now and then – Nathan knew that the situation was making his father-in-law nervous. But he was oblivious of the real struggle going on in the man's mind.

"Is there anything I can do to help?" Nathan asked, hoping the answer would be yes.

"She is getting some counseling," Kenneth said. "I think that will help her."

"Do you think if I talked to her that would help or make things worse?" Nathan asked.

Kenneth pulled in a large amount of smoke and drew it into his lungs.

"I don't think that's a good idea right now," he answered. "But you can come over and see Stephanie. She wants to see her father."

Nathan could feel a lump swelling in his throat and tears ready to burst out of his eyes. It wasn't all he wanted to hear, but it was enough, and it was a start.

"I'll head that way first thing in the morning," Nathan said.

Nathan was anxious as he drove into town to visit his daughter. It had been a long drive, and he had a long time to think. Except for short stops to eat and relieve himself, Nathan drove straight through the five hundred fifty-mile, nine-hour trip.

What had Cynthia said to Stephanie about their leaving him? He could not tell from the transcript of the restraining order hearing that he got from the court whether his daughter had been at that original hearing. If she had heard anything said there, she certainly would be wondering whether she should trust her father. Would she even want to see him?

They were questions that nagged him throughout the drive.

He liked to think he had built such a good rapport with his daughter that she would love and trust him no matter what. But he was concerned about the same being true between Stephanie and her mother. It was hard to deny that the bond between mothers and daughters was stronger than between fathers and daughters. Was the bond he had with his daughter strong enough to weather any accusations?

As he pulled up in front of Kenneth's and Jennifer's home at about three o'clock in the afternoon, he sent his father-in-law a text to let him know he was there. Nathan approached the house with trepidation. The front door opened and Stephanie was there, hugging her grandfather's waist tightly. Nathan's heart began to pound in his chest and he was afraid it might burst out of his body.

She slowly began to smile and release her grip on her grandfather. She suddenly began running toward Nathan, and when she got to him, as he dropped to one knee, she threw her arms around his neck and squeezed so that Nathan believed he might lose his breath – as much from the hug as from relief.

"I missed you, Dad," Stephanie whispered in his ear, and he could hear the crack in her voice as she spoke.

"I missed you, too, Squirt," Nathan said, his own voice unsteady. He reached up and wiped the tears from his eyes before he pried his daughter loose and looked deeply into her eyes.

"How are you?" he asked. He dared not ask the other questions that were swirling through his mind.

"I'm okay," she answered. "But I want to go home. I want us all to go home."

Nathan did not know what to say. He wanted to reassure his daughter that that would eventually happen. But he also did not want to get her hopes up. He needed to know what Cynthia really wanted to do. Was she really intent on breaking up their family? It was a question he would have to delay the answer for until he had more information.

"I want that, too," he said. "We'll have to see what your mother wants."

"She doesn't want to live with you anymore," Stephanie said. "And she wants me to live with her."

"Did she tell you that?" Nathan asked.

"No, but I've heard her talking to Grandma and Grandpa and she said that to them," Stephanie told her father.

It was at that point that Kenneth came toward them.

"Let's go inside and talk, Nathan," he said.

Nathan got to his feet and began to follow Kenneth into the house. But Stephanie grabbed his hand and gently pulled.

"Can we go get some ice cream?" she asked. She was smiling, but Nathan could see it was an uneasy, faked smile. He glanced at Kenneth and could see that his father-in-law did not recognize it as such. He again implored Nathan to go inside the house so they could talk. Stephanie gave another gentle tug on her father's arm.

"We have time to talk later," Nathan said. "Since I now can, I want to spend some time with my daughter first."

Kenneth did not agree, but he knew there was no legal way for him to prevent it. Nathan read both in his father-in-law's face. He turned toward his car with Stephanie still gripping his hand.

While they sat on the park bench slowly licking their ice cream cones, Nathan learned a lot about what had transpired in the last several days. He asked no questions of his daughter, not wanting to pry anything out of her. He did not want to appear like he was forcing her to talk about what happened. As she talked, he listened and said only enough to reassure her that nothing was her fault.

In their conversation, he learned that Cynthia had been planning her departure for several months before she actually put the plan into action. He also learned that during that planning, she had been confiding in her daughter. During that time, she had said things about Nathan that no child of Stephanie's age – or any age – should have been told about a loving and caring father.

"She said you killed people and that you had sex with other women," Stephanie said. "She also said you were a thief."

Stephanie paused for a moment. Her father could tell she had something more to say, but was having trouble finding the right words. But he did not want to press her, so he waited patiently.

"Mom said you had sex with other women," she finally said haltingly. "She said you even had sex with a man."

Nathan was stunned. Kenneth had shared that his daughter had accused him of being sexually unfaithful, but he had no idea Stephanie knew about those accusations.

"She said that was why she needed to get away," Stephanie said.

Stephanie said the plan had been to pack up their belongings and they would leave while Nathan was at work in the middle of the week after they returned from selling the house. But the wreck on the freeway had thrown a monkey wrench into her plan, and she panicked.

Cynthia took advantage of the accident and the fact they had rented two vehicles. She and Stephanie would leave while Nathan was shopping for that new car to replace the Explorer that was totaled in the crash. But during his absence, Cynthia began to get paranoid that Nathan had discovered the plan and was waiting for them to get in the car. She switched to a different plan.

"She called Grandpa to come and get us," Stephanie said. "She said he would protect us if you tried to do anything to us to keep us there."

When Stephanie seemed to be winding down her sharing, Nathan hugged her and told her everything would be okay. She looked up at him, worry remained in her eyes, and it tore at his heart. His reassurances appeared to be falling on deaf ears.

"Dad, she said she doesn't love you anymore," his daughter said. "If she can stop loving you, when will she stop loving me?"

Nathan felt as if someone reached inside his chest and was squeezing his heart with vice grips.

"No, Squirt, your mother will never stop loving you," he said without hesitation. "She's your mother, she'll always love you."

Stephanie's expression told him those words had comforted her some, but not completely. He knew this was going to take some time for his daughter to heal.

Chapter 8

Nathan sat on the end of the plush leather-covered sofa in the living room of the McAdams home. He had been there multiple times before, and nothing seemed changed.

The living room walls were of oak paneling, resembling the décor of a 1960s home. In addition to the leather sofa, there was a love seat and two over-size chairs. They were all covered in the same leather of a light gray hue. The furniture was spread around the room with a large brick fireplace on one wall. In front of the sofa was a large rectangular coffee table with both ends open and supported by four ornate legs connecting to a lower deck. In the center was a storage space with doors on each side.

He was alone in the room. Jennifer had gone to the store and taken Stephanie with her. Kenneth wanted time to talk with Nathan. He came into the room and set a tall glass of ice water on a coaster in front of Nathan, then sat at the other end of the sofa with a cup of coffee in his hand. He took a sip and set the cup on a coaster at the other end of the table.

There was a tense silence before either man spoke.

"I suppose Stephanie talked to you about her mother," Kenneth finally said. It was not a question. He knew his granddaughter would speak freely with her father.

Nathan nodded a confirmation.

"I was hoping I could explain it to you," his father-in-law said. "I really didn't want her to be in the middle."

"But since she is our daughter, she is in the middle," Nathan said. He then quickly reviewed what Stephanie had told him.

Kenneth sipped his coffee throughout without offering even a hint of a reaction.

"Is what she said accurate?" Nathan asked.

Kenneth nodded before answering.

"Yes, Stephanie gave you an accurate account," Kenneth answered somewhat business-like.

"And do you believe what she said about me?" Nathan asked.

Kenneth put his head in his hands and rubbed his face for a few seconds. When he lowered his hands, there was a pained look on his face. That unnerved Nathan, believing his answer would be yes.

"No, Nathan, I do not believe you are a serial killer, thief or gay," Kenneth said slowly.

Nathan noticed Kenneth did not address the accusation of infidelity. That made the anger rise in him.

"But you apparently believe I cheated on her," Nathan said.

Kenneth's answer came slowly and deliberately.

"Nathan, I don't believe you are that kind of man," he said, then paused for a few seconds. "But I can't completely rule it out."

His father-in-law's response did not fill him with confidence. Nathan's fidelity was a source of pride to him. There was nothing that would drive him to have sex, or even any kind of feelings of love or lust, for any woman other than his wife. Had he been that kind of man it would have happened by now, he had opportunities from time to time and had turned away from each one.

"Well, I have never cheated on your daughter – ever," Nathan said as he stood up. "I don't know how to prove that to you."

He began to leave the room, intending to leave the house and wait in his car for his daughter's return. But Kenneth stood and stopped him by gently touching his upper arm. Nathan stopped, but pulled away from his father-in-law's touch. He continued to face away from him.

"I'm sorry, Nathan, but that's my honest feelings," Kenneth said.

Not looking back, Nathan continued out to his car.

Nathan was on the road back to Nebraska and the home he and Cynthia had shared. There were things he had to take care of. While waiting for Stephanie to return to her grandparents' home, he had made some decisions about what to do now.

He had hoped to be able to talk to Cynthia before leaving, but Kenneth and Jennifer told him she was spending time in a halfway house while she received counseling. Nathan had wanted to bring his daughter with him on this trip, but his in-laws argued against it. Their stance was that if he took Stephanie, her mother would react badly. They hinted that another restraining order could be part of that reaction. Nathan did not share with them what Judge Dixon had said about the chances of another restraining order if Cynthia pulled back on her claim that she was in fear of her life.

"Let them find out for themselves if they try," he thought.

Jennifer also hinted that Nathan could very well not return Stephanie to their home. Nathan took her not-so-subtle words to mean Jennifer believed Stephanie belonged with them and not her father. That infuriated Nathan, but he bit his lip and did not argue that point.

Nathan, who thought he had every right to take his daughter wherever he pleased since there was no custody ruling by a court, reluctantly agreed. He did not want to give his wife any reason to restrict his access to their daughter.

Stephanie had wanted to go with her father, but he talked to her and convinced her it was best for her to stay with her grandparents for the time being. Since they were alone when they talked, he also shared with her one of his decisions – to move back to Illinois – which helped Stephanie accept his argument to stay. However, he asked her not to share that decision with Kenneth and Jennifer.

Nathan was nearly an hour away from home when his cell phone ringtone went off. It was his brother, Bryan.

"How are you holding up?" he asked once the greetings were exchanged.

"I'm doing okay under the circumstances," Nathan answered.

He then reviewed the latest developments and shared his near future plans. They also chatted about the rest of the family.

"Listen, Nathan, I have something I want to run by you," Bryan said with some conviction in his voice. "If Cynthia is dead set on divorce, you need to be with your daughter."

"I will be trying to get custody if it comes to that," Nathan said.

"You know how the courts are about that, they nearly always give custody to the mother, whether she is the better parent or not," Bryan said. Still a bachelor, Bryan had no first-hand knowledge of custody situations. But he had friends who did.

"I can help make sure you get her," Bryan said.

"How can you do that?" Nathan asked, not just out of curiosity. He would be grateful for any advantage he could get.

"I can go to her grandparents and say I want to visit with her," Bryan began to explain. "They know me and I think they would trust me."

"How would that help?" Nathan asked. "I don't want anyone trying to make Stephanie pick sides."

"What I can do is take her away with me," his brother answered. "I can take her to a place where no one would find us. Then I can let you know where and I can help you do the same. I have a pack trip coming up. I can do it then."

Bryan had served in the Army Special Forces and had been honorably discharged after serving two tours in Iraq. He now owned his own business as an outfitter and guide in the Rocky Mountains. He had the survival training and knowhow to accomplish the task.

Nathan pulled to the side of the road and put the car in park. He was horrified at the idea and surprised his brother did not see the flaws in the plan he presented.

"No, don't do anything like that," Nathan said. "I appreciate what you think you would be doing for me, but don't even think about it."

Bryan presented a few arguments about why it was the best option. But Nathan was adamant.

"She's been yanked out of her home, school and away from her father, I don't want to have that done to her again," Nathan said.

His brother finally agreed to not abduct his niece and Nathan breathed a sigh of relief. But for the rest of this trip and as he carried out the decisions he had made, he wondered if he had made the right choice about his brother's plan.

Nathan poked at the scrambled eggs on his plate at the restaurant he managed. The business's owner sat across from him.

"Are you sure this is what you want to do?" Armin Yablonski asked. "You are the best manager I've ever had and the place has never done so well, even in this economy."

Armin was not a hands-on owner. He relied heavily on good managers for the restaurant and the three other diverse businesses he owned in the area.

"It won't be easy, but I'll find a way to give you a raise," he went on.

Nathan slowly shook his head.

"I appreciate it, Armin. You have been very good to me, especially in the last couple of weeks," Nathan said. "But I want to get my family back, and I think my best shot is being near them."

Armin heaved a long sigh.

"As you wish," he said. "I will pay you for the time you have been away and give you your two weeks of vacation pay, plus another two weeks."

Nathan was flattered, and knew he could use the money. But he did not want to take advantage of Armin's generosity.

"No, Armin, that's too much," he said. "I know you're strapped where the restaurant is concerned, no matter how much business it has been doing."

"I won't take no for an answer, my dear boy," Armin said. "Besides, I have a selfish motive." There was a twinkle in his eyes.

Armin suddenly got up from the booth and headed toward the small office. He returned shortly and handed Nathan a check that contained all that he had promised. When Nathan pushed it back across the table toward him, Armin folded it and reached across the table and slid it into Nathan's polo shirt pocket.

"You will take it, my boy, because you need it," he said. "And I have a proposition for you."

Nathan took a half-hearted bite of cold bacon, ready to listen.

"I will be calling you from time to time with questions about the restaurant until I can find the right manager; and that might take a while," Armin said. "Each time I call you, I'll send a small stipend."

Nathan said nothing, but Armin knew he could count on him.

"And, I have some business connections over there and if you need any reference, you have them call me," Armin said before sliding out of the booth and leaving before Nathan could give back the check or refuse the consulting arrangement.

Gathering his and his family's possessions was a stressful task for Nathan. Back in their apartment with a moving truck outside, he packed items in boxes. It was difficult when he packed items that belonged to his wife. It only reminded him of her plans to divorce him and take their child from him.

Nathan was not alone in the work. Word spread during his absence from the restaurant about what was happening in his life. Throughout the day, restaurant employees who weren't scheduled to work and some of the regular customers dropped by to help where they could.

With so much help, it only took a few hours to pack the apartment items into the truck. When that was done Nathan and a few helpers went to the storage unit where the remainder of the family's belongings were in a ten-foot by ten-foot unit.

Later that evening, Armin closed the restaurant to the public and hosted a going away dinner for Nathan. All those who helped with the packing attended and several other regular customers were also there. It was an emotional event for Nathan, who was overwhelmed with all the support.

He spent the night at Armin's home and early the next morning he drove to the city's small airport to meet his sister, Carolyn, who chartered a flight so she could drive his car while he drove the truck.

"How are you doing?" Carolyn asked as they hugged in the arrival terminal. Nathan had heard the question so often lately he was getting tired of it. That was mostly because the answer continued to be the same.

"The best I can under the circumstances," he said.

His emotional state was not getting any better.

"Well, it will get better," Carolyn said. "Just give it time."

Nathan was not optimistic, but he appreciated his sister's attempt to build him up.

Nathan wanted to get on the road as soon as possible. Carolyn lived in a town about an hour away from the city where the McAdamses lived. She insisted he stay at her house until he found a job and a home of his own. Carolyn was divorced and had gotten a large home in the settlement so there was plenty of room.

The nine-hour trip was a bit grueling. It was not the first time Nathan had driven a large moving truck, as he had done so during his family's previous moves. But after so many years of marriage and with a child, it was a bigger truck this time. Add to that the stress and tension he felt over the apparent family breakup and it was hard work.

They had gone only a few miles when they made a quick stop to grab some fast food breakfast. A few hours later they made a longer stop for lunch, this time at a quaint little sit down diner along the two-lane highway. It seemed like the longest day in history by the time they parked in Carolyn's driveway.

"Do you know Dad has been calling asking about you?" Carolyn asked the next morning at her home following a restful night's sleep for both of them.

"He said he's been calling your phone but you haven't been answering," his sister went on. "He is worried about you."

Nathan had not spoken to his father in quite some time. Ever since he and Cynthia had taken Stephanie to see him shortly after her birth and he had displayed such a dismissive attitude about his granddaughter, their relationship, such as it was, slowly eroded further until Nathan had no interest in seeing or even talking to him.

Not that there had been much of a relationship anyway.

George had asked his son once shortly after he finished college and had been living in his father's home why they never had a relationship. Nathan was a little astounded at the question. Surely his father knew the answer to that.

"It just seems that over the years you seemed to have not cared much about having a relationship with me," Nathan said.

"Whatever gave you that idea?" George asked defensively.

There were any number of signs, as far as Nathan was concerned. George's refusal to go back and be introduced as Nathan's father at that last basketball game, he hadn't gone to his high school graduation, he left the state right after the divorce and remarried, his doting on his new wife's children. And then there was George's refusal to attend Nathan's and Cynthia's college graduation.

But Nathan did not want to bring all that up. He was not interested in rehashing the past. What he was most interested in was moving forward.

"There were a lot of things, Dad; but I don't want to make an issue out of any of it. All that will happen is that you will make excuses, and that's just going to make things worse," Nathan said.

George pondered that for a moment. He believed his "excuses" were valid. But it was hard to argue his son's logic. He knew the two of them had different views on life and they were both stubborn, unwilling to give an inch.

While that was strictly true of George, Nathan was a little more willing to give a little, but only if his father would reciprocate. But he knew that would never happen.

"So where do we go from here?" George asked.

"I'm open to a relationship if you want one," Nathan said. "But it has to be a two-way relationship."

His father agreed. But it hadn't worked out that way. As much as Nathan reached out to his father after that, George hardly took the initiative himself to make contact. Finally, Nathan got tired of always being the one to call, write or initiate visits.

What he did not know, even as he sat at his sister's kitchen table facing her, was that the roles he and his father had played when he was in high school were reversed. Now it was George who was desperate to gain the love and respect of his son.

"I'm not so sure he does care about me, or any of his kids," Nathan told Carolyn. "He is more devoted to his step children than he ever was to his own."

Carolyn had no answer. She shared her brother's outlook on their father's approach to his own blood children.

"But still, maybe you should give him a call," she said, without much conviction.

"I'll think about it," Nathan answered, knowing at that moment what his thoughts on the matter would produce.

Nathan wasted no time job and apartment hunting. He was out that same day.

There were a few prospects on both fronts. Not all of them were completely satisfactory. On the job front, only a few places had openings. There were two restaurants and an auto repair shop. The restaurant openings were for wait staff, while Nathan was hoping for management. His knowledge of auto mechanics was only the basics – changing oil, tire repair, things that most men knew. But he was a quick study and knew he could pick it up in time.

He left applications at each location.

The fourth option was a sporting goods store. There was an assistant manager position open and Nathan thought this was his best prospect. He also left an application there.

For housing, Nathan wanted to find a place that was big enough for his family, either an apartment or a house. While there were smaller apartments that would work better financially for his current situation, he was confident he would find a way to reunite his family and wanted to be prepared.

But the prospects in that level of housing were hard to find, and the ones available were more expensive than his budget could stand, at least until he got a job and had built up some savings.

As he was about to look at another home, his cell phone went off.

"Hello," he spoke into it.

"Nathan, you need to get back here as quickly as you can," his sister said. He could tell she had been crying, and was on the verge of another outburst of tears.

"What's wrong?" he asked.

"There is someone dead at Stephanie's school," Carolyn said.

Nathan's heart skipped a beat and a large lump formed in his throat. His knees sagged and he went into a squat, then fell forward to his knees. With the Realtor at his side looking very puzzled, but concerned, Nathan stared straight ahead as if in a trace. He felt the bile rising in his throat, but it couldn't get past the lump. Nor could the words he was thinking.

"Oh my God!"

Slowly he heard Carolyn speaking and the words finally came into his comprehension range.

"Stephanie is alive, as far as we know," she said. "But she is missing."

"What do you mean missing?" Nathan was finally able to clear the lump, swallow the bile back into his stomach and speak.

"Someone took her, Nathan," Carolyn said, then her dam burst and the tears and wailing roared out.

Chapter 9

After making the drive from Carolyn's house to Stephanie's school in forty minutes, a trip that normally took one hour, Nathan pulled into the school parking lot to find much of it taken up by law enforcement and emergency vehicles and parents' cars picking up their children.

The middle school included nearly 180 students and a staff of about 20, so it was mass confusion.

Nathan parked on the street and started jogging toward the school's main entrance. He found it and a large area around it bordered by yellow police tape. He tried to duck under the tape, but a city police officer rushed over and grabbed his arm.

"You can't cross that tape, sir, there's been an incident here," the officer said.

"I know that," Nathan shouted. "My daughter was kidnapped."

The officer loosened, but held, his grip on Nathan's arm. He asked him to produce an identification. Nathan fished out his wallet and displayed his driver's license.

"Come with me, sir," the officer said and, still holding his arm, guided him toward a large Christian County Sheriff's Office tactical trailer. He ushered him inside and followed.

"This is the missing girl's father, Nathan Wallis," the city policeman told the first deputy he encountered. The deputy motioned Nathan to an empty chair and he sat down as the city officer left the trailer. After making a quick call, the deputy took a seat across from Nathan.

"What happened to my daughter?" Nathan asked before the deputy could speak.

"It appears, sir, that she was taken by an adult male," The deputy said. "And this man killed someone before taking her."

"Oh God," Nathan blurted out, then went on. "Do you have any idea who took her? Do you know where she is?"

The deputy sighed before answering.

"No, sir, we have no suspects and we do not know where your daughter was taken." He knew that would increase the father's anxiety, but he did not want to give him false hope.

"How do we find her?" Nathan asked, holding back the tears ready to burst out.

"We are very busy investigating, but I can't share anything on an ongoing investigation," the deputy said. "But we will apprise you when we do have something to share."

The deputy stood, and Nathan knew the conversation was over. He slowly stood himself, but did not move.

"I suggest you give us your contact information so we can get back to you when it is time," the deputy instructed.

Nathan gave the deputy his cell phone number and Carolyn's address, explaining that he was staying there for the time being. But Nathan had no intention of returning to Carolyn's until he knew more about the whereabouts of his daughter. He walked to his car then drove to the McAdams home.

If Nathan had thought it through, he would not have gone to the McAdams home.

When Cynthia learned that Stephanie had been taken from the school, she left the safe house and went to her parents' home. She was in a frenzy and had one suspect in mind.

"Nathan took her," she said to her parents.

Jennifer gasped and said he was the most logical person to suspect. But Kenneth was not convinced.

"I don't think Nathan is that kind of man," he said.

Jennifer jumped in before her daughter could speak.

"Of course he is," she said angrily. "He wants that little girl all to himself. I've known it all along."

Kenneth put his hands on his wife's shoulders and spoke as calmly and gently as he could.

"I don't think that is the case," he said. "He hasn't shown anything like that to me. And you've never said anything like that before."

Jennifer broke away from his grasp and went to her daughter, putting her arm around her.

"I kept it to myself for Cynthia's sake," she snarled at her husband. "But now we see just what kind of man he is."

Kenneth shook his head. He knew he wasn't going to convince his wife to see Nathan in any other light. And in many ways, he could have predicted her attitude at this time. There had always been some uneasiness in Jennifer where Nathan was concerned.

But he had never seen that from his daughter. Cynthia had always appeared to feel nothing but love and respect for her husband. But he could see, ever since he and Jennifer had picked up the mother and daughter and brought them home, that there was a change in her. He could see that continue to evolve even now.

Without another word, Kenneth left the house and headed for the school. He wanted to find out as much as he could about the situation.

Nathan arrived at the house before Kenneth returned. He expected to see his father-in-law open the front door after he rang the doorbell. But it was Jennifer instead, and Nathan's hopes fell.

"What do you think you are doing here?" his mother-in-law snapped.

Nathan paused to push down the anger that rose in him with her terse greeting.

"I want to see Cynthia," he said.

"She does not want to see you," Jennifer said, still with the snappy tone.

Nathan noticed movement behind his mother-in-law.

"Cynthia, is that you?" Nathan asked. "I just want to talk to you."

Jennifer started to speak, but her daughter cut her off, though still remaining behind her out of Nathan's line of sight.

"I have nothing to say to you except let my daughter go," she said timidly.

Since Cynthia had already sent the message through her father that she wanted a divorce, Nathan knew there would be custody to settle.

"We can work something out, if you'll just talk to me," he said.

"No," Cynthia said much less timidly. "You bring her back here right now."

For an instant, the meaning of her statement did not register. She had taken Stephanie when she took off several days ago. Why would she now be demanding he return her?

Then suddenly that sledge hammer of comprehension pounded it into his brain.

"You think I took her from the school?" Nathan said. "I can't believe you would think I would do something like that."

"Well, we do, and I'm going to call the police," Jennifer said before slamming the door in Nathan's face.

With the events at the McAdams house, Nathan's mind was spinning, trying to figure out what was going on in his life. His marriage was in serious doubt now that his wife was claiming she wanted a divorce, his daughter turned up missing and his wife and mother-in-law, and maybe even his father-in-law, considered him the kidnapping suspect.

As he drove aimlessly around town, another thought crashed into his brain. He remembered his brother Bryan's offer to take Stephanie and hide her away until her father could join her. Nathan protested, and Bryan appeared to agree. But had he carried out his plan despite his brother's refusal?

He pulled out his phone and speed-dialed Bryan's number. After three rings it went to voicemail.

"This is Bryan. I'm either out in the woods or in the bedroom with a hottie. Leave a message and I'll get back to you."

Every other time Nathan heard his brother's voicemail greeting he had to laugh. Bryan was less active with the ladies than he wanted people to believe. But Nathan did not see the humor in it this time.

"Bryan, this is Nathan. Stephanie is missing," he recorded. "Did you take her even though I told you not to?"

He ended the call, knowing that if Bryan had done so, he would not call back. But if he did not, he would get ahold of Nathan as soon as he got the message.

Just as he ended the call, he heard the shrill screech of a police siren. Looking in his mirror, he saw the red and blue lights flashing. How long the officer had been following him he did not know, so wrapped up in his own thoughts and the frantic call to his brother's voicemail.

Nathan quickly pulled to the curb and turned off the engine. As he pulled out his wallet to get his driver's license and insurance card, he searched his memory to see what he had done to warrant a traffic stop. Nothing came to mind, and he was certain he had not exceeded the speed limit. He wondered if Illinois was one of those states that made it illegal to use a cell phone while driving.

With the cards in his right hand, Nathan pushed the button to open the driver's side window. He noticed a sheriff's deputy advancing cautiously with his right hand on the butt of the revolver in the holster at his hip. Nathan began to lean to his right to open the glove compartment to get the vehicle registration.

"Don't make another move!"

Nathan heard the distinct sound of cold, hard steel sliding out of leather simultaneous with the shouted command. He looked to the left to see the deputy with his gun drawn and pointing into the vehicle from a few feet away. He was holding the pistol in a two-handed shooting stance. Nathan turned his head so he was looking straight ahead and eye-rolled to the right and saw another deputy in the same posture on the other side of the car.

"Slowly sit up and put your hands outside the window," the driver's side deputy demanded.

Nathan complied, moving as slow as he could, but making sure the deputy could see that he was doing what he was told. When his hands were outside the car, the deputy released his left hand from the gun and took the cards from Nathan's hand. He looked at them quickly then put them back in Nathan's hand. He opened the car door.

"Please exit the vehicle," the deputy said. "Slowly."

Once Nathan was standing facing the deputy, his partner moved from the passenger side of the car to keep Nathan covered.

"Turn and face the car," the deputy said. "Put your hands on top of the car, take one step back and spread your legs."

If it weren't happening to him, Nathan would have laughed at the commands, almost exactly like what he had seen on numerous cop shows on television. But he could tell by the demeaner of the deputies that this was not the time for levity, or of making any noise whatsoever.

While the second deputy kept Nathan covered with his drawn weapon, the lead man frisked him with his left hand while keeping his pistol drawn but pointing it straight up to his right. The deputy was quite thorough, and Nathan couldn't help flinching a little when the officer's hands moved up his leg into his crotch. The reaction must have been normal, since neither officer seemed to notice. But Nathan again bit his tongue to keep from making a wisecrack about a "hidden weapon" in that area of his body – "Is that a gun in your pants or are you just happy to see me?"

The deputy then ordered him to put his right hand on the top of his head and leave the other on the car. Nathan heard the pistol slide back into the holster and felt the handcuff enclose around his wrist then his arm moved down to the small of his back. Then the left hand was moved down and secured in the other cuff. The deputy took the cards from Nathan's hand and the other deputy reached inside the car and grabbed the keys and Nathan's cell phone.

"We'll come back and search the car after we get him to the command post," the lead deputy said.

As the sheriff's vehicle drove away with Nathan in the back seat, he hoped the officers had locked his car.

Nathan sat on a hard metal folding chair in a corner of the command trailer in the school parking lot. He was still handcuffed.

Several officers, both city police and sheriff's deputies, came in and out of the trailer. Their time in the trailer was spent updating the man who seemed to be in charge seated at a small desk with a laptop in front of him on the other end of the command post. Nathan heard the officers call him sheriff.

From what he could overhear, Nathan learned that a female teacher had been killed during his daughter's abduction. It appeared she had been struck on the head. It sounded to Nathan like the teacher died nearly instantly, although that would not be certain until after an autopsy was completed.

Nathan also learned the police did not have anyone definitely identified as the teacher's assailant. There were no security cameras at the school or in the parking lot. There were no businesses in the area, but the school property was surrounded by homes. He also learned that while no one had seen the kidnapping of Stephanie or the killing of the teacher, officers were continuing interviews of students and school staff, as well as canvassing the residential neighborhood in the area.

His disappointment in the lack of progress in locating his daughter was mounting. So much so that he had not given a thought to why he had been taken into custody. The two deputies who arrested him had not said a word on the way to the school and they deposited him in the command trailer and left.

But he was about to get an education.

The sheriff stood and slowly walked to where Nathan was sitting and pulled up another folding chair and sat across from him. There was nothing in between them and the sheriff was so close their knees were nearly touching.

"Mr. Wallis, my name is Frank Martin. I am the sheriff of this county," he said.

Nathan nodded, but remained silent.

"We are doing everything we can to find your daughter, but I think you can help us with that," Martin said.

"I'll do whatever I can to get my daughter back," Nathan responded, shooting a quick glance over his shoulder and downward, trying to imply the handcuffs should be removed.

"Then why don't you tell me where she is," the sheriff said.

Nathan was stunned. How could anyone think he knew where Stephanie was at that moment. He had not seen her since he dropped her off at school several days ago in a city far from here.

"How would I know that?" Nathan asked a little testily.

"Come now, Mr. Wallis, your wife left you and took your daughter and says she wants a divorce," the sheriff said. "I've seen my share of cases where a father, knowing he's going to lose a custody fight, takes the kids."

"That's not what happened here," Nathan shot back. Obviously, Kenneth, Jennifer and probably Cynthia had laid out the details of what happened to the family in the last few days.

"And your wife and mother-in-law seem to think you took her," Martin said.

Nathan felt his heart seem to skip a beat. He remembered Jennifer saying they would call the police when he was at the house. But at the time he considered it an idle threat.

"Tell me, sheriff, in those cases you mentioned, was there any times when a mother took her children after the father took off with them?" Nathan asked with a touch a sarcasm.

"Do you think that is what happened?" Martin asked, pointedly not answering Nathan's question.

"I don't know," he answered. "But I'm not saying it's impossible."

"Are you going to tell me where your daughter is?" the sheriff asked as he leaned in closer.

"If I knew where she was," Nathan answered, starting to get angry.

The sheriff sat up straight in his chair, sighed and took a small notepad from his front shirt pocket.

"Alright, why don't you tell me your activities the last several days," Martin said with a pen poised above the pad.

"Am I under arrest?" Nathan asked.

"Not at this time," Martin said. "Right now you are a person of interest."

"Then you need to remove these handcuffs," Nathan said.

"You are not in a position to make demands here, Mr. Wallis," the sheriff said as he leaned in closer to Nathan's face.

"As long as I am in these handcuffs, I will assume I am under arrest," Nathan said. "Plus, no one has read me my rights. As long as I am cuffed, I want to have an attorney present for any further questioning."

The sheriff sat up in the chair again. He stared at Nathan for a few moments. The stern expression he had worn since he sat down began to soften. Then he reached into another pocket, drew out a key and stood up. He went behind Nathan, unlocked and removed the handcuffs and sat down in his chair again.

"Now, about your activities," The sheriff said, with the pad and pen in his hands again.

Nathan gave him an overview of what had happened before and after Cynthia and Stephanie had disappeared. He was more detailed in his summary for the past 24 hours. Nathan gave the sheriff a list of all the places he had been looking for a job and a home that day and the contact information for each that he could recall. He told the sheriff there was a list at his sister's home that included the information he could not remember.

"And why did you go to your in-laws' home today?" the sheriff asked.

"I wanted to talk to Kenneth, my father-in-law," Nathan answered.

"Why?" Martin asked.

"I wanted to talk to him. He has always been upfront with me," Nathan said.

Suddenly, he wondered just how much he could trust Kenneth to be truthful with him now. He wasn't sure if it was because of the sheriff's curiosity about it or the possibility that Kenneth and Jennifer, and maybe even Cynthia, were behind Stephanie's abduction.

But with the death of the teacher, Nathan had a hard time believing his wife or her parents would have gone so far as murder to take the young girl.

"So, you had a good relationship with your in-laws?" the sheriff asked.

"With my father-in-law for sure," Nathan said. "But I don't think my mother-in-law ever really liked me."

"Why is that?" Martin asked.

"She didn't think I was good enough for her daughter," Nathan said. "Cynthia and her brother, Bart, were pretty much given everything they wanted by their parents."

Martin made a few notes on the pad, then sat pensive for a few moments. Then a female deputy came into the trailer and got his attention.

"Sheriff, we've got some information from the canvass of the neighborhood," she said.

Martin excused himself, telling Nathan to stay where he was for the time being. He gave the deputy a gesture to stay in the trailer and keep watch.

When the sheriff returned, he walked right past Nathan and to the small desk at the other end of the trailer. He was followed by two deputies who sat in chairs on the other side of the desk. The sheriff listened as the deputies shared some information with him. However, they spoke in near whispers and Nathan could not hear any details from the conversation.

Finally, the two deputies got up and walked the length of the trailer to the door near where Nathan was sitting. Nathan noticed they did not look in his direction.

The sheriff made several phone calls, keeping his voice low enough that Nathan could not hear his side of the conversations. After about ten minutes, the sheriff walked over and sat down in the same folding chair across from Nathan.

"It seems all of the contacts you gave us verified that you were at their location this morning," the sheriff said.

"So that means I'm free to go then," Nathan said. Having sat in the command center for more than an hour with no conversation and with the female deputy staring at him constantly, he was quite edgy. He tried to keep the anger out of his tone, but he was only partially successful.

"The fact that your activities were verified only tells us that you were not directly involved in the abduction of your daughter and the murder of the teacher," the sheriff said with a bit of an edge in his voice. "That does not exclude the possibility that you could have had someone do it for you."

Nathan wanted to protest his innocence again. But he could feel the anger boiling up inside him and he did not want to give any of the law enforcement gathered at the school any reason to further suspect him – or worse.

"Am I to stay in custody then?" he asked.

The sheriff mulled the question for a few moments. He looked Nathan over from head to toe, as if he were sizing up a steer at the auction house.

"You are no longer in custody," the sheriff finally said. Nathan began to stand up, but the sheriff put his hand on his shoulder and eased him back onto the chair.

"But your car is still being processed and checked for any evidence," he told Nathan. "And I would like you to stick around here until it is ready."

"But I can get my sister to pick me up and you can let me know when my car is ready," Nathan said. "All you need to do is give me my cell phone back."

The sheriff shook his head.

"Here's the thing, Mr. Wallis," the sheriff said. "Until we can positively exclude you as a suspect, we consider you a flight risk."

Nathan began to protest, but the sheriff held up his index finger to indicate he had more to say.

"That being the case, officially we should put you in jail until that is determined," he said. "But, if you are involved or not, I believe you can be a help in this investigation, so I want you close at hand."

The sheriff indicated the female deputy.

"Deputy Barnes here will be your shadow while you are on these premises, or anywhere else we want you to be," the sheriff said.

Deputy Dawn Barnes' only reaction was to give the sheriff a slight nod.

Nathan could see that the sheriff was giving him some leeway. It was possible the sheriff believed he was not involved in the crimes. Nathan only hoped he was right about that.

Chapter 10

Frank Martin was four months away from completing his fourth year as county sheriff. Prior to that, he had been a city policeman for ten years before being elevated to the chief's position for another ten. In those twenty years, he had never been part of a murder case.

Neither had he been part of a kidnapping case, although there had been plenty of custody disputes between divorcing parents. On the surface, that part of this case looked like another custody dispute.

He sat in the command post, still roosting in the school parking lot, going through the evidence that had been collected so far. There was still more to gather, but so far it was slim pickings.

There was a certain amount of pressure to solve this case and do so quickly. Some of that pressure came from the fact that in four months county voters would elect a new sheriff, and Frank was on the ballot, most likely for the last time. Blowing a big case like this meant he would be on the unemployment lines for the first time since college. But more likely it would mean his plans for a long overdue retirement would be pushed forward by four years.

At 62 Martin was ready for retirement. He only put his name on the ballot with the idea that one more term as sheriff would mark four decades in law enforcement for him. He liked the idea of that round number. But if he didn't make it there, that would be okay, too.

Pressure also came from the fact that the kidnapping victim was the maternal grandchild of Kenneth McAdam, a big fish in the city. Kenneth did not have a direct line of communication to Frank, but he did have the city police chief's ear. And he kept calling him to get updates and the chief, in turn, pestered Frank.

It made concentrating on the task at hand difficult.

"I understand the pressure you are under with this guy," Frank told Chief Bob Talbott in their last telephone exchange just twenty minutes earlier. "But I can't give you what I don't have."

"It's not just for Mr. McAdams that I am asking," Talbott protested, then thought better of it. "Well, actually, it is. But the guy keeps bugging me and I need to give him something."

This was the part of the job that Frank, and Talbott, hated the most – dealing with pushy people aways wanting to know the intimate details of cases. Sharing the details of ongoing investigations was frowned upon by nearly all law enforcement agencies. But people, especially families of victims, just did not understand.

"Doesn't he understand we can't just share our information willy-nilly? Doesn't he understand how that can undermine investigations?" Frank asked.

"I believe he does, but he's got his own pressures to deal with," Talbott said. "His daughter's got him by the ear and his wife has him by the balls."

Frank nodded to himself. He understood the type. In fact, in his 16 years as county sheriff, he was well acquainted with the McAdames. He had had his own run-ins with them over the years.

Now poring over what little evidence his deputies and city police officers had gathered so far, he felt his own frustration rising. With nothing much to go on, the logical place for him to look for a suspect was the father who was facing the real possibility of losing his only child in a custody battle. How many times had he seen parents – both mothers and fathers – take their children in a fit of panic, thinking spiriting them away would guarantee the children would remain with them.

That was rarely how it worked out.

While on the surface Nathan was the most logical suspect, Frank was not certain he should be. To start with, because all the whereabouts and activities Nathan had given the officers were verified, Frank was having a hard time putting together a timeline that would put Nathan at the school at the time of the kidnap and killing.

And if it were a custody kidnapping, there were plenty of other suspects to go around. For starters, there was the other parent. It was entirely possible that Cynthia had hidden her daughter somewhere with the hope that she could join her very soon in some undisclosed location. Her parents certainly had the financial means to help her make that happen.

Then there were Cynthia's parents. In an interview with Nathan's sister, Carolyn, one of the deputies reported she had told how Stephanie was the McAdamses' only grandchild, and how Cynthia's brother, Bart, and his wife had no plans to have their own children.

"They were always so possessive of Stephanie," Carolyn had told the deputy. She added how one Christmas the Wallises were having trouble with the only vehicle they had, so much so that it looked like they would not be able to make the trip to the McAdamses' for the holiday. Kenneth, following his wife's urgings, was in the midst of buying Nathan and Cynthia a new car. But when the salesman from the dealership in the city where Nathan and Cynthia were living at the time called Nathan to come down and take possession of the vehicle, her brother had refused. When he called Kenneth to tell him, in no uncertain terms, he did not want the vehicle purchased for them, he cancelled the deal.

"They did not go to Nathan's in-laws that Christmas, and Jennifer was so distraught about it, she had a nervous breakdown," Carolyn told the deputy.

Nathan's siblings were also not above suspicion. Bryan, who lived and worked in Colorado, was interviewed by a policeman in his city and Tessa was also interviewed by an officer from the New York Police Department.

Frank considered taking Bryan and Tessa off the suspect list because they were too far away to have committed the crimes. But it was possible they could have enlisted someone to kidnap their niece. However, an endeavor like that would take time to plan and set up. Even considering that Nathan had told his brother and sister

91

about Cynthia's desire for divorce as soon as he learned of it, the sheriff was not convinced there was enough time to put such a plan in motion.

But it was not impossible. So, they remained on the list.

Because of her proximity to the city in which Stephanie's school was located, Carolyn also had plenty of opportunity. Reading over the reports of the respective officers' interviews with Carolyn, Frank saw there were windows of opportunity in her activities of that morning for her to have abducted the girl. They were very tight windows, but they were possibilities.

But Frank was having a hard time making a connection with the girl's abduction and the killing of the teacher.

He was trying to puzzle that out when one of his deputies dashed into the trailer.

"Sheriff, we've got something," he said a little out of breath.

The sheriff and two of his deputies, along with the city police chief, sat around the small desk in the command center with a laptop connected to a seventeen-inch monitor.

During the canvas of the residential neighborhood, officer found one house that had a door bell camera and another that had security cameras. Both were positioned in a way that the school entrance was in the background.

However, the fisheye nature of those cameras did not allow for a clear shot of the school. The majority of the images they were watching showed the front yards of the residences where the cameras were located and the streets in front of them.

The doorbell camera was located right across the street from the school's main entrance. The other was located on a right-angle street. The doorbell camera images had some blockage from parked vehicles, but about 70 percent of the entrance could be seen. The video from the other camera showed the entrance more clearly, with nearly 100 percent of it visible.

The officers were disappointed before they even began viewing the videos.

"We're not going to see much from these," the city police chief said, throwing up his hands and leaning back in his seat.

Frank looked to the other end of the trailer to the empty chair where Nathan had been sitting. After the deputy announced there was a new development, the sheriff had Nathan removed from the trailer before the nature of the development was revealed. He did not want a potential suspect, even one he was considering taking off that list, to hear details about the investigation.

"We have some software that will help enhance these videos," the sheriff said. "But in the meantime, I want each of you individually to review each video.," he added, indicating the two deputies.

"While you do that, I'll talk to some tech people I know who might have something more sophisticated that could help," he added.

The sheriff shut down the video that was loaded and removed the thumb drive it was stored upon. He handed it to one deputy and another that contained the other video to the other man. They took them out to their patrol vehicles to view on their laptops.

"Where are you on suspects?" Talbott asked.

"We're ready to eliminate two of the father's siblings because there is no way they could have been directly involved," the sheriff answered. "But we're still looking into whether they were involved behind the scenes."

"And the father?" the chief asked.

"We've checked on all his activities in the last few days," Frank said. "And at the time this happened, there is a potential window of opportunity for him to have been at the school, but it is extremely thin. He was an hour away and for him to have gotten here when this happened, he would have had to go 90 miles an hour non-stop to make the timeline."

"What you're saying is that it could have happened, but not likely," Talbott said.

The sheriff nodded.

"What about the rest of the immediate family members," the chief asked.

Frank looked at his list.

"They all, on both sides, are still viable suspects," he said. "But we are still checking things on most of them."

Talbott leaned forward and placed his face in his hands.

"This is so complicated," he said through his fingers. "It's sure not like the stuff we normally deal with."

"Yes, it is," Frank said. "But it's early in this investigation. I suspect things are going to start popping soon."

Talbott uncovered his face and looked at the sheriff. Frank sympathized with the look on his face that nearly screamed, "*I hope so.*"

Nathan sat in the back seat of a county sheriff's patrol car parked a few feet away from the command trailer. He had followed the sheriff's request to go there without protest at first. But the longer he sat there alone, the more frustrated and restless he became.

Because there was no way to open the back doors from inside the car when they were closed completely, to prevent detainees' escape, the driver's side back door in the unit in which Nathan sat simmering was closed but not latched. He could get out of the car and stretch his legs, which he had done twice since being sent there. But there was a deputy sitting in the driver's seat of the car monitoring his radio and laptop – and to make sure Nathan did not go anywhere without an escort.

Deputy Barnes, who had been assigned to shadow Nathan, was nearby, but not in the car.

The deputy had the radio volume turned down in an attempt to keep Nathan from hearing the chatter. The sheriff had instructed the man to avoid letting Nathan hear about any of the investigation's progress. But at the same time, he needed the man to perform some tasks.

There were four sheriff's districts in the county and this one had the largest area to cover. As with most government agencies, the sheriff's department was undermanned. Not that there was a shortage of funds, but because the politicians were not the best at using common sense in prioritizing taxpayer money. Law enforcement, first responders and other human services were lower on the priority list than things like government infrastructure, welfare programs and perks for those in elected office.

Sheriff Martin had twenty sworn deputies to patrol the district, and half of them were now directly working this case. The other half were either on patrol or had time off to save on overtime. But even those on active patrol elsewhere were assigned certain tasks for this case.

Martin could not afford to leave any on duty officer sitting idly watching a suspect if he wanted to close this case quickly.

The radio volume in the car where Nathan sat was low, but not so low that he could not pick up a few tidbits here and there. From those snippets of chatter he learned that all his siblings were interrogated, as well as his mother. He also heard that no one was entirely eliminated as a suspect, although Bryan and Tessa were very low on the list. He heard nothing about his own standing in the investigation.

What he did not hear was that his wife, her parents and her brother had been interviewed in connection with the case. He was sure they had been, not from anything he heard from the little bits and pieces of the radio traffic, it just seemed to be common sense.

But it still irked him a bit. Were they not being considered as suspects? If not, how were they different than he and his family? The McAdams' money, he supposed.

The speculation that was running through his head was giving Nathan a headache, and it seemed stuffy in the patrol car. It was time to stretch his legs and get some clean air in his lungs. He tapped the window to get the deputy's attention and motioned that he was going to step out of the car. The man motioned him to go ahead and then both stepped out at the same time.

"It's getting stuffy in there," Nathan said, just for some conversation.

"I understand," the deputy answered, very business-like. He kept his eyes on Nathan.

"I don't suppose there's anything you can tell me about what is going on," Nathan said.

"Only that they are still looking for your daughter," the deputy answered in his monotone voice. He offered Nathan a water bottle and he drank several mouthfuls of the warm water.

Nathan nodded and smiled as he handed the bottle back to him, trying to let the deputy know there were no hard feelings. He understood that he was just doing as he was told. Nathan's real frustration was aimed at Sheriff Martin for keeping him in the dark.

"Where the hell is my granddaughter?"

Nathan recognized Jennifer's voice and turned to see her and Kenneth, trailed by Cynthia, about ten yards away. There was desperation in her voice, but overriding that was an accusatory tone.

Nathan was speechless for a moment, partly stunned from seeing the three of them after the confrontation at their home, and partly from the implied accusation.

"I don't know," was all he could muster.

Jennifer started to advance on him, a fire in her eyes. The deputy took one step away from the car and put his left arm across Nathan's chest to keep him from moving toward his mother-in-law. The gesture irritated Nathan, since he had not moved an inch. The deputy held out his right arm toward Jennifer and held up his hand, palm out, indicating she should stop, which she did after another two small steps. Deputy Barnes saw the interaction and came to stand with the other deputy.

"Let's all stay calm," the male deputy said, looking at Jennifer, but clearly hoping they all got the message.

While Jennifer halted her advance, she did not halt her words.

"Why did you take her away from us?" his mother-in-law said, now raising her voice.

Now Nathan could feel the anger rising in him. He wanted to check it before it became the rage he knew that it could. But it was difficult in the face of the tension that had been building ever since Cynthia had disappeared with Stephanie.

"If I took her, do you think I'd be here instead of with her?" he said sternly.

"You have her hidden away somewhere," Jennifer hissed. "Or one of your inbred, redneck family took her for you."

This time Kenneth stepped forward and put a hand on his wife's shoulder to try and calm her. She shook it off, but he replaced it, this time holding on a little tighter. Jennifer turned and gave him a look that could have melted a steel beam.

"That's enough," Kenneth said.

"Maybe he's finally growing some balls," Nathan thought to himself, biting his tongue so he didn't say it out loud. *"Small ones, but...."*

"Where is she, Nathan?" Cynthia's voice was barely audible, but enough that they all heard it.

"I don't know, Cynthia," Nathan said, working hard to keep his voice calm. "If I did, she would be here with us right now."

"Liar," Jennifer breathed, elongating the word.

Kenneth spun her around to face him.

"Enough," he said in a tone Nathan had never heard him use with his wife. Cynthia either, judging by her expression.

"You and Cynthia go wait in the car," Kenneth instructed.

Neither mother or daughter moved a muscle.

"Now," Kenneth demanded.

Jennifer huffed and shook herself free of Kenneth's one-handed grip. She glanced over her shoulder at Nathan. Her facial expression spoke more loudly than the words that remained in her mouth, *"You bastard!"*

She then strode past her daughter, who glanced at Nathan before turning and following Jennifer.

"I hope you're telling the truth," she said as she turned away.

"So do I," Kenneth said, hanging his head and walking to the command trailer.

Nathan had just settled back into the deputy's cruiser when Sheriff Martin stuck his head out the door of the trailer and motioned for the deputy to come talk to him. With Deputy Barnes remaining at the car with Nathan, the sheriff spoke to the male deputy briefly, then the deputy walked back to the cruiser and opened the back door.

"The sheriff wants you inside," he told Nathan.

Once inside, Nathan saw the sheriff, the police chief and his father-in-law standing around the small desk at the other end. The sheriff motioned for him to join them. He gestured for him to take a seat in front of the laptop with the external monitor to the side.

"Please watch this video and tell us what you see," the sheriff said, double clicking on a video icon he had copied from the thumb drive then pressed play.

Nathan concentrated on the screen as it began to play. It was from the doorbell camera across the street.

He could tell the image had been enlarged. The images were blurry, but some detail could be distinguished.

For about two seconds, there was no movement. Then a car drove past on the street. Nathan thought he recognized the type of car, a two-door sporty vehicle that looked to be gray or a dull green. The car went off the screen to the right and for a few seconds there was no more movement. He looked back at the sheriff, standing behind him, but Frank pointed at the screen.

After another couple of seconds, a person walked into the frame heading for the school entrance. The person entered the building. The person could only be seen from the back. It appeared to be a man, based on the build. The person wore a ball cap, which appeared to be tan in color, so it was difficult to see if the hair was short or long. It appeared there was hair on the back of the neck extending down below the shoulders, but Nathan believed it could have been just shadow.

There was a noticeable skip in the video showing that it had been edited down. Nathan had no idea how long the person was in the building, but after the skip the same person came out the front door holding the hand of a child. Although the video had been enhanced, the image was still blurry. But Nathan knew it was Stephanie.

The pair had only taken a few steps out the door when another figure appeared behind them. The adult leading Stephanie out the door turned a head to the right then back ahead. Something may have been said to the person following, who may have been a woman. Then the other adult turned to the right again and swung the right arm around, striking the following person in the neck. The blow knocked the follower to the right of the screen and Nathan could see the head strike a thick column supporting a cover over the entrance.

The striker hesitated for a moment, staring at the person on the ground. Then Stephanie, who was also staring, was scooped up and the striker ran off the frame to the right. Shortly, the same car he had seen earlier crossed the frame right to left at a higher rate of speed than before. This time Nathan recognized it as a Dodge Challenger that was olive drab green in color.

Something nagged at Nathan about the person who took Stephanie. There was something familiar, but he could not dredge it up from his memory.

The sheriff then ran the footage from the security camera at a right angle from the previous view. This one, also enlarged, showed the school entrance more clearly, and the resolution of the image was higher. At the far right, Nathan caught a glimpse of the car heading down the street away from the camera and after an interval he saw the figure walk toward the school's front door.

This time Nathan could see a little more detail. The person was wearing a green jacket with a patch on the shoulder, which was not detailed enough for Nathan to make out what kind of patch it was. But the profile shot showed the person had short cropped hair, so it was either a man or, less likely, a woman with a buzz cut. The man's head was turned slightly away from the camera, so Nathan could not see any features.

When the man came out, he was walking faster than when he went in. Nathan could see his daughter on the man's left, then the woman – yes, this time he could see it was a woman – following them out. The man turned his head and clearly said something.

Again, that nagging familiarity, only this time it seemed right on the verge of recognition.

Then the man turned again and swung his arm, striking the woman in the neck. This time Nathan did not see her head strike the column, because when the man turned to swing his arm, he was stunned because he was sure he knew who it was.

"Oh my God," he muttered, then louder. "Oh, my fucking God!"

Chapter 11

When it initially dawned on Nathan that Cynthia had left with Stephanie, he called all his immediate family members to tell them. The last call was to his father.

He left his father to last because he wasn't even sure he wanted to talk to him about it. The two had been somewhat estranged for so long he wasn't even sure his father would be interested in what was happening in his life. And considering his reaction when he first saw his granddaughter, Nathan was certain his father had even less interest in what had happened to Stephanie.

In the end, Nathan decided it would be the polite thing to do to inform his father of what appeared to be a big development in his life. Little did he know just how big it would become.

Nathan was a little relieved when it was George's voicemail that picked up.

"Hello dad. I just wanted to let you know that Cynthia left me and took Stephanie," he told the voicemail, choking up a little as he spoke the words. "I don't know what this is going to lead to, but it's possible she's going to leave for good and take Stephanie away. Anyway, just wanted you to know, if you are even interested."

When George listened to the message a few hours later, he began thinking about what he could do to make things better for his son. Nathan's parting shot – "if you are even interested" – stung like a bullet passing through his shoulder.

George Wallis was interested in and cared for his children very much – in his own way. He was not the type of man to wear his emotions on his sleeve, so his children never got a hug, never heard their father say "I love you," rarely saw an expression of pride when he talked about his children or was there to see their accomplishments or the rewards from them.

Part of that was because of George's military background and part was because that is what he saw in his own father. He knew no other way.

But he was proud of his children and what they had grown to be, even if he wasn't a part of their growing years.

And he was very proud of Stephanie.

Although he rarely saw her face-to-face or got any direct information about her from Nathan, he had kept up with her life from the things her parents posted on their social media. While Stephanie's parents kept those platforms shared only with family and friends, Nathan had accepted George's friend requests out of courtesy. He had no idea his father would follow his family there as closely as he did.

George was not into social media and had started a Facebook page only because his step daughters talked him into it. In the beginning, he was rarely on it. But one day he saw something on his news feed that Cynthia had posted about Stephanie. He immediately sent friend requests to both of them.

George had also hoped that some day he and his son would find peace and develop a better relationship, although he still did not recognize that it was his actions – or lack thereof – that was the largest reason for the rift.

But as the years went by, George became more eager – even desperate – to get closer to his children and share in the family he had developed. He had talked with Bryan and Carolyn, but those visits were usually initiated because he or his son and daughter wanted information. George and Tessa never spoke. She was the most bitter of his children over the family split.

So as George ruminated over Nathan's voicemail, he began to formulate a plan that he hoped would mend some fences between them.

George Wallis flew over four states and rented a car to drive to the city where Cynthia had taken Stephanie. It was not hard to figure out where they were, since George knew her parents lived in Illinois. It was an educated guess that would be where she went, but the odds were heavily in his favor. He knew the close-knit nature of Cynthia's family, although he did not know the intricate details.

He was driving an olive drab green Dodge Challenger. He had wanted something a little less conspicuous, but it was better than the compact and electric cars and minivans that were the only other vehicles available.

He had traveled and rented the car under his own name. He would have preferred to make his reservations under an assumed name, but with all the restrictions set up since September 11, 2001, that would be impossible for an ordinary citizen. If he had been still active military, it might have been different.

However, being retired military, and a senior citizen, did allow him a few discounts that helped keep the cost of the trip down. Not a lot, but enough. But the expected end result of this mission would have been worth any cost, in George's mind.

After picking up the car, he found a quiet park and settled into the parking area to do some research. Being former military did help him in this area as he still retained his classified status and access to some search engines not available to the everyday citizen.

First, he found the address of Kenneth and Jennifer McAdams. He had never been to their home and knew very little about them from a personal perspective.

He was also certain her mother would have wanted to get Stephanie back into school as soon as possible. While he had no clue where she would be enrolled, he was sure the school would not be far from where the mother and daughter were staying. His search for schools in the area showed one public school within three-quarters of a mile from the McAdams' home. There were two private schools in the city, but only one within a mile of the grandparents' home.

So, it would be a fifty-fifty shot as to which school she attended.

Considering Nathan's and Cynthia's financial status, his first thought was the public school. However, what he did know of the McAdamses was that they were very well-to-do. So, the private school was a possibility. Checking the policies of both schools on their respective websites revealed that the public school was open enrollment while the private school encouraged enrollment at the beginning of each school year.

But George knew that exceptions would be made if there was enough money in it.

"Money talks and bullshit walks," he muttered aloud.

Now, with no clear choice, his task would be to do a little reconnaissance. But it was too late in the day now for that. He went to a fast food restaurant and got a quick meal, then drove back to the park to plan things out for the following day.

George's military training had hung with him through the years, so much so that without an alarm he always awoke at four o'clock in the morning. Age had not changed that and like clockwork his eyes fluttered open at exactly that time. He grabbed a clean towel from his field pack and had a G.I. bath at the water fountain nearby. He also brushed his teeth and dry shaved, rinsing his face afterward.

He found another fast food restaurant whose drive-thru window was open twenty-four hours and ordered two breakfast burritos to eat on the road. He made the ninety-minute drive to his destination. He pulled up to the curb on a street a block away from the private school.

It was still an hour before students would be arriving. But George did not want to miss anyone. His location gave him a clear view of the school's main entrance. But being a block away, he needed help getting close up looks of students as they came in. Regular binoculars would have attracted too much attention, so he used a small single ocular spy glass that fit in the palm of his hand.

He parked so that he would have to look to his right, across the passenger side of the car. He placed his laptop on the passenger seat with it open to a major national daily newspaper's website. If anyone, especially police, came to check out why a man was parked a block away from a school, he could spin a story that he was passing through and was taking time to read the newspaper online before he moved on.

As it turned out, he didn't need to use the cover story. Although he got a few stares from passersby, no one approached the car to challenge him.

But when all the students had entered the building, he had not seen Stephanie. That meant he would go to the public school and repeat the surveillance when school was dismissed for the day. He was prepared to do the same the next day, or longer, until he found his granddaughter. But that was not going to be necessary. He spotted Stephanie being escorted from the school by her mother and another woman he assumed, by the resemblance and difference in age, to be Jennifer McAdams.

But his plan had been, once he identified the school she attended, he would approach her at the end of the school day after she left the building. Since her mother and grandmother were with her, he had to alter the plan. That meant spending another night in the car.

George was across the street from Stephanie's school. This time he had parked the car around the block and walked to the designated street to where he had seen a bus shelter. He sat on the bench with his laptop in front of him, again open to a business publication's website, and with the spy glass in his palm.

From his observations the day before, he knew what vehicle to watch for, so he had an advantage this time. As soon as he saw the beige Crown Victoria pull into the school parking lot, he knew they were there. Again, Cynthia and the woman George assumed was her mother escorted Stephanie into the building. Clearly, they were making sure the girl got inside the school safely. They were obviously concerned about her father making contact.

Their overprotectiveness confirmed the plan he had worked out the night before. It would help make it more believable. He reached into his inside jacket pocket and pulled out a black leather bi-fold identification holder and opened it. His old Navy ID was inside under a plastic cover. He pulled from another pocket the six-point star badge he had purchased from a dollar store and pinned it to the side opposite his ID. He closed it, then using just his right hand practiced opening it and closing it as quickly as he could.

He let an hour pass after the final bell before walking back to the rental car. He drove around the block and entered the school parking lot. He pulled into the bus lane and parked directly in front of the main entrance doors.

George took a few deep breaths to calm himself. He was getting in full mission mode. Then he swung the door open and headed for the school lobby.

Inside to his right was a long counter with a work space then some offices behind it. There was no glass partition extending from the counter to the ceiling, like one might see in a police station or title loan office lobby. There was one woman behind the counter working at a computer terminal. She was young, about mid-twenties. George guessed she had attended some college but did not have a degree. Maybe she was working at the school to save up money to return to college.

No matter. Her youth and possible inexperience worked in his favor.

She looked up as he approached the counter. George took out the ID wallet and flashed it open then closed. Long enough for her to see the badge but not long enough for her to see it or the ID in detail.

"Hi. I'm Deputy Tanner from the county sheriff's office," George said calmly, in control. "I'm here to see Stephanie Wallis."

The young girl stayed at her desk. George glanced around the area and could see no one through the half-wall windows and doors of the offices behind the work space. That was also working in his favor.

"I'm off duty," George said, noticing the girl looking at his casual attire – jeans, a blue polo shirt under a green leather jacket and a blue ball cap with an American flag and the inscription, "United We Stand" underneath. On the right sleeve of the jacket, just off the shoulder, was a circular patch with an anchor and "United States Navy" embroidered inside gold braid around the outside of a navy blue background.

"Stephanie's mother and grandmother are concerned about her father coming to take her," he told her, assuming – correctly – that school officials had been informed about the potential divorce and custody battle. "They hired me to help keep an eye out for him. But I wanted to meet Stephanie so she knows who I am."

The girl cocked her head to one side, obviously working something out in her head.

"Well, they were just here and they didn't say anything to me about that," she said.

"It could be that they discussed this with the principal but it hasn't filtered down to you yet," George said, trying to not sound condescending. "After all, these arrangements were just made this morning."

The girl seemed to take that explanation in stride.

"OK, let me call her teacher," she said, and consulted her computer screen. She then picked up the phone and punched in a few numbers. "Miss Stewart, there's a county detective here that wants to speak to Stephanie Wallis. Can you bring her to the main office?" She listened for an answer then hung up.

"She'll be right down," the girl said, then began typing on her computer keyboard.

George started to feel his nerves tingle as he stood by the counter, but not leaning on it. This was the part of the plan that worried him the most. It was a stroke of luck that the young girl was the only one in the lobby when he entered the school. It meant less time telling the county deputy lie, less chance of him slipping up.

But the more time he spent there waiting, the more it was possible that someone else would come into the area and start asking questions. Maybe even the school principal would stumble upon him and it would be harder to sell the story to her. He knew that any kind of extra outside security on the campus would have to go through the principal.

Then he heard the distinctive *clack, clack, clack* of women's heels on polished tile floors coming from down the hallway leading to the lobby area. He tensed up a little, running his story through his mind and putting together scenarios that would explain his presence without the principal's knowledge.

The heels on tile got slowly louder until suddenly, about thirty yards down the hallway he saw a woman round the corner. She was in her late-twenties or early-thirties, slender with curly brown hair extending past her shoulders. The hair was bouncing up and down as she walked. She was dressed in a white blouse with the top two buttons open and a light gray skirt that went to her knees. She had a confident stride.

Holding the woman's right hand was Stephanie. She wore basic red tennis shoes, bright blue long pants and a flowered shirt. George had seen enough pictures of her on Facebook to recognize her immediately. She was average height for an eleven-year-old. Her light brown hair, bordering on dark blond, was long and wavey. Once a bit chubby, Stephanie had thinned out, and she was pretty. George imagined that when she grew into her twenties she would be a heartbreaker.

When the pair was just ten feet away, George pulled out his ID wallet and flashed it like he had to the young girl behind the counter.

"I'm Deputy Tanner with the sheriff's department," he began. "Stephanie's mother and grandmother ...." He was not able to finish the spiel.

"Grandpa George, is that you?" Stephanie asked innocently. "What are you doing here?"

The jig was up. George knew he now had to switch to mission improvisation.

In all his planning and rethinking the mission, this was a contingency George had not considered.

His granddaughter had not seen him since she was two years old. She had asked her father about her Grandpa George, and Nathan shared the barest of basics with her. Nathan had very few photos of his father, and all of them were taken while George was still married to Mary Anne. There was no way Stephanie could have recognized him from those photos.

But George had made an error of social media ignorance. While he had followed his granddaughter's development through her parents' social media platforms, he never considered the reverse would be true.

Stephanie started out looking through her parents' social media accounts under their supervision. When she was ten, Nathan and Cynthia agreed to let her have her own platforms, but under their supervision and they were set for family and friends only, not public. The deal was that Nathan and/or Cynthia had to approve any "friends" she added to her lists.

One day, Stephanie stumbled onto George's Facebook page during a few moments when her mother was preoccupied and not paying attention to what Stephanie was viewing. Her grandfather's page was set for family and friends, so she could not view much on it unless they were friends. She looked around to make sure her mother was not watching and sent George a friend request. A day later he accepted, and Stephanie was able to view it all.

George rarely posted photos of himself, but his wife, Barbara, was not as bashful about posting photos of her husband she had taken. Whenever she could steal an unsupervised moment, Stephanie went to her grandfather's page and looked through his photos, and those Barbara shared, and read his few postings.

Even though he was unprepared for Stephanie recognizing him, which blew his cover, George was good at thinking on his feet. The Navy instincts were still sharp. But in this instance, he panicked.

George grabbed Stephanie's right hand with his left and headed for the door. Miss Stewart was caught off guard and Stephanie's hand slipped from hers. She followed the pair.

"Call the principal and the police," she called over her shoulder to the young girl behind the counter.

She had already sent an email to the principal while George was waiting, just to confirm the situation, so she went straight to the phone and dialed 9-1-1.

George burst through the front door with Stephanie in tow and Miss Stewart right behind them.

"Just stop," George turned his head and shouted, then rotated his head back to front view.

The teacher was right behind him and reached out her arm to grab his shoulder. George felt her fingers trying to get a grip and he instinctively swung his right arm in a circle behind him. He felt the back of his hand contact her neck and, without looking back, was aware she had pitched to the left.

Stephanie screamed the teacher's name. Looking back as best she could as she was being pulled forward, she saw the teacher's head strike the pillar quite hard. She saw her fall to the sidewalk.

The girl tried to stop her grandfather's advance, but he was too strong.

"Miss Stewart is hurt, we have to help," she wailed.

Without breaking stride, George scooped Stephanie up and at the same time opened the Challenger's passenger door. He placed her roughly into the seat and swiftly fastened her seat belt. He ran around to the other side and got in, just as Stephanie snapped out of the seat belt.

"You need to keep this on," he said, and clicked it back into the latch.

"But we have to go back and help Miss Stewart," Stephanie said.

The trauma of the moment had her focused on only one thing – the welfare of her teacher. She did not even consider why her grandfather was taking her from school or where they were going. That would come later.

"No," George shouted. "We need to get out of here."

"But….."

"But nothing," George yelled, leaning over nearly nose to nose to the frightened little girl. "You need to behave and do as you're told."

Stephanie could see the rage in his eyes. After seeing what had happened to her teacher, she was afraid the same could happen to her. She slouched in the seat, trying to merge into the upholstery, thinking that would protect her.

George straightened up in the seat and gunned the big V8 engine and they roared out of the parking lot and sped up the street the way he had come.

George had purchased a roundtrip ticket for himself and added a one-way for Stephanie when he originally booked the flights. He paid extra to have the return flights open-ended, meaning they could be used on a non-specified date, as long as they were used within thirty days.

As they waited for the flight to board, George tried to calm and reassure his granddaughter, who was obviously very scared and acting nervous. He was afraid someone might spot the behavior and people would start asking questions. He had no idea how long it would be before the authorities were able to identify him as the abductor. They needed to complete this flight before that happened.

"Everything is going to be alright, Stephanie," he said to her as calmly as he could. "I'm trying to protect you."

She did not respond. The image of George striking Miss Stewart and seeing her head smack the pillar was still fresh in her mind, as was her grandfather yelling at her in the car.

"I'm sorry I yelled at you back at the school," George said, and Stephanie recognized the regretful expression on his face. It reduced her fear, but not by much.

"I would never hurt you," her grandfather said.

"I want to go to my Mom and Dad," Stephanie whispered.

"And you will, eventually," George said. "But right now your mom wants to take you away from your dad. We have to fix that first."

Having overheard a lot of what her mother said to her parents, Stephanie knew her family was in danger of being split apart. But the reasons her mother had given were confusing. Some of the things that were said about her father were hard for her to reconcile. From her perspective, he had always been very loving and caring toward both herself and her mother.

"How are we going to fix it?" she asked.

"I'm still working on that," George said. "But I think if you help me, we can do it."

Stephanie wanted nothing more than to keep her family together. She was ready to do what she could to make that happen.

"OK, I'll help," she said. But while she was agreeable to do what it took to keep her family together, there was still a grain of fear and distrust she could not shake.

Their flight was called for boarding and within thirty minutes they were in the air. Their plane was on its final approach to the Boise, Idaho airport at the same time Nathan was viewing the surveillance video of his daughter's abduction.

Chapter 12

Once Martin was able to get Nathan out of his stunned stupor, he had an ID on the person who took Stephanie from the school.

"That was my father on the videos," he said, still trying to process it in his mind. He barely heard Kenneth mutter under his breath.

"Holy shit."

Martin and Talbott immediately sprang into action. They called for their officers who had interviewed people at the school and canvassed the neighborhood, who had yet to give full reports, to come to the command trailer. Within thirty minutes they were all there.

The receptionist, though still rattled by the experience, had given a detailed description of the man. It matched the man on the videos. She even recalled that Stephanie had called the man Grandpa George. She had seen the man strike Miss Stewart and watched her head slam into the column.

She was the only eye witness to the abduction and attack. But officers canvassing the neighborhood heard from several residents about a dull green Challenger in the area two days straight – once as school let out and again the following fateful morning. Two residents got the license plate number of the car.

Within an hour, they tracked the car to the nearest airport and were able to get the rental records. They confirmed it was George Wallis who rented the car. A check of flights that day showed Wallis had used an open-ended ticket for himself and young girl. But not only had the flight already taken off, it was already at its destination.

Martin had not ushered Nathan and Kenneth out of the trailer while these facts were gathered, so they heard everything. Kenneth had taken a seat next to Nathan, who continued to process all the information. He was vaguely aware of Kenneth's voice and turned to face him.

"Did you know he was going to do this? Are you involved in any way?" his father-in-law was asking.

Nathan stared at him, a blank expression on his face. Was he involved in his own daughter's abduction and a murder? What an absurd question.

"Well, were you?" Kenneth asked with a little more intensity in his voice.

"Of course not!" Nathan said, a little louder than he had intended. "Why would I have anyone kidnap my daughter? That's a ridiculous thing to ask."

Just then, Martin appeared across the desk.

"That may or may not be true, Mr. Wallis, but it's a question that must be asked," he said. Nathan turned to face the sheriff, and Kenneth smiled with satisfaction that he and law enforcement were on the same page.

"So, I'm officially asking you, did you have your father take your daughter? Were you involved in any way?" Martin said calmly.

"Hell no, and hell no," Nathan answered. "My brother offered to do it, but I told him not to. I didn't want to uproot her a second time."

As soon as those sentences left his lips, he immediately regretted it. He was worried it might intensify suspicion on him as a suspect, but worse he was dragging Bryan into it, which he did not want to do.

"We'll check that out," Martin said. "How can I contact your brother?"

Nathan reluctantly wrote Bryan's cell phone number on a sticky pad and handed it to the sheriff. He also provided his satellite phone number in case he was out of cell tower range, explaining Bryan's work as an outfitter.

Martin left the trailer to make the calls. He got no answer on the cell phone and left a voicemail, saying Bryan needed to contact him as soon as possible. He then dialed the satellite phone. It rang five times before there was an answer.

"Is this Bryan Wallis?" the sheriff asked. When the voice answered in the affirmative, he went on.

"Do you recall a conversation with your brother about his daughter?" he asked.

"There have been any number of those, to what are you referring?" Bryan asked, and the sheriff could hear caution in his voice.

"I'm talking about a specific conversation you had about taking Stephanie from her mother," Martin said.

There was a pause while Bryan considered his answer.

"Yes, we had such a conversation," he said. "I offered to take Stephanie to a secure location until he could get custody."

"And what was your brother's response?" Martin asked.

"He told me not to do it. He didn't want Stephanie uprooted a second time," he said, then went on before the sheriff could say anything else. "What's this all about?"

"Your niece was abducted from her school and someone was killed in the process," Martin said.

"Well, it wasn't me, I've been on a pack trip in the mountains in Colorado for three days," Bryan said. "And my brother wouldn't have done it, for the reason he wouldn't let me do it."

"But your father would," the sheriff explained. "He has been positively identified as the man who took Stephanie."

There was silence on the other end of the satellite link and Martin thought the call had dropped. Then he heard a muffled voice but couldn't make out what was said.

"I'm ending this trip and I'll be down there in the morning," Bryan said, then the link was broken.

Sheriff Martin sat at his desk at the district substation, Nathan sat across the desk from him.

The office was small, about the size of a small bedroom. It was sparsely decorated with a few certificates, photos of vehicles and a small bookcase filled with law books, three-ring binders and some novels. There was also a four-drawer gray vertical filing cabinet in one corner.

The sheriff shuffled some papers on his desk, made a quick check of his emails and the contents on a few pink "While You Were Out" message slips.

All the while, Nathan wondered what he was doing there. The sheriff looked up and paused a few seconds before speaking.

"I am inclined to believe that you had nothing to do with your daughter's abduction and the killing at the school," he finally said. Nathan raised his hands, palms up, to about shoulder height and gave the sheriff a look that screamed, *"I told you so."*

"But it's still possible your brother or your sister assisted your father, so until they are cleared, they will remain on the suspect list," Martin said.

"You're kidding, right?" Nathan said.

"No, Mr. Wallis, I am not," the sheriff said. "But I won't be leading this investigation any longer."

He picked up one of the messages and looked at it.

"This was a simple custodial interference case until your father took Stephanie out of state," he explained. "Now it is a federal matter, so the FBI will take the lead."

Nathan looked puzzled. Was that a good thing or not? Wouldn't the FBI have more resources at their disposal than a county sheriff's department? Martin understood his puzzlement.

"They are better equipped to deal with this kind of thing, and kidnapping is a federal crime so it is their jurisdiction," he said. "One of their agents is on the way. In fact, judging by the time on this message, he should be here any time now."

"Does this mean the sheriff's department and city police are off the case?" Nathan asked.

"No, we'll assist as much as we can, or as much as the FBI wants us to," Martin said. "I want you to be here when their agent arrives. You know your father and that could be helpful."

"But I don't really know him that well," Nathan said. "We haven't seen each other or spoken much over the years."

"But you know him better than any of us," Martin said.

Sheriff Martin had just returned from the sub shop up the street with sandwiches for himself and Nathan and they were just getting started eating their lunch when Martin's phone buzzed. He hit the speaker and Deputy Barnes' voice came through.

"The FBI agent is here," she said.

Barnes remained Nathan's "shadow," but waited in the station's bullpen while Nathan was with the sheriff.

"Send him in," Martin said through a mouthful of bacon, lettuce and tomato on wheat.

The office door opened and in walked a tall, slender woman in a conservative black suit with a white blouse under the jacket. The top two buttons were unfastened and Nathan and the sheriff could see the hint of cleavage. Her reddish-brown shoulder-length hair was down and framed an egg-shaped face with skin so unblemished it had the appearance of a mannequin.

She strode confidently in front of the sheriff's desk and extended her hand. Martin hesitated in mid-chomp, then swallowed the mouthful down his throat, feeling it catch there. He held up his index finger and took a few large sips of his soft drink to clear it through. He then stood and took her hand and shook it.

"Special agent Susan Blastmore, FBI," she said in a voice so sultry both Frank and Nathan felt their hearts skip a beat.

"Sheriff Frank Martin," he said, then motioned to Nathan. "This is Nathan Wallis, the abducted girl's father."

Nathan stood, setting his pastrami and Swiss sandwich on the table between his chair and the other in the office, and shook her hand. Her piercing blue eyes burned through Nathan like Superman's heat vision. Without waiting for an invitation, Blastmore slithered into the other seat and the two men sat back down.

"So, can you brief me on what we've got?" the agent asked, actually more of a polite order.

Martin gave a brief summary of what had happened up to that point. He then keyed up on his laptop the videos of what took place at the school. He and Nathan waited silently while she watched. Nathan turned his head away through much of it, and Blastmore couldn't help but notice.

"Do you have an ID on the unsub?" she asked the sheriff.

Martin did not answer right away. He glanced over at Nathan. Blastmore noticed and followed his eyes to Nathan, who slowly turned his head back to the laptop screen.

"It is my father, George Wallis," he said.

The FBI agent saw the look of anger in Nathan's eyes, but she also noticed some sadness and worry there as well.

"Is there a concern about the girl's safety?" she asked, looking first to Nathan then to the sheriff. "Her name is Stephanie, right?"

Nathan nodded, but then quickly spoke so the FBI agent did not get the wrong idea.

"Yes, her name is Stephanie," he said. "But I don't really think my dad would do anything to hurt her."

"Physically, you mean?" Blastmore asked.

"In any way," Nathan said a little defensively, which surprised him.

Susan took in a short breath and held it while she contemplated just how to say what she needed to say next. She did not want to offend the father, especially since she did not know the family dynamic.

"Well, Mr. Wallis, the truth of the matter is that being taken away like that, even by someone she knows, and seeing what she must have seen happen to that woman is going to do some damage to her psychologically," she said.

It was not something Nathan had thought much about in the past hours. But what he was hearing from the FBI agent was very possible. He nodded his head in acknowledgement but said nothing.

"Are your daughter and father close?" she asked.

Nathan shook his head, then explained his relationship with his father and how little his father had actually seen Stephanie during her lifetime.

"I can count on one hand with fingers left over the times he has seen her," Nathan said, with a little bitterness in his voice. "And there has been no phone calls or any other correspondence that I know of."

Blastmore made mental notes of it all, things she would put to paper later on. But she wanted Nathan to see that she was paying full attention to him at this time.

"So, what happens now?" Nathan asked.

The sheriff also looked to Blastmore for a direction on the case.

"We're going to have to follow him out there, and if we can't find him, we'll have to canvas his neighborhood," she explained. "Is he single?"

Nathan shook his head.

"Then we'll also need to talk to his wife. That's assuming we don't find him and your daughter at home."

"We would want you to keep us in the loop," Martin said.

"Oh, we will," Susan said as she stood up. "In fact, I want someone from your office to accompany me on this trip."

"I'll assign a deputy to go with you," the sheriff said. "I'll stay behind to coordinate things here."

Susan turned to Nathan.

"And I'll want you to come along, too," she told him. "Will that work for you?"

Nathan stood and faced the FBI agent, who looked to be about an inch taller than he was.

"I can go. I'll do whatever I can to help get my daughter back," he said.

"Good," Susan said. "We could use your knowledge of your father to help us find him. The two of you may be estranged, but you have insights we don't have, and could miss."

The two bid the sheriff farewell and left the office while he picked up the phone to make the deputy assignment.

Nathan walked toward the white Gulfstream jet idling on the runway. Except for the tail number and black and gold stripes running horizontally from nose to tail, there was no way to tell it transported FBI agents. The jet had been chartered for this mission as domestic flights were all booked. The FBI had it on a running lease, meaning the agents had it at their disposal while they were in the field until the case was completed.

Agent Susan Blastmore led the way and Deputy Dawn Barnes followed Nathan. He couldn't shake the feeling of being a prisoner with two guards making sure he didn't make a break for it.

Sheriff Martin had told him he was no longer considered a suspect by the sheriff's department in his daughter's kidnapping and the murder of the teacher. But he could tell that Agent Blastmore hadn't dismissed him as a participant in the events on some level. It's nothing she had said, but there was something in her manner, the way she spoke to him, the fact that she had shared nothing concerning their trip with him. All he knew was they were headed for his father's home in Idaho.

And the FBI agent was not the only one who continued to hold Nathan under suspicion.

After traveling to his sister's, with Deputy Barnes along both as his continued shadow and the deputy assigned to go with the FBI, to gather up some extra clothing and his travel kit, they found Kenneth, Jennifer and Cynthia at the sheriff's substation before they headed to the airport.

"Why isn't he locked up?" Jennifer demanded.

"He is not a suspect in your granddaughter's kidnapping and the event at the school," Sheriff Martin said as calmly and politely as he could. He was tired, and a little suspicious, of Jennifer's attitude and demands. She had made constant calls to the office wanting to know the progress of the case and when Nathan would be arrested.

"He is involved. He and his father cooked this whole thing up," she insisted.

Kenneth reached forward and put his hand on her shoulder, but she shrugged it off, throwing a look over her shoulder at her husband that could melt the nuts off a steel bridge. Kenneth threw up his hands in disgust and sat in a chair. Cynthia stood passively by her mother's side.

"I want some action taken," Jennifer almost screamed it.

Agent Blastmore stepped forward and identified herself to Jennifer. She tipped her head back slightly and regarded the agent down her nose. It's a gesture Nathan had seen many times. So, too, had Agent Blastmore during her career.

"Mrs. McAdams, we are taking action," the agent said. "We are doing everything we can to find your granddaughter."

Jennifer pointed at Nathan and opened her mouth to speak, but Susan cut her off.

"You can do one of two things," she continued. "You can keep your mouth shut until we ask you for information, or you can be arrested for interfering with our investigation."

Jennifer blew out a hurrumph of contempt, but stayed silent otherwise.

"Thank you for your cooperation," the agent said to Jennifer, then motioned for Nathan and Barnes to follow.

Cynthia stepped forward demurely.

"Please bring my daughter home safely," she told the agent, pointedly ignoring her husband.

"We will do our best, Mrs. Wallis," she answered.

Now Blastmore had met all the players, except the victim and the abductor.

Stephanie walked into her grandfather's garage to find him packing items into a silver Jeep Wrangler. She couldn't see what was in the vehicle, but she recognized a rifle scabbard leaning against the right rear fender and a handgun in a holster lying on the floor.

It was after dark when they arrived at the house about two hours ago. Before coming out to the garage, Stephanie heard her grandfather arguing with his wife in the house. The wife was very upset and begged him not to continue what he was doing.

"Send her back, turn yourself in," Barbara Wallis said.

"I can't do that. She needs to be with her father," George said. "Besides, it went a little too far out there."

"What do you mean?" Barbara asked.

"Someone got hurt," he said.

Stephanie heard Barbara gasp, and then George went out to the garage.

"Where are you going?" Stephanie asked from the side doorway. The main garage door was closed.

George was startled as he was so intent on his tasks that he did not realize she was in the garage. He turned slowly to face her.

"We're going on a little trip," he said, then picked up the weapons and placed them carefully in the Jeep.

"I want to go home," Stephanie said. "I want to see my parents."

He turned again and sighed.

"You will see your father. I hope that is soon," he said.

"I want to go now," she said.

George's frustration was growing. But he did not want to lose his temper with Stephanie as he had after taking her from the school.

"Please be patient, Stephanie," he said as calmly as he could. "This should be all over soon."

She doubted that. But there was nothing she could do but go along and hope she was presented with an opportunity to change the situation.

Chapter 13

When they boarded the FBI jet there were, in addition to the pilot and co-pilot, two others on board. Blastmore introduced them as agents Phillip Mason and Bernard Vallow. They all quickly took their seats and the co-pilot pulled up the door/ladder combination and secured the door.

During the four-hour flight, Nathan and Susan sat in seats facing each other and she had him repeat all the details of his activities from the day Cynthia left with Stephanie up to boarding the plane they were on now. She went over it with him three times, and his recitation never wavered.

While they spoke, Mason did a deep dive into Nathan's cell phone, checking his phone calls, texts and internet searches. There were many phone calls and texts, the majority to his family, immediate and extended, and the few calls to and from Kenneth McAdams. While they could not know what was said on the phone calls, the texts appeared to show a man in distress, looking frantically for his family, then when it was learned where they were, expressions of extreme hurt and of missing his wife and daughter.

There was nothing in the texts or internet searches, what few there were on his phone, to indicate Nathan colluded with anyone to abduct his daughter.

"This is not to say there were not other ways for you to communicate with an accomplice or accomplices," Agent Blastmore said as the jet was making the final approach to the destination. "But I'm inclined to believe you did not."

Nathan heaved a heavy sigh, both of relief and vindication.

"I'm sorry to put you through all the scrutiny, but until we have evidence to the contrary, we suspect everyone," the agent said.

"Does that include my wife and her family?" Nathan asked, his voice dripping with bitterness, more for his mother-in-law than anyone else. Her accusations in the school parking lot and the sheriff's substation still rang in his ears.

"Yes, Mr. Wallis, even them," Blastmore said. "Their backgrounds, phone and computer records are being checked as we speak." She paused for a beat. "As are those in your family."

Nathan wasn't quite sure how to take that, but he nodded his acknowledgement.

The interview with Barbara Wallis was a bit awkward at first. She was quite surprised to find an FBI agent and another woman at her door, but even more surprised to see Nathan with them.

She and Nathan first met face-to-face not long after George had married her. The newlyweds had been in town to pick up the last of George's possessions he had left in storage after divorcing Mary Anne. Nathan was unaware they were there until they inadvertently ran into each other at a local restaurant.

At that time Barbara, ten years George's junior, was an attractive blond with a model's figure. But living with George had changed her. He saw that when he lived at his father's home during college, but it was even more pronounced now. The woman Nathan now saw was a faint shadow of her former self. Her silky blond hair had gone gray and was coarse. There were many more wrinkles and lines on her face than should be there for a woman her age. And she had gained about fifty pounds, Nathan judged. The model's figure was gone, and he could see much of her self-confidence had gone with it.

Shaking off her surprise, she invited them in. Mason and Vallow remained on the plane, chasing down the background and alibi checks of Nathan's and Cynthia's families. To Nathan, it seemed a waste of time as it was clear who was behind the kidnapping and killing. But Agent Blastmore said it was necessary to eliminate each family member from any involvement – or to find out if any existed.

After the introductions and other pleasantries, Blastmore, who sat on the opposite end of the sofa from Barbara, got down to business.

"Mrs. Wallis, we are looking for your husband, do you know where he is?" she asked.

"He said he was going to spend some time with Stephanie," Barbara said without hesitation. "He doesn't get to see her very much."

That got the hair on the back of Nathan's neck to stand up. Deputy Barnes, sitting on a chair nearby, tensed, ready to intervene if Nathan got out of hand.

"He hasn't made an effort to see her before. Why now?" he asked. Susan held up her hand, silently telling Nathan to let her ask the questions.

"What about that, Mrs. Wallis. Why now?" she asked.

"I don't know, he didn't say," Barbara answered a little sheepishly. George had not kept anything from her about anything in his life, Barbara claimed. But it was clear to Blastmore that had come to an end with his granddaughter.

"Do you know where he took her?" the agent asked.

"All he said was he wanted to spend time with her," Barbara answered.

"Why didn't you go along with them?" Susan asked.

"I wanted to, but he said no," Barbara said, not masking her irritation with being left behind, especially now that the FBI was in her home. She wondered what her husband was up to and what kind of mess he had gotten her involved in.

Nathan was feeling a little restless and squirmed a little bit in the armchair in which he was sitting. They were getting nowhere with Barbara. Either she was covering for George or she was truly in the dark about his activities out-of-state. He wanted Blastmore to ask more pointed questions.

"Do you know how Stephanie came to be in your husband's company?" Susan asked.

"He told me his parents gave their permission for her to spend a couple of weeks here," she said, looking to Nathan for confirmation. When he shook his head, the color drained from her face.

"Didn't you think that was odd, since it was in the middle of the school year?" Blastmore asked.

"I did think it was strange, especially since he hasn't spoken to Nathan in quite a while," Barbara said. "But he's never lied to me before."

Blastmore looked to Nathan, then to Barnes. The deputy got up and repositioned herself beside Barbara, who looked up at her. Barnes was not in her deputy's uniform. Without all her law enforcement accoutrements she was more attractive than when Nathan first met her in the command trailer. Her straight strawberry blond hair hung on her shoulders. She was quite shapely, and had a face very much like the Tinkerbell character in Disney's animated adaptation of "Peter Pan."

"Your husband kidnapped Stephanie Wallis," Blastmore said slowly. "And a young teacher was killed in the process."

Barbara stood up abruptly and Barnes put a hand on her shoulder. Barbara tried to duck under it but Barnes gripped her shoulder tighter. Continuing to look at Blastmore, Barbara's mouth opened but no words came out. The agent stood, opened her laptop, keyed up the video from the school, stepped forward and held the computer up for Barbara to see.

As it played, she recognized George and tears began to roll down her cheeks. When the video showed George swinging his arm around and the teacher's head snacking the pillar, Barbara fainted and fell back onto the sofa, despite Barnes' grip on her shoulder.

Back on the plane, Blastmore, Mason, Vallow and Barnes put their heads together to try and figure out where George might have gone with Stephanie.

When Barbara fainted at her home, Barnes quickly called 9-1-1. When paramedics arrived they revived Nathan's step-mother with smelling salts. When her head had cleared, Blastmore peppered her with questions, but she claimed to know nothing about where her husband could have taken his granddaughter.

One of Vallow's tasks while the others were interviewing Barbara Wallis was doing a search to find out what properties George Wallis owned, either in his name only or in a combination deed with his wife. He found that in addition to the home on the outskirts north of Boise, he owned 26 acres within the Boise National Forest. It was only his name on the deed, and Vallow's research showed the land had been owned by George's ancestors before the forest was established and the family ownership was guaranteed by the Homestead Act of 1862. The land was handed down from generation to generation.

Clearly, George may not have lied directly to his wife, but he omitted certain things.

It was the same for his son, as Nathan had no idea his father owned the land.

"I remember going up into the mountains when I was very young, we'd go to the same place several times," Nathan explained to the law enforcement officers. "But I had no idea my dad owned the land."

He said during his childhood visits there he recalled a small cabin on the property.

"But I've never been back there since shortly after I started grade school," he attested.

They all consulted the map Vallow had pulled up on his laptop. The property in question was highlighted by a yellow outline. It was located in a remote part of the forest and accessible only by a logging road.

"I did some checking with the Forest Service," Vallow explained. "That road hasn't been used for logging for at least ten years."

"That means if we are going up there, chances are the road has not been maintained regularly," Mason said. "We'll need some specialized vehicles."

"We can get those," Blastmore said. "We'll also need someone who knows the area."

Mason tapped a few keys on his laptop.

"I've already contacted the Forest Service and they are sending over a guy who is in that area regularly," he said.

George drove through the nearly deserted streets of the small suburb and Stephanie rotated her vision from straight ahead to her right. She was trying to memorize the streetscapes in the hope that if she had an opportunity to get away, she would know how to get back to somewhat familiar surroundings. She saw plenty of storefronts and residences. But what she was hoping to see – a police station – never materialized. Nor did she see a police patrol car. If she had, she would have made an attempt to signal them that she was in trouble.

Her hopes of an escape began to fade as George drove out of the town. The farther he went, the darker it became as the street lights and other ambient light of the town slowly diminished to eventually be swallowed up by the darkness. Even the dim lights from homes off the highway were fewer and farther in between.

After they had traveled about ten miles, George took a right turn onto a smaller paved road. But the asphalt did not last long. Several miles later the pavement ended and they were on a graded dirt road.

From the time they left the garage, George had not spoken. In between her glances out the windows to orient herself to the cityscape and countryside, she stole a few glances at her grandfather. He never took his eyes off the road and kept both hands on the steering wheel. He looked very much like a man in super concentration.

As they continued along, Stephanie could tell they were going uphill. It started as a slight tilt to the Jeep but slowly increased.

Stephanie could see nothing past the sides of the vehicle. It was pitch black. And through the windshield she could see nothing past the range of the headlights. Eventually the road became rougher.

Stephanie began to understand there was no way she would be able to find her way back without some reference points. As this realization took hold, so did fatigue from the trying day she had experienced. She could feel her eyelids getting heavier. She tried to fight off the sleep, but without the motivation of memorizing her surroundings, she finally drifted off.

When she awoke, she found herself lying in a bed covered under a sheet and what felt like several blankets. She felt the upper side of them and they were a bit scratchy. She opened her eyes fully and looked around.

At first, it was completely black. But as she looked around, she could begin to see a little bit as her eyes became more acclimated to the darkness.

She was in a one room structure. In addition to the bed, she could make out the shape of a couch and a recliner nearby. There was also a wooden table with four wooden chairs around it. On the other side the of table and chairs was a small cook stove and a sink.

There were three windows – one near the door, one over the sink and a third on the backside wall directly opposite the door. Each of the windows were covered entirely by black cloth. The entirety of each window was covered, allowing no light to come in – if there was actually light outside to get in. Stephanie had no idea how long she had slept.

She was alone in the structure.

"Grandpa, are you there?" she asked hesitantly.

There was no answer. In fact, there was no sound at all.

Agent Susan Blastmore got three four-wheel-drive vehicles from the Ada County Sheriff's Office, and drivers to go with them. They were parked on the Boise airport tarmac near the chartered jet on which they had flown to Idaho. Nathan tried to do the math to determine how much it was costing to keep the plane at their disposal, and the pilot on call. The total daily cost he guessed made his head spin.

Before securing the vehicles, the FBI agents returned to George's home for a thorough search. Barbara wasn't thrilled about having her property searched, but she had little choice.

The search turned up next to nothing useful. It was clear that George had covered his tracks well. They did find some clothing that would have fit a pre-teen. They were a mix of types of girls' outfits and shoes. Barbara said they were items her daughters had worn and she had packed away after they left home with the idea she would give them to the girls for their own children.

But Barbara told Agent Blastmore that about half the clothing she had packed were missing.

"Do you think your husband took these clothes for Stephanie?" she asked.

"I suppose so, since Stephanie only had what she was wearing when she got here," Barbara said.

"And that didn't raise a red flag for you?" Susan asked.

"I really didn't think about it," she answered a little testily. "I was pretty surprised that she was here at all. My husband did not tell me he was going to be bringing her here."

Blastmore also learned from Barbara that George had taken at least two weapons with him, a rifle and a pistol.

When asked what kind of guns they were, Barbara produced a sales slip with a description of the rifle, which was purchased within the past two years. It was a Mauser M18. Blastmore had heard of the rifle. It was described as the most accurate deer rifle for the money. It had a three-lug action, good trigger and the stock was finished in the classic American style. The sales slip also included a high-power scope.

The pistol was a Sig Sauer P226, according to an older sales slip Barbara produced. While the weapon is most commonly used by Navy Seals, some other officers and non-commissioned officers like the gun as their personal side arm. That was the weapon Blastmore used.

"Where is the ammunition for these weapons?" Blastmore asked. They had found no other guns and ammo during their search.

"I don't know," Barbara said. "He keeps all that in the garage. The only time I have anything to do with it is when we're out in the field hunting."

"Do you hunt?" Blastmore asked.

"I go with him most times when he goes," Barbara answered. "But I don't shoot the guns. They bother me."

"Why is that?" the agent asked.

"Because I don't know enough about them to be safe with them," she said.

"Hasn't your husband taught you about firearms?" Blastmore asked.

"He's tried, I just don't get it sometimes and he gets frustrated," Barbara said.

Susan hesitated before asking her next question. In a way, she was afraid of the answer she might get. It could indicate Stephanie was in danger of being hurt by her grandfather if she did not cooperate with him.

"Has he ever gotten so frustrated that he yells at you or strikes you?" she finally asked.

Barbara's answer came quickly, too quickly for Blastmore's tatste.

"Never."

The two women stood looking at each other for a moment. Susan could tell she was holding something back. Under Blastmore's stare, Barbara crumbled a little.

"That is not to say I haven't been concerned about that sometimes," she said.

"Does he have a violent temper?" the agent asked.

"He gets frustrated easily, and when that happens, he raises his voice and looks menacing," Barbara said. "But I suppose that comes from his days as a drill instructor. It's part of the way he got recruits' attention, I guess."

Blastmore could see the logic in that. But it also confirmed her concerns that Stephanie could place herself in danger if she did not conform to her grandfather's instructions.

That made finding them that much more critical.

Stephanie carefully got out from under the covers. Even with her clothes on, she felt the cold air. It was much colder than when she got up in the mornings at the McAdams house, or even the family's home before her mother took her away.

She stood at the side of the bed for a few moments, letting her eyes continue to get used to the dark interior. She was starting to make out more detail.

She could see the couch was older and a bit worn in some places. She couldn't tell whether it was covered by cloth or leather. But she believed the recliner was a leather one. The table and chairs appeared to both be made of wood. They were old and scuffed.

Stephanie stood very still for a few seconds, trying to hear any noise. There was none.

She took one step ahead toward the couch and recliner directly across from the bed. Four steps later she was feeling the couch. It was definitely covered with cloth. She moved to the recliner and confirmed her earlier impression that it was covered in leather. It, too, was worn. She could feel cracks in the leather on the seat and back portions.

She then moved to her left to the door. It was a regular door but as she felt it, she could tell that it was rough wood, not smooth like the doors in homes she had been in. She reached out and grabbed the door knob and turned it to the right. But when she pulled on it, the door did not budge. She did not see a deadbolt knob or latch. She knew she was locked in.

Stephanie went to the window behind the couch and felt around the edges, trying to determine how the cloth was attached. She discovered the cloth was very thick and was attached by large nails driven into the walls next to it. She tried to get her hands under the edge of the cloth, but the nails were spaced too closely together to allow her to get a grip to pull the cloth away from the wall. And the nails had large enough heads they wouldn't just allow her to pop the cloth away from the wall even if she could get a grip.

Now she knew she was truly trapped.

The girl began to get scared. Had she been dropped off somewhere and left to slowly die? Was there food in this place? If so, how long would it last? Was there water? Would she ever see her family again?

But one questions was uppermost in her mind. Was this man who had taken her really her grandfather? She knew very little about her dad's father. When at his home she saw no pictures of herself anywhere. Wouldn't a grandparent have pictures of their grandchildren? The McAdamses had a lot of pictures of her in their home.

That last question increased her fear.

She flopped down in the recliner and began to sob. But after a few minutes she stopped suddenly. She thought she heard a noise outside. With even the slightest move in the recliner, the creak of the leather made her wonder whether she had actually heard something outside or if it was just the chair.

She stood up and took a step away from the chair. She cocked her head to one side and strained to hear. There it was again! But she could not tell what the noise was. The sound seemed to get closer to the structure. Then she recognized the noise as footsteps. And she noticed something else – the sound of heavy breathing, like she did after she had been running.

Then the footsteps stopped, but not the breathing. Then she heard the sound of metal against metal and she realized a key was being inserted into a lock. Stephanie turned toward the door and stood transfixed in fear.

Chapter 14

The door opened inward towards Stephanie, who had retreated to a spot in front of the sofa. No one entered for a second or two, then a large stainless-steel container came inside enough for her to see half of it before it was set down to the side of the door. Then another entered, then a third.

Fear and adrenaline started mixing within her.

George then entered the structure, breathing heavier than he was outdoors. He stood just inside the doorway for a moment, catching his breath. He looked over at Stephanie.

"There is no running water here," he said, then took a deep breath. "This is what we'll use." Another breath, this one more shallow. He was getting his breath back after carrying the three water containers inside.

"Where did it come from?" is all Stephanie could think to ask.

"The river about a half mile away," George answered, taking one final long, deep breath. He had recovered from the exertion.

"Where are we?" she asked.

George shut the door, moved to the table where he lit a small candle, much like the candles Stephanie's parents put on her birthday cakes. The room was bathed in faded light. Before George shut the door, Stephanie saw no light from outside. George turned back toward the door and Stephanie could make out a skeleton key in his hand. *"So it is still nighttime,"* she thought. She heard the key turn in the lock, and again she was trapped inside.

"We are at my cabin in the mountains," George said, then pulled out one of the chairs and sat down.

"Why are we here?" she asked, still rooted to the same spot on the wood floor.

George released a long, heavy sigh and put his head in his hand, resting his elbow on the table. He was still trying to work that out in his own mind. He knew taking Stephanie from the school was going to mean law enforcement would get involved. But when he struck the teacher and heard her head hit the pillar, he knew things were going to escalate.

He was sure the teacher could be seriously injured. But until he saw a news report when they landed at the airport announcing a teacher had been killed in a kidnapping, he did not know it already had gone to another level.

He had originally planned to keep Stephanie at his home until Nathan contacted him. He would then assure his son that he would return his daughter to him once he was awarded custody of her. It wasn't a perfect plan, but he believed it would give Nathan some leverage. With the death of the teacher, any leverage that may have been available disappeared. Now he was improvising.

"I'm trying to get you back to your dad," George said, with his face still buried in his hand.

"And Mom?" Stephanie asked hesitantly.

"No," George said.

"Why not?" she asked, he tone turning angry.

George snapped his head toward her and banged his fist on the table. Stephanie jumped at the sound and took a step backward.

"Because you need to be with your father," George yelled.

But seeing the frightened look on Stephanie's face, he spoke in a calmer voice.

"Your mother wants to take you away from your father," he told her.

She knew what her mother planned to do, because she had confided it to Stephanie. She had also overheard her mother telling her parents all those horrible things about her dad. She didn't believe them, of course. She was convinced her father could never have done the things her mother was accusing him of. But Stephanie knew divorce and her mother gaining sole custody was something that was entirely possible.

Stephanie wanted the family to stay together. She was convinced that once her parents had a chance to talk about it, they would come to the same conclusion. She was just biding her time until that could happen. Then she would provide her input. She was certain that would seal the deal and keep them all together.

Up to this point, she had given no thought to the idea that the separation of her parents was going to be permanent.

"Is my father coming here?' she asked.

"Possibly," George said. "But others will probably come first."

"You mean police," Stephanie said. It was not a question.

"That's right," George said, standing up and facing her. Then he turned to the water containers and drug one over to the sink. He took a kerosene lantern from a shelf and lit it to provide more light in the semi-darkened cabin.

"You need to clean up. Use this water," George instructed, then unlocked the door and went outside, locking the door behind him.

When George came back in with two duffel bags, Stephanie was at the sink washing her face and hands from a large bowl full of cold water and a wash cloth she found in the small cupboard. He tossed one duffel on the couch and another on the bed.

"There are clothes in there for you," he said, pointing to the bed. "I'm going outside for a little while. Clean yourself all over and then change clothes. Dress in warm clothes. Put the clothes you have on in that duffel bag."

Stephanie did not look around the whole time, but she heard the skeleton key turn in the lock and knew that her grandfather was no longer in the cabin.

It was still dark when the convoy of three county sheriff's Ford Explorers headed out of town. But the sky to the east was beginning to take on a lighter shade of blue along the horizon. As the vehicles turned right onto the paved side road, the horizon had taken on a bright orange glow in the nearly cloudless sky. One point was nearly white, indicating the sun was right behind it.

FBI Agent Susan Blastmore rode in the first Explorer in line with a sheriff's deputy at the wheel. They had not spoken since climbing aboard and setting out. Blastmore was intent on the GPS map tracker on her cell phone. She had programmed in the coordinates of the cabin on George's land and was following their progress.

Agents Mason and Vallow rode in the third vehicle in line with their deputy driver. Nathan and Deputy Barnes, sitting in the front passenger seat with Nathan behind her, were in the middle vehicle with another deputy doing the driving.

Before setting out, the group talked about their objectives. Blastmore explained this would be a reconnaissance only to determine if George had actually gone to his cabin.

"I'm sure he is smart enough to realize that we would find out about his ownership of this land and know that would be one of, if not the first place we would look," she said. She stole a glance at Nathan who nodded in agreement.

However, she wanted the team to be prepared for other contingencies.

According to George's wife, he had only taken two weapons – the rifle and handgun – and a lot of ammunition for them. Barbara was certain those were the only two guns her husband owned. But Blastmore was not convinced that he may have possessed more but had kept them hidden from her. It was also possible he had a stash of additional weapons at the cabin.

The FBI agents and the deputies, including Barnes, had their side arms. The three local deputies also brought their assigned .223 semiautomatic patrol rifles.

"If we do encounter George and the girl, there is to be no gunfire except on my order," Blastmore said.

"And what if we are fired upon?" one of the local deputies asked.

"Only on my order," Blastmore said firmly. "Understood?"

The deputies and Mason and Vallow nodded in agreement.

"I don't want to take any chances of hitting Stephanie," Blastmore said, with a glance at Nathan. His look of relief was only half-hearted.

The agents and deputies each had Kevlar vests packed in the vehicles. Blastmore talked the sheriff out of an extra one for Nathan, just in case he needed to be with the law enforcement personnel if they were confronted. But she had no intention of allowing that except as a last resort.

Eventually, the paved side road turned into a gravel road which later gave way to a bare dirt road. It was also graded, but was rougher than the caked gravel roadbed. Just after getting on this section of roadway, they saw a sign that told them they had entered the national forest. It was not the large monument type sign, but a small brown and gold shield on a post. That indicated this road was a secondary entry point to the forest, rarely used by the public.

The sun had topped the horizon some minutes before and lit up the area in harsh light that created stark contrasts on the surroundings as they rolled by the vehicle windows.

They were going through a section a flat land with prairie grass and scattered bushes and sagebrush on either side of the road. The tree line loomed ahead of them, thin at first but getting more dense as the trees ascended the mountain like thousands of climbers striving for the summit.

After entering the tree line, the road became less of a road and more of a set of parallel rut trails.

Nathan began to have vague flashbacks of familiarity. He knew his father had taken him to the woods when he was very young. No distinct memories came to his mind, but the nagging feeling he had been here before would not leave him.

As the fir, pine and cottonwood trees rolled past his window like an old-time movie viewer, the sun's rays peeking through the trees made it seem as if a strobe light was blinking into the vehicle. The effect was a bit hypnotic, and Nathan turned away from the window.

The line of Explorers droned on, going ever slower as they climbed the mountain on the ever-deteriorating path. The slap of high grass could now be heard impacting the underside of the vehicles.

Suddenly, the lead vehicle came to a dead stop and the others, in turn, did the same. Blastmore stepped out of the Explorer and motioned for the rest of the party to join her.

"The GPS says we are about a half mile from the cabin," she explained. "We're going to walk the rest of the way."

She handed Barnes a hand radio and slipped another one into the utility belt she borrowed from the sheriff's department.

"You and Nathan stay here until we've scouted it out," she instructed.

Nathan started to protest, but Susan stopped him with an upturned index finger.

"You need to wait here until we secure the area," she said. Her tone was commanding, but with a hint of understanding.

Nathan was not happy as he watched the agents and deputies don their Kevlar and begin walking, in two single file lines, along the trail.

Forty-five minutes later, Barnes' radio chirped.

"Barnes," he heard Blastmore's voice say. The deputy put the radio to her ear. "Barnes, come back."

"You two can come ahead on," Blastmore said. "Leave your vests there."

Nathan could hear the disappointment in Susan's voice. A sense of dread came over him and he began running up the trail before Barnes could close the communication with Blastmore.

The FBI agents and sheriff's deputies advanced along the trail, one line in each track. The timber was so thick on either side of the trail it was like they were walking along a hallway.

Initially, they went at a normal walking pace. They slowed when the trail curved about 45 degrees to the right, making sure there was nothing ahead of them as they made the turn. After about twenty yards, the trail curved back to the left, but only slightly. They slowed their pace even more.

When Blastmore caught sight of something ahead, she signaled for a halt. She backed the columns up a few paces and turned to the others. She signaled for the column on the left – hers – to advance through the trees on that side of the trail and the other group to go into the trees to the right. Blastmore had two of the deputies with her and Mason and Vallow had the other. They advanced at a snail's pace, trying not to make a sound. It wasn't easy as they serpentined between tightly grouped trees and walking through downed limbs. Every sound was magnified in the woods. They were fortunate it was the spring, and early in the morning, and the ground, along with the debris on it, was damp.

As they moved forward, a vehicle slowly came into view. It was parked in the trail facing in their direction. Drawing closer, they saw it was a Jeep Wrangler. Behind it was a small cabin surrounded on three sides by the trees, just like the sides of the trail. The log exterior was weathered, a dull gray. This structure had obviously been here for years.

Blastmore caught sight of the other group and motioned for them to stop. She took a few minutes to appraise the situation and come up with a plan for further investigation. She could see a window near the front door. She saw nothing but blackness through the window.

Susan gestured for Mason alone to circle the cabin on the right and she assigned one of the deputies to do the same on the left. After ten anxious minutes, they returned to their groups.

The deputy whispered to Blastmore that he found a window in the back and Mason had seen one on the right side. They were both dark, as if they were covered from the inside. She considered their options, then gave instructions to the deputy and motioned for Mason to meet him in back of the cabin. Mason returned to his group, whispered instructions then returned to the rear of the cabin. He and the deputy took positions at opposite corners of the structure.

Blastmore motioned for Vallow and another deputy to proceed. They, Susan and the last deputy stealthily advanced to the front door. She slowly took hold of the door knob and turned. She could tell it was locked.

"Breach," she whispered to the deputy.

He stood in front of the door and gave it a mighty kick just below the old-fashioned metal box that housed the door knob. The crack of old, dry wood echoed through the forest and the door swung open. Blastmore crossed the threshold from left to right followed by Vallow in the opposite direction with the deputy going straight in.

"FBI! Put your hands on your heads," Blastmore yelled.

Nathan ran as fast as he could, faster than he had run since high school, along the mountain trail. He was in the left-hand track. His mind was on what was ahead. So much so that he did not hear the footfalls behind him. Deputy Barnes was slowly gaining on him.

When Nathan made the second turn on the track, he saw the Jeep ahead straddling the center "median" of tall grass. He also saw the cabin behind it and suddenly had that feeling of familiarity again.

As he came even with the Jeep, he felt a hand grab his right arm and pull. It slowed but didn't stop him right away, but Barnes was strong, stronger than she appeared, and had more training. She ground him to halt just as he got to the passenger door of the Jeep.

"Slow down, Mr. Wallis," he heard Dawn say over his shoulder.

Nathan tried to call his daughter's name, but he was struggling for breath and couldn't get the word out. Agent Blastmore appeared in the doorway of the cabin and walked to him.

"They are not here," she said. But he tried to break Deputy Barnes' grip. She gripped tighter and he felt a little pain.

Blastmore put her hand on his left shoulder and gave it a squeeze.

"There is no one inside," she said to him a little louder, but she was not yelling.

He stared at her dazed for a moment.

"I thought...." He started to say, but could not bring himself to speak aloud his worst fears after overhearing the radio call.

"I know what you must have thought," Susan said, giving his shoulder another squeeze. "And I apologize if I frightened you. We were all a little disappointed."

Nathan took a few deep breaths until he had filled his lungs with air. They were high enough in the mountains that the air was a bit thinner than what he was used to. He glanced at Deputy Barnes and saw that she was breathing normally.

"Must be the training," Nathan thought to himself.

"We are searching the cabin and we are treating it like a crime scene," Blastmore said, but added when she saw worry creep back into Nathan's face, "But we haven't found anything that indicates anything more than that your daughter and father were here."

Nathan's sigh of relief was audible to the FBI agent and deputy.

"I want you to come inside and look around, you might see something we might miss," the agent said. "But please don't touch anything."

Nathan nodded his head in agreement and followed Susan to the cabin door. On the way he saw a sheriff's deputy at each of the front corners of the cabin facing into the woods and scanning back and forth.

Nathan stood in the doorway and made a quick survey of the one-room structure. Even with the front door standing open, there wasn't much light inside because all the windows were covered. He saw the shape of the recliner and couch to his left, the bed against the left back wall, the cook stove on the right back wall and the sink on the right. The table and chairs were in the middle of the room.

Mason and Vallow were checking every inch of the inside with their penlights. Mason was near the bed and Nathan saw some clothing on it. They were the same clothes he had seen Stephanie wearing when she was taken from the school. He walked to the bed and reached his hand out to touch them. But Blastmore put her hand gently on his arm.

"Not yet, Mr. Wallis," she said. "We need to examine them for DNA and fingerprints."

He nodded and turned to walk outside. He sat down on a stump on the side of the cabin. Within minutes, Blastmore sat on a stump nearby.

"Did you see anything in there that might be helpful?" she asked.

Nathan slowly shook his head.

"It looks like Dad pretty well cleaned it out before he left," he said.

"Yes, except for your daughter's clothes," she said, more to herself than to Nathan.

Chapter 15

Stephanie and her grandfather were hiking up a slight rise. He was in the lead, with a very large backpack that extended past his head and below his butt, colored in the shades of green, black, gray and brown of military camouflage, stuffed full with clothing, food, first aid supplies and a variety of other items, including ammunition. The only thing Stephanie could see of her grandfather was his sturdy legs striding evenly over the rough ground and his arms swinging in opposition by his sides.

Secured to the back of the pack was a rifle scabbard containing his Mauser M18. He wore a utility belt on which hung the Sig Saur P226 in a leather holster on his right hip and two canteens full of water on his left. Perched in a shoulder holster, she had seen when they set out, was a Glock nine-millimeter pistol.

Stephanie also had a pack slung on her back. It was much smaller than her grandfather's, about twice the size of the book bag she carried to school. In it were two extra sets of clothing and more food. Her pack was also decorated in military camo colors, only this one was shades of black, gray and white.

She was a little less steady in her strides on the forest floor. In the first one hundred yards of their hike, she felt her feet tip several times, nearly twisting her ankles as she stepped on fallen branches and animal tracks left in the soft earth, most of which were disguised by the wild grass that covered the ground.

"Watch the ground where you are about to step," her grandfather instructed after having to stop and wait for her a few times.

That helped, and as they progressed, it became easier.

It wasn't that Stephanie had never been in the outdoors. She and her parents hiked often in the flat wooded areas near their home. They also occasionally went camping. But this was more intense than she had yet experienced.

Once she got use to the uneven ground and the dried branches on the ground, she was able to keep pace with George. They were now advancing faster than in the beginning.

The pair had been hiking since the sun started to peek over the horizon about an hour ago. As the sun filtered brighter through the trees, Stephanie also found the going easier.

At the start of their trek, George had re-entered the cabin telling Stephanie to get dressed and beckoned for her to come outside while grabbing the two duffel bags and going out again. Stephanie quickly retrieved the clothing she had been wearing from under the bed and put them on the top of the bed, throwing the blankets over them.

She then hurried outside, lest her grandfather come back in and see them. But he did go back in with one of the duffels, which he had emptied its contents into the back of the Jeep. Stephanie's anxiety rose, thinking he would discover her clothing on the bed. When he came back out five minutes later the duffel appeared full and he tossed it into the back of the Jeep.

He said nothing about her clothing.

But since they began their hike up the mountain, Stephanie worried that he had found them and put them in the duffel with whatever else he had filled it with.

Nathan stood in the airport terminal watching his brother, Bryan, walking toward the exit from the checkpoint area. As Nathan and all but two of the FBI/sheriff's team drove off the mountain around noon, he received a voicemail from his brother telling him he was flying in that afternoon.

The group, including Blastmore, two local deputies, Vallow and Nathan, stopped by the airport to check in at the chartered jet the FBI agents were using. It was then that Nathan and Deputy Barnes, continuing her orders to shadow Nathan, went to meet Bryan.

"So that's your brother, huh?" Barnes asked when Nathan pointed him out as he strode toward them. "He's kind of hot," she added in a low whisper, hoping Nathan wouldn't hear. The roll of his eyes told her he had. She blushed a little.

Bryan came out of the checkpoint area and gave his brother a big bear hug.

Although just over a year younger than Nathan, Bryan was taller and built more like an athlete. His curly brown hair was medium length and he sported a full, fluffy beard, The blue eyes pierced right through to the soul of the person he happened to be addressing at the moment.

Bryan released his brother from the massive, long hug and held him at arm's length.

"You look like shit," he said with a twinkle in his eye.

"Well, I did just come off a mountain," Nathan answered.

"Yes you did," Bryan said, inhaling the smell of dirt, pine needles and sweat. It was exactly what made him feel at home.

Bryan glanced over at Barnes and nudged his brother in the ribs.

"Didn't waste any time finding a new babe," he said. "I'm impressed."

Barnes blushed lightly again. Nathan gave his brother a good-natured punch in the shoulder.

"This is not a new babe," Nathan said. "This is Deputy Dawn Barnes. She was assigned to babysit me until they officially clear me as a suspect in all this."

Bryan looked her over from head to toe.

"Sorry, big brother, but this is a babe," he said. "And I see there is no ring on that left hand."

"I'm on duty," was all Barnes could manage through her increasing blush.

"Well, we'll have to talk when you're off duty," Bryan said, picking up his carry-on duffel bag and small backpack. "But right now, we need to go to baggage check. I had to check my fire arms."

At the baggage claim area, Bryan collected and signed for a long, padded case that held his rifle and a small, desert tan backpack that contained three different pistols. There was no ammunition, as it was not allowed even in checked baggage.

"We'll need to go to a sporting goods store and stock up," he told his brother as they headed for the tarmac and the FBI's chartered jet.

"Why bring so much hardware?" Nathan asked. "And for that matter, why did you come at all?"

Bryan gave Barnes a quick glance.

"I hadn't heard from you since after you and I talked last and I wanted to know what was going on, so I called Sheriff Martin from the mountain," Bryan explained. "That was the day before you and the FBI and Deputy Hottie here left to come out here looking for Dad."

Nathan stole a glance at Barnes, who was two steps behind them. Her face was a little flushed, but there was also a look of satisfaction. She was beautiful, she knew it and she liked when men noticed. But the little redness in her cheeks each time Bryan eluded to it was telling.

But Nathan put that aside for the moment.

"So why didn't you just call me?" he asked his brother.

"You would have himed and hawed about it and told me everything was under control," Bryan said. "I wanted to know what was really going on."

"But things are under control, as far as I can see," Nathan said.

"And what have you and the FBI found so far?" Bryan asked.

"You mean here?" Nathan asked.

"No, in your search for the holy grail," Bryan mocked. "Here's yer sign."

Nathan took a playful swipe at this brother's head, caught the upper part of his brown Wyoming Cowboys ball cap and watched it fall to the floor. Bryan barely broke stride as he bent and picked it up.

"Nyuk, nyuk, nyuk," Bryan said while jabbing two fingers towards Nathan's eyeballs in perfect Three Stooges style. Nathan yanked his head backward and cried out in faux pain. Barnes shook her head, thinking, *"Couple of knuckleheads."* But the brothers were starting to grow on her, especially Bryan.

Nathan quickly turned back to serious mode.

"We were on the mountain this morning and found a cabin," he explained while Bryan listened intently. "Dad's Jeep was there and we found the clothes Stephanie was wearing the day he took her."

Bryan considered this as they neared the door leading to the tarmac where the jet was parked. Barnes showed her law enforcement ID to the guard there and they began to go through. Bryan stopped and turned to the other two once they were all outside and the door closed behind them.

"Because if he is going where I think he's going, you're all going to need my help," Bryan said.

"Why is that?" Barnes asked.

"Because I have been there," Bryan said. "With him."

Barnes was a little surprised at the revelation, but looked on it as a positive step in the investigation. She could not wait to share it with Agent Blastmore. She headed for the jet, but Nathan was rooted to his spot, looking at his brother with his mouth agape.

George and Stephanie had been hiking for more than an hour since they left the cabin. While the sun was higher in the sky, it had not topped the tall pines and spruce that towered over them. But as the sun filtered through the trees the contrast of bright light and shadow was still quite stark.

While Stephanie could feel her calves tighter than when they had started out, she was not tired. Several times George stopped ahead of her. She thought he was taking a break as she stopped just a couple of feet behind him. However, each time he first glanced behind himself to make sure she was still there, then he scanned the maze of trees in almost a three hundred-sixty degree arc. The first time this happened Stephanie started to ask what he was doing, but he quickly shushed her, a bit rudely, she thought. But then she recognized that he was listening. But for what?

As they continued to ascend the mountain, Stephanie worried that the farther up they went, the less her chances would be to make an escape attempt. She did not want to try it during the first hour because it was still dark and she knew even if she did get away she could not find her way back to the cabin in the dark.

Plus, George's frequent stops to check her progress and their surroundings made it difficult for her to know when the best time would be.

Then during his last stop, Stephanie could hear that his breathing was heavier. They walked on for another fifth yards until they came to a stump with another tree directly behind. But it wasn't actually two trees, it was a single one that had split into two upward shafts. Stephanie knew from her school studies that it took trees hundreds of years to reach the height of these.

The stump was not ragged, as if that shaft had broken away and fallen. Rather, it was flat and smooth. Someone had cut the one portion of the tree. It was just the right height from the forest floor to serve as a chair and her grandfather sat down upon it. He leaned back against the other tree shaft and let his head rest on the rolled up sleeping bag tied to the top of the pack. The other, tied at the bottom, fit neatly into the space between the stump and the base of the other shaft.

George looked very comfortable sitting there. So much so that Stephanie guessed that it was he who cut the tree forming the chair in the forest.

She stood several feet away from him. He had not invited her to sit. There were plenty of fallen tree trunks in the area for her to do so. Then he closed his eyes and within seconds his breathing became heavier.

Stephanie waited about five minutes, not moving a muscle. Then she started to hear her grandfather's breath begin to rattle softly. She slowly turned away from him and, keeping her eyes on the ground so as to avoid any dry twigs, began to slowly walk downhill.

She had gone about twenty yards, having been so quiet with her steps she could hear her own heart beating rapidly, and suddenly heard a voice behind her.

"Stephanie, stop right there. Don't make a move," George said softly.

She tilted her head up and was about to turn it in his direction when she caught sight of movement directly in front of her. What she saw at first frightened her, but then she was filled with wonder and excitement. Standing about ten yards away was a small bear.

Its fur was jet black. Its snout was a medium brown, getting darker above and alongside its eyes and mixing with black at the forehead. The rounded ears reminded her of the Mickey Mouse hat ears she had seen on television. It was about the size of an adult springer spaniel.

The bear had its front paws on a fallen tree truck and was sniffing the air.

"Stephanie, very slowly, start walking backwards toward me," George instructed. "If the bear starts coming toward you, don't panic and keep moving backward very slowly."

She wasn't afraid, but she followed her grandfather's instructions. She had taken three slow steps when she suddenly heard something to her left. It was first a variety of grunts, then loud blowing noises. She slowly turned her head and saw another black-furred bear about twenty yards away. This bear was much larger.

Stephanie had continued to move backward when she looked over at the new visitor. She felt her heel come in contact with something and even though she was moving very slowly, it made her lose her balance and she fell backward and landed on her rump. Not hard enough to hurt, but with the pack on getting up was going to be a challenge.

Stephanie heard a loud thump behind her and looked over her left shoulder in time to see her grandfather, sans his pack, running to take a position between her and the bear.

"Stephanie, go up to the stump," George said.

She got to her feet and walked briskly up the hill, stopping to grab her grandfather's pack. It was much heavier than the one she had on her back and she struggled to lift it. But she was able to get it up enough to carry it, with the bottom sleeping bag dragging along the ground, to the stump.

George adjusted his position so as to keep himself between the larger bear and his granddaughter. The bear continued its grunting, and began to move toward the smaller bear. The two animals grunted back and forth then moved away, disappearing into the thick forest.

George returned to the stump and put his pack back on.

"We need to move on," was all he said and began walking up the mountain. Stephanie followed, a little closer behind him this time.

Twenty minutes later, George halted the hike where the trees thinned out against a rock face. He told Stephanie to wait, and this time she picked out a spot and sat down. The sudden encounter with the bears left her a little rattled, and curious.

George took off his pack and leaned it against a tree, then walked the twenty yards to the rock that jutted up as high as a two-story house. It stretched fifty yards wide. He went to an opening in the cliff, oblong in shape horizontally with the bottom about two feet off the forest floor. He checked the opening thoroughly, then he crawled inside.

The first part of the cave was small, just big enough for a bear to turn around in. But George could see that it extended into the mountain and opened to a slightly larger cavern. George crawled into the larger area and looked around, using the flashlight he had brought with him.

Along the walls in the entrance chamber, he noticed claw marks on the walls. There were none in the inner chamber. The floor of the cave was rock, but there was some dust and in it he saw a few bear paw prints.

George crawled out of the cave and brushed off his clothing. He looked around and listened. There were just the wind blowing gently through the tops of the trees and an occasional chirping of birds.

He walked to his pack and put it back on.

"We need to keep going," he told Stephanie. She stood and adjusted her pack.

"Thank you for saving me from the bear," she said hesitantly. She felt funny thanking someone who had kidnapped her.

"She probably wouldn't have hurt you, so there was no saving to it," he said.

She didn't move even though her grandfather had turned and taken a few steps to go around the rock face. He stopped and turned toward her. The puzzled look on her face was mixed with curiosity.

"She was just protecting her cub," George explained. "As long as you stayed away from the cub they would have walked away."

Stephanie started moving toward her grandfather and he, in turn, returned to the direction he was going initially.

"So why did you get in between us?" Stephanie asked.

"Just to make sure, sometimes they will charge," George said. "But only to try and scare you."

"But I've read about bears attacking people, and I've seen it on TV," Stephanie said.

George sighed as he walked.

"This was a black bear," he said. "They don't usually attack people unless they feel threatened."

"But....," she started.

"You've read and watched some bad information," George said a little angrily. "Grizzlies will attack, not black bears."

"Are there grizzlies around here?" Stephanie asked with a touch of fear in her voice.

"Some," George said, then stopped and tuned toward his granddaughter. "That's enough talking. Let's get where we're going."

He turned and continued. Stephanie followed silently.

Chapter 16

With the flurry of introductions of Bryan, the FBI agents and sheriff's deputies gathered inside the jet, then the mutual briefings, Nathan had no time to talk to his brother until they were headed back up the mountain.

In the jet, Agent Blastmore gave Bryan the basics of the case so far. Until she knew just what Bryan was doing here and what he could offer the investigation, she was not going to share it in detail.

"So why are you here?' she finally asked Bryan.

"First, may I say that if you are as good an agent as you are a looker, we'll have the case solved in no time," Bryan said with a glint in his eye. Nathan rolled his eyes and nudged his brother. Blastmore stood as stoic as a statue, showing no emotion. *"Oh boy, another one of these guys,"* she thought.

"No, really," Bryan said. "Even in those FBI TV shows they don't have agents that match you in looks," Bryan said, looking to Nathan for validation, which was not forthcoming. Nathan put a hand to his forehead and shook his head.

"And if what you can offer this investigation is anything like your ability to shovel bullshit, I'd say we're screwed," Blastmore said, giving Bryan a look of disdain.

Bryan let Susan's words echo through the silent jet for a beat or two. Then he lost his cavalier attitude and looked her dead in the eye.

"Have you been up in that forest?" he asked, then looked at everyone gathered there for an answer. None was offered, even from the local deputies.

"I didn't think so," Bryan said.

"We rarely go up into the forest unless we are called in by the forest rangers," one of the local deputies finally said. "I can count on one hand the number of times we've been called up there in the 11 years I've been with the department."

Bryan flashed a triumphant look around the jet's passenger cabin.

"There is one person here who has been up there," he said. "I've not only been in this forest, I know exactly where my father is likely to go."

"And how do you know that?" Blastmore asked, feeling a little chastised, but wanting to regain control of the conversation.

"Because he took me on a tour of all his favorite places up there," Bryan said. "Twice."

Blastmore was not entirely comfortable with a civilian having so much control over an investigation, but she had to admit that Bryan most likely had information that months of research couldn't produce and that he would be an asset. She also knew that she and her agents were out of their element in the wilderness and because he was a professional outfitter, he had skills they lacked.

"We would appreciate your help," Blastmore said graciously, but through mentally gritted teeth.

She then took Bryan by the arm and led him to the cockpit and closed the door. The pilot and co-pilot were inside the terminal, waiting to be called back to work, so they were alone in the cramped space.

"While I agreed to let you help us out, you need to understand that I am leading this investigation," she said. "Do not go off the rails, everything goes through me. Understood?"

Bryan fixed her with a steely gaze.

"All kidding aside, Agent Blastmore, all I'm interested in is getting my niece back safely. So, whatever it takes," he said.

"And your father?" she asked.

"I am totally focused on Stephanie," he said slowly. The implication was clear. If George got in the way of his goal, he would be collateral damage.

Blastmore nodded and turned to leave the cockpit, but she paused at the door and looked back at Bryan over her shoulder.

"So, you were only kidding when you said I was a looker?" she asked, throwing him a seductive look.

"Oh no, you are super hot," Bryan said with a smile.

"Don't let it interfere with our mutual goal," Susan said, dropping the seductive voice and back into the voice of authority. She opened the door and marched into the passenger cabin.

"Super hot," Bryan thought, licking his finger, touching it to his buttock and whispering a sizzling noise.

The brothers were headed up the mountain alone in a four-wheel-drive Ram single cab pickup borrowed from the sheriff's department after Blastmore vouched for them. The vehicle was a stripped down model in the reserve role in the sheriff's motor pool. While it still had the sheriff's department decals and other markings affixed to it, there was no light bar, siren or other special equipment except the radio, which was in working order.

As the day was nearly half over and darkness was within hours, FBI Agent Blastmore decided there was no opportunity to track George and Stephanie at night. Bryan had agreed. But he wanted to go up the mountain and stay the night at the cabin to allow him to scout things out a bit before they started a search the next morning.

She agreed, and instructed him to send the sheriff's deputy that was left there back down the mountain when they got there. However, she wanted Mason to stay there with them to have an FBI presence. Using her satellite phone to Mason's, Blastmore gave him instructions, especially to not allow Bryan and Nathan to strike out on their own. She wanted a full team involved in any continued search.

As the brothers, with Bryan at the wheel, drove through town heading for the mountain cabin, Nathan began peppering his brother with questions like a bulldog detective in an interrogation.

"So, when have you seen Dad?" he asked.

Nathan knew that each of his siblings, when they were younger, grew tired of being the ones who initiated contact with their father while he never called, wrote, texted or emailed. They all decided to stop making contact in hopes it would spur him to get in touch with them.

Their ploy did not work, and eventually they all became estranged from their father. Or so Nathan thought.

"It's only been a few times over the last twelve years or so," Bryan said.

"I never knew you were in contact with him," Nathan said. There was a bit of bitterness in his voice. "How come you never said anything?"

"I got in touch with him when I first started thinking about becoming an outfitter," Bryan said. "I figured with his military background he could give me some tips on survival in the wild."

"Okay, I can understand that," Nathan said. "But there weren't any others you could turn to?"

Bryan sighed. He understood Nathan's consternation with his decision to contact their father. All four siblings had talked about their individual decision to not contact him, hoping that would force him to contact them. He was the only one to break that trust – at least he thought he was the only one. With Nathan's questions now, he knew his brother had not really betrayed the siblings' agreement. His contact with his father was for a specific, career-oriented reason. Nathan decided he could live with that.

"Yes, I talked with a few outfitters I met. But none of them had military experience, and they all told me they wished they had," Bryan explained.

"But what's so important about that?" Nathan asked.

"The survival training they go through is quite intense," Bryan said. "It really adds a dimension to what an outfitter can do to not only give his clients a great experience, but also keep them safe."

"But why Dad?" Nathan asked.

Bryan used the turn onto the side road as an excuse to think about his answer. It could be tricky.

"It was kind of a natural," Bryan said slowly, choosing his words carefully. "Even though we hadn't spoken in a while, there was that family connection. I figured it would be easier than talking to a stranger."

"And was it?" Nathan asked, this time curiosity being the driving factor for the question.

"Well, not right away. It was awkward at first," Bryan said. "But once we got past that part, it was easier to talk to him than I expected."

Nathan was silent for a few moments, thinking it over. Bryan let him think. He was hoping his brother wouldn't ask any questions about any other reasons he had chosen his father to gather advice from. For Bryan, being the younger son, there was a desire to have a connection with his father. And while he was not aware his brother felt the same, Bryan wanted to make his father proud of him.

"But you said you had been up in these mountains with him," Nathan finally spoke. "How did that come about?"

"He asked me to come out here and we spent a weekend on the mountains," Bryan said. "He taught me things I would never have learned on my own, or from outfitters."

"When was this?" Nathan asked.

"About ten years ago," Bryan said hesitantly. How upset would his brother be that he kept this secret so long?

Nathan said nothing for a few minutes, and his face was expressionless. Bryan could not get a read on whether or not he was upset.

"You said you were here twice," Nathan said evenly.

"I came out again about five years ago, after I had been running my business for a couple of years," Bryan answered. "After taking out a bunch of people, that brought up some more questions I wanted answered."

Nathan was silent again.

"I went into both visits as a way of gathering information, nothing more," Bryan said, but the last part was a white lie.

"Has there been any other contact?" Nathan asked.

"That's the thing. Between the first and second trips out here and since the second, we have not spoken," Bryan said. "I did not contact him just like before, thinking maybe he would get in touch with me. But he never did."

Nathan shook his head and fell silent again just as the whine of tires on pavement transitioned to the crunch of gravel under rubber.

"Why is he like that?" Nathan asked, half just to himself. Then to his brother he asked, "Do you think he just doesn't like his own kids? I mean, from what I've gotten from Mom he doted on his step-daughters."

Bryan shrugged his shoulders.

"I don't know," he said. "Maybe it was just that four of us was too much for him to handle, and since there are only two of them, he could keep up."

"Maybe," Nathan said.

Then both brothers fell silent until they reached the cabin.

After leaving the cave, George led Stephanie up the mountain for another thirty minutes.

While they slowly walked through the still dense forest, she kept remembering the encounter with the bears. The cub had not frightened her. She saw it as harmless because she knew it was a young bear, still learning its way in the world, much like she was a few years ago.

But when the mother bear appeared, fear took hold of every fiber of her being. She was sure she was going to be mauled to death. Even the explanation her grandfather gave her about the nature of bears didn't lessen her fear much.

But that was a good thing.

With that encounter fresh in her mind, she decided there would be no more attempts to escape. George's actions in getting between her and the mama bear proved to her that he had no intention of hurting her. It also showed her he was her best bet for survival in this environment.

She had gone camping with her parents before. But their camping excursions were much different than this. There were amenities, like restrooms and showers. Even when they went "wilderness," it was much different than this. For one thing, they drove to their campsite and the only hiking was short walks into the forest.

With each step up the mountain, this was much different than she had ever been through. But in a strange way, she was enjoying it. Stephanie was aware that in reality she was a prisoner of sorts. Her grandfather had taken her from her school and brought her to a place she was totally unfamiliar with and she was in a situation she had never experienced. But the newness of it all did create some excitement in her.

It also brought out her competitive side, her desire to prove she could handle anything and do it well.

Not long before they came to a stop in this latest leg of the journey – to wherever they were going – she had dropped a few steps further behind because she was looking at their surroundings very carefully, taking in the beauty of the forest.

"Step it up, girl," George said sternly. "Don't want any bear coming out and eating you."

She glanced around quickly, momentarily allowing the fear of the mama bear to surge through her. Then she recognized her grandfather's statement as a challenge. Possibly playful, possibly irritated that she wasn't keeping up. Whichever was of no concern to her.

Stephanie quickened her pace and gained on him quickly. She went past him and opened a ten-yard gap between them. She glanced over her shoulder and saw him watching her as he trudged along.

"C'mon, Grandpa, the bears are gonna get you," she said.

Stephanie thought she saw a slight smile curl the corners of his mouth upward. But it was fleeting as the determined look returned to his face and he picked up his pace until he was back in the lead.

Eventually, they came to a small clearing, about the size of the gymnasium at Stephanie's school. The open area was covered in grass, and a small stream ran through it in a wavy line. The stream left the clearing and went into the trees about fifteen yards away from them.

George led her to a spot about ten feet into the trees and about the same distance from the stream. The small waterway was on a slight incline, so Stephanie heard a faint gurgling sound as the water traveled over dips and humps and collections of rocks scattered in the stream bed.

They stood in front of a fire pit and behind it was an enclosure made of logs of varying sizes. It was enclosed on three side, with the open side facing the fire pit, and the top included more logs covered by a tarp tied securely at multiple spots on each wall.

"We'll spend the night here," her grandfather said as he shed his pack and began to unpack some items.

In the dense forest, very little light got through. But when she looked into the clearing Stephanie could see plenty of light shining brightly. She had no watch so could not check the time. But she was certain only about half the daylight for the day had passed. Except for some energy bars before they left the cabin, George and Stephanie had not eaten all day.

"Are you hungry?" he asked her. She nodded her head.

George pulled out from his pack a light brown package and handed it to Stephanie, then pulled out another. He then took out two more packages, cartons with a greenish bag inside. He slid her package inside the carton above the greenish bag, added water and leaned one end on a rock beside the fire pit. He did the same with the others.

"What are those?" she asked.

"These are flameless heaters," George said pointing to the cartons. "They use a chemical reaction to make heat."

She eyed the cartons.

"We will be eating MREs," he said.

"What are MREs," she asked, wrinkling her nose.

"It stands for Meals Ready to Eat," he said. "It's what soldiers eat when they are in the field."

"What do they taste like?" Stephanie asked.

"It depends on what menu you have," her grandfather explained. "You'll be having cheese tortellini in tomato sauce and I'm going to have chili and macaroni."

Stephanie had had tortellini before, and she liked it, so her meal didn't sound so bad. When they were warm, George tore hers opened and handed it to her with a plastic spoon.

"Don't throw your spoon away when you're done, we'll wash them and use them again," he told her.

Stephanie took a big spoonful and put it in her mouth. The smile on her face told George she liked it.

A few miles down the mountain, Stephanie's father and her uncle had settled in at the cabin. The sheriff's deputy took the vehicle they had come up the mountain with and headed back to town shortly after they had arrived. Mason then briefed them on what had taken place since the others had left earlier, but there wasn't much to tell.

Nathan gave him Blastmore's instructions about staying overnight at the cabin and the rest of the team would join them in the morning.

Mason went outside to check the surroundings again. That left the brothers alone to talk.

"So, what's going on with you and Cynthia?" Bryan asked. "I thought you two were a great couple. I like her."

Nathan shrugged. It was something he had been trying to figure out for days.

"I don't know," he said. "She's never said anything about wanting to leave before in all the years we've been together."

"Do you think there's someone else?" Bryan asked.

Nathan had considered that but rejected it. She was not the kind of woman who would be with another man while she was married. Or so he thought. These days he couldn't really be sure.

"I don't think so. But who knows," he said.

"Something like this doesn't just come out of the blue," Bryan said. "How do you get along with your in-laws?"

Nathan had considered this even before Cynthia had left with Stephanie. He believed his relationship with Kenneth was good. But Jennifer was a different story. And since Cynthia had run to their home, she had dropped any pretense of how she felt about Nathan.

"Her mother really doesn't like me," he said. "I could tell that almost from the beginning, but I didn't really know how bad it was until Cynthia left."

"You do know mothers have quite a bit of influence over their daughters," Bryan said.

He had never been married, but Bryan had a succession of girlfriends, with no relationship lasting more than a year. He could speak to this subject from first-hand experience. Many of the mothers of his girlfriends did not care for his choice of professions or his carefree lifestyle. They convinced their daughters they could find someone better.

"Yes, she does like to stick her nose into just about everything, and she is very controlling," Nathan said. "And she has her husband by the dick."

"They usually do," Bryan said, drawing a disapproving look from his brother. "But not you, of course."

Nathan wasn't quite so sure of that, considering the last week or so.

"But hey, at least I don't have to deal with the McAdams up here," Nathan said. "They are states away."

Chapter 17

The sun had just started peaking over the horizon when Susan Blastmore, Bernard Vallow and a sheriff's deputy parked in front of the forest cabin in three separate vehicles in single file behind the Jeep Wrangler. Nathan and Bryan stood in the doorway as Blastmore and Vallow exited from the driver's side of two older model Chevy Suburbans, one tan and the other light blue in color, and Barnes got out of the passenger side of the lead vehicle. The deputy behind the wheel of the sheriff's department Ford Explorer stayed put.

"Where the hell have you been?" Bryan asked. He had been raring to go hours earlier.

"I'm not in the mood," Blastmore said, her voice as icy as her stare as she walked past the brothers into the cabin.

"You got trouble comin'," Vallow whispered to Nathan as he followed his boss inside. Nathan and Bryan looked at each other, an unspoken, *"What the fuck,"* passing between them. Then they went inside.

A kerosine lantern bathed much of the cabin in light, but eerie shadows were thrown against the walls from the bodies in the room. It darkened the mood even more than Blastmore's expression.

"You need to get back to town," she said to the sheriff's deputy.

The brothers gave her the same questioning look they'd given each other.

"You and your cohort outside need to get back to your station," Blastmore said.

The deputy hesitated, giving Blastmore a questioning stare, but saying nothing.

"Get out of here and off this mountain," she yelled with a volume that made everyone gathered in the small room wince.

The deputy strode to the door, went out and straight to the sheriff's vehicle and climbed into the passenger seat. The other deputy started his vehicle and started the laborious task of turning it around. It wasn't easy in the cramped space available, but it was finally accomplished and the Explorer slipped past the Suburbans with barely an inch to spare then headed down the road.

Inside the cabin, Barnes and Vallow sat down in chairs at the table. They knew what was coming.

"What's going on?" Nathan asked a little testily.

"Your freakin' in-laws, that's what," Blastmore said.

Nathan was confused. They were states away. What on earth could they have to do with sending the sheriff's deputies in another county, another state, back to their station when their assistance was necessary in finding and returning his daughter alive?

"What do they have to do with this?" Bryan asked, his brother too stunned to ask himself.

"Your in-laws apparently have some pull in some very high places," Blastmore said, still angry and snapping the words out like Indiana Jones' whip. "They got the sheriff's office here pulled off the case."

She looked over at Deputy Barnes.

"Barnes is supposed to be at the airport to go back to her duties also," Agent Blastmore said. "But she is apparently disobeying orders. She insisted on coming back up here."

With Blastmore's back turned to her, Barnes pointed at Nathan, then herself then tapped her thumb to her fingers several times. Nathan understood immediately they would talk later when they could get a few moments alone.

"So, what now?" Bryan asked. "If law enforcement is getting pulled off this, that's going to make it more difficult for Nathan and I to find my niece."

"This is an FBI investigation and no one is pulling us off," Blastmore said defiantly.

"So when do we leave?" Bryan said. "We've lost too much time already."

"Then let's haul ass," Blastmore said, and headed for the door.

Blastmore, Mason and Vallow put on their Kevlar vests and loaded up utility belts they brought from the chartered jet with gear. They checked their weapons. Barnes did the same. Susan got Nathan fitted into a spare FBI vest, but Bryan refused one.

"I can't let civilians go on an op without protection," Blastmore said. "You really shouldn't be here in the first place."

Bryan pushed the vest she offered him aside.

"If I put that thing on, I'll lose my mobility," Bryan said as he checked his own gear.

"I must insist," she said.

Bryan stopped what he was doing and looked her deeply in the eye. She could see the determination there.

"I'm telling you, G-woman, if I go up that mountain with that extra weight on, I won't be very effective," he said. "Besides, my dad will not shoot me."

"Fine," Blastmore said. "Suit yourself."

She began to walk toward the end of one of the Suburbans to finish with her gear. But halfway there, she turned and pointed a finger at him.

"But if you get shot, don't come crying to me," she said.

Bryan couldn't help but notice the wink she gave him.

When they were all geared up and ready, they set off up the mountain.

Blastmore had refused to give Nathan a weapon. But as they were setting out, Bryan slipped him his German DWM P08 Luger pistol.

"Use it only if you have to," he whispered. "And don't lose it or I'll take it out of your hide."

Bryan double-timed to get ahead of Blastmore and the other agents. Nathan and Barnes followed behind them. After a few steps Barnes put her arm across Nathan's chest indicating he should slow down. When they were about twenty yards behind the others, they returned to their normal stride to maintain the distance.

"Your in-laws and your wife are in town, they came in last night," she began to explain. "They apparently have some political pull. The state's governor ordered the sheriff's department to back off the case."

Nathan shook his head. He knew the McAdamses had money, but he was not aware how far their influence went. He speculated aloud that they must know the governor in Illinois and convinced him to get the Idaho governor to intervene.

"That's the gist of it as I overheard," Barnes said.

"Were you called off also?" he asked. "If so, why are you here?"

"I was supposed to head home, but Sheriff Martin texted me to continue my assignment," she said.

"But why pull the sheriff's departments off the case?" Nathan asked. "The FBI will continue to investigate."

"They are trying to get the FBI called off also," she said. "But they are federal. That's going to take more juice."

"But why would they want to stop the investigation? Don't they want to get their granddaughter back?" Nathan asked.

"They hired their own investigators," Barnes said.

Nathan did not respond. He could not figure out what they hoped to accomplish with that tactic. He was trying to work it out in his mind when he heard his brother's voice.

"Quit your lollygagging back there and get your asses up here and help us search," he hollered.

Bryan had them set up in a straight line abreast search pattern about five yards apart. He was in the middle with Blastmore to his left and the other FBI agents to her left. Nathan and Barnes were to the right.

"What are we looking for?" Nathan asked.

"Anything that is out of place," Bryan explained. "Anything that doesn't belong in a forest, Twigs and limbs that look stepped on; just anything that looks odd."

Blastmore and her agents, and even Barnes, had been on searches before. They were aware of the procedure.

It only took a couple of times for Nathan to call for Bryan to check something out and be told it was nothing for him to start understanding what to ignore. He was not exactly a novice to the woods, but he had never been on a search before. And with his daughter's safety at stake, he wanted to get it right. Bryan understood that and was patient with him.

The searchers continued their slow trudge up the mountain, scanning the ground. Bryan not only checked out the ground in front of him, but every few minutes rotated his head 180 degrees on a level view watching for any movement. He didn't want to miss any human presence, but he was also concerned about wildlife.

They had been on the move for almost two hours when Nathan suddenly stopped dead in his tracks without alerting the others. Luckily, Barnes noticed out of the corner of her eye and ordered the others to stop. The look on Nathan's face told her this was no false alarm this time.

Nathan squatted down on his haunches to get a closer look at an object in the grass. It was a silver plain bracelet. He reached down and picked it up. He caught the movement of his brother walking up to his side.

"What is it?" Bryan asked, watching Nathan finger the bracelet gently.

"It's a bracelet I gave to Stephanie on her birthday last year. She never took it off," Nathan said.

"And it was laying on the ground right there?" Bryan asked. Nathan nodded and stood up, still staring at the bracelet.

"Everyone stay right where you are, don't move," he ordered, then did a slow, methodical search of the area in a ten-yard radius of where the bracelet was found. He then returned to his brother's side and motioned everyone to join them.

"I found some bear tracks over there," Bryan said, pointing to the right of the group. "They pick up again down there a little ways." This time he pointed at the direction they had come.

"Anything else?" Nathan asked, the increased worry evident in his voice.

"The tracks don't come this way, it looks like the bear, an adult, was coming this way then veered off and headed down that way," Bryan said.

"What does that mean?" Blastmore asked.

"Between the bracelet and the behavior of the bear, it's pretty clear Dad and Stephanie came this way," Bryan answered.

"You don't think the bear attacked them?" the lead agent asked.

"There's no blood, shred of clothing or anything else that suggests an attack," Bryan said. "If it was a black or brown bear, it probably got spooked by seeing humans and went another way."

"What if it was a grizzly?" Nathan asked, still worried.

"The tracks are too small for a grizzly," Bryan said.

Everyone but Bryan looked around the area.

"So, if they were here and came across the bear, they most likely changed direction," Blastmore said. "But which way?" The last part was rhetorical.

"Nope, they kept going up, the same direction they had been," Bryan said.

"How can you be so sure?" Blastmore asked.

Bryan pointed up the hill to a spot about twenty yards from their position. The others looked in that direction.

"You see that stump?" he said, and she nodded. "My dad cut that tree down years ago. He called it his resting chair."

Bryan started up the hill in the direction of the stump and the others followed. When they got there, they gathered around the stump. This time it was Blastmore who noticed something out of place. She nudged Bryan and pointed to the back of the stump where it was touching the other tree.

Bryan bent down and grabbed an item and stood up. He held it out in front of him, inspecting it. The item was a wooden match.

"See, they did come this way," Bryan said.

"That could have been dropped by anyone, it doesn't prove they were here," Vallow said. Blastmore held up an index finger to shush him.

"No, it's not the kind of proof you look for. But for anyone who spends time in the woods it is a tell-tell sign," Bryan said. "When you're up here for more than just a stroll, you protect your matches like they are gold. This match has not been used." He pointed to the red tip.

"That could have been up here for weeks, or months," Vallow said. Again, Blastmore raised the index finger, and added a stern look at the agent under her charge.

"This match is only slightly wet, surface dew," Bryan said. "If it had been out here more than a day or two, it would be soaked through, even if it hadn't rained."

He put the match in his pocket and surveyed the group.

"My dad puts his matches in zip-lock bags to make sure they stay dry," Bryan said. "The only way this could have gotten here was if someone opened the bag and took one out."

"But why?" Blastmore asked, but she was forming a few theories.

"There's any number of possibilities," Bryan said. "But the two most plausible are that Dad or Stephanie left it here to signal to searchers they had been here."

"But if he's trying to get away, why would he leave clues behind?" Nathan asked.

"Exactly," Bryan said. "Remember her clothes at the cabin when everything else was cleaned out? Now the bracelet and this match. I think Stephanie is leaving clues behind like bread crumbs."

Blastmore nodded her head. She had formulated the same possibilities.

"But where do we go from here?" she said. "They could have gone in any direction."

Bryan shook his head and pointed up the mountain, in a straight line lining up with the direction they had taken so far.

"They are headed that way," he said. "Dad has several more resting places in that direction, and that direction only."

Nathan was amazed that his brother had learned so much about their father's habits in the woods. But he was also realistic enough to recognize that by his own admission it had been five years since

Bryan was here with his father. In that time George could have created other nooks and crannies as resting places.

But he kept silent, trusting his brother knew what he was doing.

Bryan crawled out of the cave, brushed himself off and stood looking around the entrance. After a few moments, his silence was grating on everyone.

"Well?" Blastmore asked the question that was on everyone's mind.

As if coming out of a trance, Bryan blinked his eyes and looked at each of the five faces staring at him.

"I saw bear sign and human sign inside there," he said.

When he offered nothing else, Blastmore pressed.

"Was it them?" she asked.

"There was only one person in there," Bryan explained. He noticed his brother's face go white and he knew what was going through his head.

"That doesn't mean anything," he said. "The human sign was for an adult. And the person and bear weren't in there together. The bear sign is older."

That didn't seem to sooth his brother's escalated worry.

"It's likely Dad went in there to scout it out and Stephanie stayed outside," Bryan said. He saw some color – very little – return to Nathan's face.

Susan saw Nathan's reactions and felt for him.

"This can't be easy on him," she thought. *"I'm surprised he's held up as well as he has."*

"So where do we go from here?" Blastmore asked.

Bryan scratched his head. He knew there was no guarantee his father caused the human traces he saw in the cave. There was nothing there that pointed to any one person. But it's not something he wanted to share with the others just yet. He wanted to find something that indicated George and Stephanie actually were at this location.

He opened his mouth to say something, but a voice stopped him.

Mason and Vallow had begun searching the area when Bryan said Stephanie could have stayed outside the cave. They remembered the clothing in the cabin, the bracelet and the match and thought there might be something else here to indicate her presence.

"Got something," Mason said as he headed for the rest of the group. He was holding, pinched between his thumb and index finger, the corner of an energy bar wrapper. Bryan took it from him.

"Be careful," Vallow said. "You'll spoil any fingerprints we can get from it."

Blastmore gave him a look that said, *"Really?"* He sheepishly went silent.

"This is Dad's favorite brand," Bryan said, ignoring Vallow.

The wrapper was opened only at one end by pinching either side and pulling outward to pull the adhesive apart. Bryan looked inside and saw that one or two bites of the energy bar were still inside the wrapper. He turned the wrapper upside down and let the remnant fall into his bare hand. He nibbled one corner of the chunk and let it settle on his tongue for a few seconds.

Each of the FBI agents made a disgusted face. They had all seen the pool scene in "Caddyshack" where Carl, in full hazmat suit, finds what everyone thinks is a turd on the bottom of the drained pool, takes off his protective gas mask and takes a bite. Nathan had the same image in his head, but instead smiled.

"This is fresh, no more than a day old," Bryan said. "Show me where you found it."

Mason led them to a spot along the rocky outcropping about fifty yards to the left of the cave and pointed to a rock jutting up out of the ground.

"It was beside this rock," he said.

"Show me exactly how you found it," Bryan said.

Mason took the wrapper and set one end on the ground and leaned it against the rock. It was facing away from the cave. Bryan studied it for a few moments from various angles.

"Do you think Stephanie left this for us to find, like the other things?" Nathan asked his brother.

"Very likely. It certainly wasn't Dad," Bryan answered. "She may be trying to let anyone know she's been here."

Bryan looked at the wrapper then along the line of the outcropping that continued away from the cave.

"What else?" Blastmore asked.

"What do you mean, what else?" Bryan asked.

"There's something else you are thinking, I can see it in your face," she said.

He gave her a blank look, but she wasn't buying it.

"Profiler," Mason said, pointing at her.

Bryan nodded his head. *"I'll have to be careful about what I'm thinking if this chick can read my mind,"* he thought.

"Okay, Dad has resting spots in both directions from here," he said, pointing first to the right of the cave then the left. "But this tells me they headed for the lean-to that is in that direction," as he pointed again to the left.

"How is this eleven-year-old girl able to leave clues along the way without her wilderness-experienced grandfather noticing?" Vallow asked.

Bryan looked at Blastmore.

"Is this guy new?" he asked.

"Fresh out of the academy," she answered.

"Well, newbie, it's quite simple," Bryan said looking at Vallow disdainfully. "When she gets time to herself, she selects something to leave. Dad is leading the way and she's walking behind him. That's when she drops or sets down the items."

Nathan smiled with pride.

"Maybe she could be an FBI newbie some day," Bryan said. "She's smarter than this guy."

"Fuck you," Vallow said.

"Really?" Blastmore said, giving Vallow a reproachful look.

Chapter 18

George and Stephanie sat in front of the lean-to munching on granola bars for breakfast. The sun was just starting to peek through the trees surrounding their little camp. The fire pit was alive with flames.

While her previous camping experienced with her parents hadn't been quite as primitive, Stephanie settled into this different environment with little effort. She slept inside the lean-to while George slept next to the camp fire. During the night, she woke a couple of times to noises nearby, only to find her grandfather stoking the fire. Between that and the military surplus mummy bags he had brought along, they were comfy warm despite the temperatures dropping below forty degrees at their lowest.

"Where are we going next?" Stephanie asked as they ate.

George sat silent for a few seconds while he finished a bite of granola bar he had just taken. He then washed it down with a drink of water from his canteen.

"We'll move to another place later today," he said. "First, we'll give your dirty clothes a quick wash and let them dry."

"Yours too?" she asked.

"No, mine are good for now," he said, finishing his granola and taking another swig from the canteen. "But I'm sure you are used to clean clothes every day, so go change your clothes and hand me your dirty ones, including what you had on at school."

Stephanie's heart skipped a beat. She had left those clothes at the cabin. What would his reaction be when he found out she didn't have them?

"It's okay, we don't need to wash those," she said hurriedly. "I won't wear those again in the forest."

"No, we need to wash them so they don't get everything else in your pack smelly. There's food in there, too," George said as he stood up. "Now go in there and change."

Stephanie remained rooted to the block of wood she was sitting upon. George stared down at her.

"C'mon, girl, get to it," he said, his voice starting to take on the tone of the drill instructor he had been.

That only heightened Stephanie's fear and she jumped up and bolted for the lean-to as George was tightly rolling up his mummy bag. When he was done, he took the plastic liner that he had laid out underneath the bag when he slept and walked to the front of the lean-to. He fastened each end to the little structure so it covered most of the open side.

Once it was in place and she heard her grandfather's footsteps move away from the lean-to, she quickly removed her clothing, slipped on new underwear, two pairs of pants and two shirts – a T-shirt and a long-sleeved shirt. She shivered a bit from the cool temperature until she had her new set of clothing on.

She stepped out of the lean-to with her clothing in her hands. She handed them to George and turned to go back to the shelter.

"Where are the others?" he asked.

"I couldn't find them," she answered without turning around or slowing her advance toward the lean-to.

"Why couldn't you find them? They were in your pack," George asked, suspicion creeping into his voice.

"They weren't in the pack," she said as she disappeared behind the liner into the shelter. Almost instantly she heard the liner being torn from the lean-to and tossed aside. It startled her and she whirled around to find her grandfather's stocky body blocking the entrance.

She could tell he was now angry. His face had taken on a reddish tint and his fists were clenched. For the first time since seeing her teacher struck down in the school entrance, Stephanie was truly frightened. She took a step backward and bumped her head on the shelter roof where it started to slant down. She dropped down onto the ground and cowered.

Suddenly, as if struck across the face, George stood up straight and the normal color started returning to his face. He realized he had balled up his fists and quickly opened his hands. He softened his voice when he spoke to her again.

"Did you leave those clothes at the cabin?" he asked.

"I must have, but I didn't mean to," she lied.

All those years training sailors gave George an insight into people and their intentions. His gut instinct was that she was not telling the truth, that she had left the clothing intentionally. But that previous experience was with adults and while his experience with young children was limited, he had learned that up to a certain age children rarely lied. It was only after years of watching that character trait from adults did they begin to emulate that behavior.

George began to turn away from the shelter, but something caught his eye and he looked closer at the young girl.

"Didn't you have a bracelet on yesterday?" he asked as calmly as he could.

Stephanie nodded her head and looked at her right wrist. Seeing nothing there, she looked at her left, and again found nothing. A panicked look took over her face. She grabbed her pack, still open, and rummaged through it. But she did not find the bracelet. Her panicked look morphed into one of loss and sorrow.

That put George's mind somewhat at ease. *"Surely she couldn't have faked that reaction,"* he thought. He turned and went to the stream and began washing her clothing. When he was done, he draped them over a line of heavy string tied to the shelter at one end and a stout tree several yards away. The line was located in such a way that the sun's rays would be on them for a few hours as it rose in the sky.

Dan Feller had been a city policeman for seven years before he was elected sheriff of Ada County two years ago. In those nine years he had been involved in a wide variety of situations, including robberies, domestic disputes, assaults, trespassing, drug raids and any number of other crimes. He had also been involved in two murder investigations, three rape cases and even suspected terrorist activity in his first year as sheriff.

But at no time had he ever dealt with a privileged, caustic, controlling woman leading her husband around by his dick and with a daughter on a tight leash.

Jennifer and Kenneth McAdams and their daughter, Cynthia, were in his office shortly after arriving from Illinois trying to get information on the sheriff's department's activities regarding their granddaughter's abduction.

"I want all the information you have on what's been done to try and find my granddaughter, and I want it now," Jennifer demanded.

Feller couldn't help noticing she said "I' not "we," and Kenneth's irritated look also did not escape his notice.

"Ma'am, to start with, we are not the lead agency on this case," Feller said. "The FBI is heading this up, we are just assisting when they ask."

Jennifer opened her mouth to speak again, but Feller cut her off.

"In the second place, it is the policy of this department, as it is with most law enforcement agencies, to not release information about an ongoing investigation."

Jennifer huffed, Kenneth nodded his head but his wife didn't see and Cynthia cowered behind her mother.

"Well by God I'm going to get what I want, even if I have to go to the governor of this state," Jennifer yelled.

"You can call the president of the United States for all I care," Feller said, starting to lose control over his frustrations with this woman. "My accountability is to the residents of this county, the state and U.S. constitutions. The governor cannot make decisions for this department."

Jennifer pointed a manicured finger at Feller and shook it at him.

"We'll just see about that," she said, then turned and left the office, her husband and daughter following like ducklings after their mother.

Two hours later Feller got a phone call from the county commission chairman.

"Dan, I need to ask you to give the McAdamses the information they are looking for," he told the sheriff.

Feller was beside himself. The chairman knew the way the sheriff's department worked, and he knew quite well the policy about not sharing information for an ongoing investigation. But here he was asking for that policy to be ignored in this case. It was something that had never happened on his watch, nor with any law enforcement agency he knew of.

"You know I can't do that," he said. "That will compromise this investigation. And since the FBI is the lead agency, it could very well create problems with them."

"We are working on the FBI," the chairman said. "We want them and your department to pull back, take no further part in this."

Feller was speechless. Jennifer had already told him they hired their own investigators to find Stephanie. But in the past two hours Feller and his deputies had researched the McAdamses' financial dealings and found the group they had hired were paramilitary mercenaries.

"So you want us to step back so this woman can fill the woods with trigger happy military wannabes?" Feller said. "That means people are going to get hurt on that mountain, or worse, sir." He laced the last word with as much sarcasm as he could.

"Sheriff, the governor made this request of me, and when I made the same arguments, it became less of a request," the chairman said. "If you and your people don't provide the information she wants and pull your people off, the governor will cut our state-shared revenue. And when I have to cut our budget to deal with that lost revenue, the first place I will look to cut will be your department."

Feller squeezed the telephone hand set so tight he thought it might shatter.

"You do realize we not only have a missing girl up there but a murder suspect, as well," he said through gritted teeth.

"I am well aware of that," the chairman said. "But I still want that information turned over and your people off the case."

"This is the smelliest kind of bullshit I've ever had to deal with in nine years in law enforcement," he yelled into the mouthpiece.

He slammed the phone down so hard it turned every head in the outer office toward the noise.

After a few moments, Feller's undersheriff came into the office.

"What's up, boss?" he asked.

"Copy all the files we have on the missing Wallis girl and her grandfather and send someone up to get our guys off that mountain," Feller ordered.

"Boss?"

"Just do it," Feller said. He then sat at his computer to draft a resignation letter.

Jennifer McAdams stood facing a large man made larger by the body armor he wore and the heavy cargo pants with equipment and supplies stuffed in every pocket. Aside from the pistol attached to the military utility belt, also loaded with equipment, he had no fire arms. His pants and the long-sleeved shirt he wore were a green, brown, gray, black camouflage pattern, as was the ball cap on his head. It had a small brown shield on it with "54 Squad" in small black lettering.

The man towered over Jennifer at six feet four inches. He was solidly built, his arms straining the fabric of the shirt. His barrel chest was accentuated by the body armor.

Behind him on an open field just outside of town was a UH1 Huey helicopter, painted olive drab green with the same shield as the man's cap on the nose of the aircraft. The rotors were idling and nine men could be seen inside sitting on bench seats facing each other. The men were outfitted similarly as the man talking to Jennifer, but they all had AR-15 rifles.

"I want my granddaughter back alive, understand," Jennifer said, looking past the man, eying the weaponry inside the chopper.

"I understand, lady," he answered.

Jennifer bristled at the use of the word. Most people used it in a derogatory way. She also saw it as dismissing her authority as his employer.

"I'm not kidding. If anything happens to her, I'll bury you and all your men," she said.

Joe Bantum just nodded. He was not excited about working for a woman. And since their first contact he was especially unhappy about working for this woman. Her demanding and controlling nature had been evident from the start. He thought about not taking the job, but he needed the money to keep his company afloat. Business had been particularly slow lately. With hardly any worldwide conflicts going on, there wasn't much call for hired mercs.

"What about the guy who took her?" Bantum asked.

"I don't give a damn," she snapped. "Do to him what you have to get my granddaughter back."

"And you got all the law enforcement off the mountain?" he asked.

"The sheriff's deputies were ordered off and I saw them come back to the station," Jennifer said. "But the FBI, the deputy from our county and my son-in-law was not with them. I can only assume they are still up there."

"Then I can't guarantee no collateral damage," Bantum said. "With the exception of your granddaughter, of course," he added with a hint of sarcasm.

Jennifer sneered at him.

"Then you need to make sure there is none," she spat at him. "Otherwise, I won't need to bury you. The FBI will."

"We'll do what we have to do to get your granddaughter back and protect ourselves," Bantum said firmly. "Outside of that, there are no guarantees."

He started to turn toward the chopper but even over the whine of the idling engine he heard Jennifer get the last word in.

"You just make sure she comes back alive. If you screw up things for yourself, that's on you," she hollered.

Bantum gave her a dismissive wave and began to jog toward the bird. The whine of the engine and the thump thump thump of the two rotor blades become loader even before he heaved himself up into the back cabin, settled in on the bench seat facing forward and put on a set of headphones.

Jennifer just stood there and watched as the aircraft slowly lifted off the ground. She shaded her eyes as the spinning blades kicked up dust and small pebbles. When the chopper's nose dipped forward and it began to head up the mountain, she turned and walked to her rented car.

"I don't like this, Jennifer," Kenneth said as she slid into the front passenger seat beside him. "We should leave it to the FBI."

"Those people couldn't find their ass with both hands," Jennifer said.

"And what if things go wrong and Stephanie gets hurt, or worse?" he asked. He heard Cynthia gasp from the back seat.

"It won't," Jennifer said, and waved her hand for him to drive away.

Chapter 19

George was sitting on a block of wood near the fire pit. Stephanie was in the shelter. Both were eating another granola bar.

Stephanie was still smarting from the exchange with her grandfather earlier. She wasn't sure what to make of his outburst. There was a little fear in her as well. She remembered what happened to the teacher when he took her from the school. Would she suffer the same fate if he lost his temper with her?

But beyond that, she was worried about the clothing she left behind, the match she left out and the empty energy bar wrapper she had left near the cave.

He seemed to accept her story about the clothing. And he seemed to believe that she was genuinely surprised to find her bracelet missing, which she was. She had been rethinking the last couple of days to try and figure out where she had lost – or left – the bracelet. But she was certain she had it on when she dressed before leaving the cabin. So, she had to have lost it somewhere on the trek up the mountain. But she could not figure it out.

She glanced out of the shelter toward her grandfather, but did not look directly at him. Out of the corner of her eye she saw him sitting there, the hand holding the half-eaten granola bar resting on his thigh. He was very still and was looking off to one side as if he were in a trance.

George thought he had heard a familiar noise, but not one that belonged in the forest. He had moved his head from side to side, trying to direct his ears in all directions to get a better take on it. He found the right angle from which he could clearly hear the sound.

It was faint, but after a few moments he recognized it. The thump thump thump was a sound he had heard many times before.

"Huey," he said aloud.

Stephanie had not yet heard the noise and her grandfather's one word utterance confused her. The only Huey that came to mind for her was one the of the Disney duck brothers. Surely her grandfather wasn't thinking of that. And if he was, she thought, he might be going senile. That added another level of fear to her thinking. If he was losing his mind, she would never find her way off this mountain.

George stood up and focused his attention on his belongings. He quickly packed what was still out into his pack. George walked to the line holding Stephanie's clothing. They were still a little damp, but it could not be helped. He gathered them and gave them a quick, not so neat folding. He then walked to the shelter and leaned in. Stephanie scooted back until she could go no more.

"Gather up your things," he said as he handed her the clothes. He then took the plastic liner that covered the dirt floor of the lean-to and began folding it. "We have to go. Now."

He then took her mummy bag and began rolling it up, not quite as neatly as he had done his. Stephanie stepped out of the shelter and slipped on her backpack, with the still damp clothing stuffed inside. Finished with the liner and mummy bag, George heaved his pack onto his back and motioned for Stephanie to follow him. While they started to follow the stream, staying within the dense forest, not going out to the clearing, George cocked his ear upward as he heard the helicopter again. This time it was slightly louder, and from the sound of the rotors beating the air, his military hearing told him it was heading in the opposite direction it had been before.

This time Stephanie heard the distinctive noise.

"What's that?" she asked.

"A helicopter," he answered.

"What's it doing up here?" she asked.

"They are doing a search pattern," her grandfather answered, with the tone most adults get when children keep asking questions.

"What are they searching for?" she asked.

"Us," George answered.

Stephanie had no more questions to ask. She followed her grandfather as he was trotting along the stream, heading uphill.

From the cave, the Wallis brothers and their law enforcement entourage hiked for another fifteen minutes, took a rest then went another quarter of an hour. Finally, Bryan called a halt and told the others to relax.

"We'll stop here for the day," he said.

"Don't you think we should go on a little more," Blastmore said, gesturing at the sky above the tall trees. "We still have some daylight left."

"I'll be using that daylight to do a little scouting," Bryan said, setting down his equipment.

"What for?" Mason asked.

"We're about a half mile from one of my dad's other rest stops," Bryan explained. "I want to go up there and see if they are there. If we keep going as a group, we might spook them."

Bryan snapped a holster to his hip that contained his Glock nine-millimeter and slung binoculars around his neck. They hung at the level of his pecs so they did not swing loosely back and forth as he walked.

He stood and looked at his brother. He could tell Nathan wanted to go with him. But though he knew his brother had spent plenty of time outdoors, Bryan knew he would make better time and be more stealthy on his own. He shook his head and mouthed, *"Trust me."*

Nathan's disappointment still shown like a neon highway billboard, but he gave Bryan a quick nod.

"I should be back in an hour," Bryan said, then turned and disappeared in the dense forest.

There was no conversation among Nathan, Barnes and the FBI agents during Bryan's absence. Almost seventy minutes later, Bryan appeared very suddenly out of the forest. There had been no noise leading up to it, and his sudden appearance startled each of the five who had been waiting for him. The agents and Barnes drew their pistols, but relaxed when they saw it was Bryan.

He sat down on a fallen free trunk facing them.

"They are there," he said.

"So, let's go get them," Blastmore said, standing up.

"Hold on there, G-woman," Bryan said. "There's plenty of time for that."

"But we still have some light," she protested, still standing.

"But it will be gone in less than half an hour," Bryan said. "They are not going anywhere tonight."

"What do you mean?" Nathan asked, but he had a pretty good idea already.

"They are at a spot with a lean-to shelter Dad built some years ago just off a clearing," he explained. "They are camped for the night."

"So, what's the plan?" Blastmore asked, sitting back down.

"We get some shut eye and get up with the sun," Bryan said. "There is a stream that runs by that little camp. We'll hike to a spot upstream of that camp and move in on them. I suspect Dad feels a little safe there, so he'll hang out there until he sees something that tells him they need to move on."

"And what if he takes off in the other direction?" Vallow asked.

"Because, Newbie, unless you know what you're looking for, that camp is well hidden," Bryan said. "He won't go toward the clearing because then he would be exposed."

"Alright, we'll follow your lead," Blastmore said, cutting Vallow off before he could get another word out of his mouth.

Few in the search party got much sleep during the night, except Bryan and Nathan. They were both used to the outdoors and sleeping under the stars. Bryan was prepared for the cold night with long underwear, heavy wool socks and a down-filled jacket. He had brought extras of each for his brother, guessing correctly that he had not anticipated going up into the mountains overnight.

The others had their moderate FBI jackets, but little else in the way of warmer clothing.

It was spring and the weather was starting to warm up. But at night in the higher elevations, the temperature could drop quite low.

That night it wasn't so bad, in the upper 40s. But Barnes and the FBI agents were not prepared and slept restlessly in short spurts.

Bryan was awake even before his brother and all the others were in one of their short periods of sleep. He decided to scout his father's camp again, just to make sure they had not moved during the night. He thought this unlikely, because moving at night, especially with a young girl, would have been extremely risky. But his father was in a desperate situation, and that could change equations quickly and drastically.

He went to his previous observation spot, just off the clearing directly across from his father's camp site. Through his variable power binoculars, he could see, between the trees that hid it from any casual hikers, that it was still occupied.

With the sun just starting to creep over the horizon, it shed some light into the camp. Because of that, Bryan would normally only make out shadows and silhouettes. But there was a fire alive in the pit in front of the lean-to and he could see his father's and niece's faces clearly in flickering light. They were eating granola bars. He also noticed his father's gear was not fully packed, so they seemed in no hurry to move on.

His father and niece were conversing in whispered tones. He could not make out what they were saying. Then Stephanie went inside the shelter, in what seemed like a rush. George rolled up his mummy bag and took a plastic liner from the ground and used it to cover the entrance to the lean-to. Not long after Stephanie emerged with a bundle in her arms.

Bryan was just about to leave to return to the others, but he heard his father's voice rise – and he could make out most of the words. He was talking about clothing left at the cabin, then he heard him ask Stephanie about a bracelet. He settled back in to watch a little bit more. Things went quiet again while George took the bundle Stephanie had carried out of the shelter and took them to the stream and began washing them.

That told him what he needed to know. George planned to stay at that camp site at least a few more hours to allow the washed clothing time to dry. He stood and silently made his way back to where the others were all awake.

"Where have you been?" Blastmore demanded.

"I scouted out my dad's camp again," he said. "They are still there, and it looks like they'll be there for a while."

"How do you know that?" Vallow asked.

While this was a sensible question, Bryan was getting tired of the rookie and his doubts. He could tell by the look on Susan's face that she was also.

"Because he washed some clothes and he'll hang them to dry," Bryan said. "That will take..."

He stopped in mid-sentence and titled his head. Vallow opened his mouth to say something and Blastmore, standing right beside him, put her hand over his mouth. Then they all heard what Bryan was listening for.

Thump thump thump.

It was faint. But Bryan could tell it was moving up the mountain some distance to the east. They stood and listened as the sound tracked north and started to fade. But then it began to get slightly louder and the sound was tracking south.

"What is that, we heard it earlier, just before you came back?" Blastmore asked.

Because he was concentrating on the return to the other searchers, the sound had not registered with Bryan until he was standing there among them.

"Grab your stuff and let's go," Bryan said quietly as he got his own pack and threw one strap over his shoulder and held it with his left hand. He began jogging through the trees with the others hot on his heels.

Bryan stopped short just at the edge of George's camp site and motioned the others to halt. He looked over the camp carefully.

In the fire pit, the charred wood was covered with dirt. On the ground around it there were no boot prints of an adult or shoe prints of a smaller person. He looked to the string tied up as a clothes line and saw there were no clothes hanging on it. He carefully skirted the camp site to go over to the line. He ran his hands across it. There was moisture on it, but it could have been dew. But when he looked at the wild grass underneath, he saw more moisture there than could be accounted for with morning dew.

He looked eastward and heard the helicopter as it made another pass. But it was much closer this time. He could not see it through the trees. He moved to where the trees and the clearing met. He saw the chopper come to a hover about a half mile away. He put the binoculars to his eyes and focused on the aircraft.

The Huey was head on to him and had started to descend. But then it stopped and rotated until he saw a broadside view. One of the men seated on the aft bench was pointing his AR-15 straight at him. The man looked at someone on the opposite end of the bench then turned back and raised his rifle.

Bryan quickly dropped to his knees and did a half roll to put a tree between him and the aircraft. As he dropped he thought he heard a faint pop, and almost immediately thereafter a gasp from the area where his brother, Barnes and the FBI agents had been standing.

"Holy shit!," he heard Nathan shout. "Bryan, get over here."

Bryan darted through the trees and found four people squatting in a rough circle with another person in the middle. He saw Nathan was one of the squatters and breathed a sigh of relief. He then saw Agent Blastmore lying on the ground. The left arm of her Navy blue FBI jacket on the underside from just above the elbow was matted and a darker color than the rest.

"Who the hell shot me?" she asked.

"I don't know," Bryan said as he grabbed his pack and unzipped a pocket. He drew out a first aid kit. "How bad is it?"

"It was a through and through," Susan said as she started to stand. Bryan put a hand on her right shoulder and settled her back down.

He took a thick gauze pad and placed it where the blood seemed to be the heaviest. Blastmore nodded her head to indicated he had the right location for the wound. He extended the gauze to cover both the entrance and exit wounds. He had Nathan hold it in place while he used a blue and white patterned handkerchief to tie it down. Blastmore grimaced as he did so.

He shook out four Advil from a small bottle in the kit and shoved them into her mouth. He gave her a few sips from a canteen.

"Now you can get up because we've got to get the hell out of here," Bryan said.

He levered her up by the right shoulder and led them all through the forest, keeping close to the stream.

Following the shot, the Huey slowly dropped into a small clearing, just big enough to allow the rotors to fit snugly, a half mile from the larger clearing adjoining George's camp. When it was about five feet above the clearing floor, the ten men in the cabin jumped to the ground.

Bantum pointed his finger up, then south toward the town, signaling the pilot to go back and refuel. He would radio the pilot when they were ready for evac. He then signaled his men to fan out with about five feet between them and they walked into the trees. He gave instructions to the man to his left that when they got to the next clearing the man would take the four men on his side and skirt the clearing to the left until they found George's camp and he would do the same with the men to the right of him in the opposite direction.

When they converged on the camp, with Bantum's group first to arrive, they assessed it from the trees, much as Bryan had. Because no one from the searcher group had entered the camp site, Bantum found exactly what Bryan had. Bantum stepped into the camp proper and ordered four of his men to search the surrounding area.

"It looks like no one has been here," his second in command said. "But we all saw someone watching as we started to drop into that clearing."

"Yes, it does," Bantum said, with a hint of appreciation in his voice. "Our boy is using his military training well. But they were here, no doubt about that."

Then one of his men called out from just outside the camp.

"We've got blood," he said.

Bantum ran over to the spot and saw a small stain of blood on the grass. He bent down, took the tactical glove off his right hand and touched it with his index finger. He rolled the substance against his thumb. It was slightly thicker than water and not sticky.

"It's still fresh," he said. "Someone was hit with that shot but only wounded."

Bantum wiped the blood from his finger and thumb on the unstained grass, then swiped them on his pants just to get any residue off them. Putting his glove back on, he instructed his men to look for any signs of direction of travel.

The men found tamped down areas of grass that appeared to be footfalls. There were so many there was no way to tell how many people had made them. But they could tell it was more than two. That took a little thought.

"We're looking for two people," Bantum said. "But we also know there is another group up here looking for them, too."

He stood silent for a moment.

"Is it possible that other group found them and are headed back to town?" his second in command asked.

"I doubt it," Bantum said. "These appear to be going further up the mountain, not down."

One of two of the men who had followed the tracks came back to the main group.

"Sir, the tracks continue on for about eighty yards then lead into the stream," he said. "They don't come out directly on the other side."

Bantum didn't have to think about this very long.

"Alright, they're trying to mask their trail," he said. "We'll put five men on each side of the stream and follow it until we see the tracks come out."

Chapter 20

Bryan followed the foot impressions on the forest floor for about eighty yards then into the stream itself. They waded another fifty yards in the shallow water then he brought them to a halt.

"Nathan, I need you to take Deputy Barnes and head off in that direction," he said, pointing to the right of the stream. "They're looking for two people, an adult and a child."

Nathan understood what his brother had in mind. Barnes, at five feet three inches, was a smaller woman than most and her footprints could be mistaken for a child, especially by vague boot prints in the forest grass. He also knew that splitting up would throw their pursuers off.

"What good is that going to do? Vallow asked.

"It will make them make a decision about who to follow," Blastmore said.

"We don't even know how many there are," Vallow said. "And what if they follow us instead of them?"

Bryan started to move toward him. He was ready to punch him out. Blastmore put her hand on his chest to stop him. She had had enough herself, but since Vallow was under her command, she was going to deal with it.

"I've had it with you, Vallow," she said in an angry whisper through clenched teeth. "While were on this mission, you will get with the program. And unless you have something constructive to say, you keep your mouth shut until we get back to the office. Then we'll deal with your performance."

Vallow stood with a blank stare on his face.

"Is that understood?" she demanded.

"Yes, sir," he said, sounding quite chastised.

Susan turned to Bryan.

"We will continue in the stream for a while, then we'll need to get out and head to our next destination," he said.

"Which is?" Susan asked.

"Another one of Dad's hideouts," he answered, then waved Nathan and Barnes on their way.

They exited the stream and headed through the trees at a brisk walk. The remaining four turned and continued upstream.

Bantum stood over the trail Nathan and Dawn had left when they left the stream. He studied the foot impressions left in the wild grass carefully. They left two distinct tracks to the right of the stream. The flattened grass clearly showed that two people walking side-by-side made the impressions.

One set of impressions was a bit bigger than the other. They could have been made by an adult and a child, he thought. But they could just as easily have been made by a man and a small woman. For all he knew, it was just as possible these impressions were made by a father and his son out hiking.

But he doubted the latter. These impressions were fresh and they had seen no other similar footfalls. In fact, they hadn't seen any indications there was anyone else in the area except George and his granddaughter, and the law enforcement group that was apparently also tracking them.

Bantum sent four of his men, two on each side of the stream, on up the mountain to see if any other tracks left the stream. He ordered the rest of his men to remain where they were while he followed the pair of tracks for a short distance. He was hoping to find some confirmation this set of tracks was George and Stephanie.

He had not gone far when he found a small patch of ground devoid of grass. It was about the size of a softball, but the morning dew made it moist and whoever was leaving the larger track had stepped right into it. It left a very defined print. Bantum looked at it closely, then lifted his left leg to look at the bottom of his boot.

The print was not left by a tactical boot. It looked more like a civilian hiking boot.

Bantum looked at the smaller tracks hoping to find another spot of bare ground that was stepped upon. But he saw nothing in the immediate vicinity.

He touched his throat mic and called to one of the men left at the stream.

"Send two men upstream to join the others and the rest follow these tracks until you find me," he ordered.

Bryan led Blastmore and the other FBI agents upstream until they came to a waterfall. It was not a large one, but enough to end their time wading through the stream. He led them to the left and up a short hill to the top of the waterfall.

The hill was actually a granite outcropping that jutted upward almost completely vertical. They had to use what hand holds and foot holds they could find during the fifteen-foot climb.

When they topped the hill, they were met by more dense trees. But the smell of the forest was a little different. Mixed in with the pine, moss and dry wood scents was the smell of water – a lot of water. There was also the sound of water gently lapping against solid ground.

Bryan led them ten more feet and they broke out of the trees to find themselves standing on an embankment about five feet above a short sandy beach studded with ever increasing sized rocks until they met the granite embankment. To their right, cut through the embankment by thousands of years of erosion, was the beginning of the stream. They could hear the water from it cascading over the falls they had just encountered.

Spread out in front of them was an enormous lake, it's water a deeper blue than the cloudless sky. The noonday sun made little flashes on the rippled water, which was so clear they could see rainbow trout swimming near the shore. They could see the lake bottom in clear detail extending out about 20 yards before the bottom slanted down sharply and the water took on the dark blue hue.

The lake was bordered on two sides by mountain slopes covered by pine and juniper trees. There were also cottonwoods scattered here and there in the green carpet of the mountains. At the far end of the lake, the mountains there were like the ones to the sides, except about two-thirds of the way up they changed to bare stone, reaching up to form three distinct cone-shaped peaks. They had snow sprinkled on them like powdered sugar on a cream puff.

They all stood and took in nature's beauty for a few moments. The FBI agents, who worked mostly in the metro areas and small towns east of the Mississippi River, were awe-struck, having not seen this kind of natural wonder before in their lives, except in photos or on jigsaw puzzles. Bryan, who was no stranger to this kind of environment, inhaled the air in full, deep breaths. His eyes were closed and there was a smile on his face.

"I never get tired of this," he said softly, so only Susan, standing right next to his right shoulder, could hear.

He took one final large breath and opened his eyes and looked to his left.

"There is a small cabin about a quarter way around the lake in that direction," he explained. "I'm sure that's where Dad is."

"How can you be sure?" Blastmore asked.

"Because he took me there the last time I was here and he told me it was his favorite place," Bryan said.

Blastmore swiveled her head to take in the scenery one hundred-eighty degrees from left to right.

"I can't blame him," she said.

Bryan turned toward the tree line and started walking.

"We should stay in the trees so he doesn't see us coming," Bryan said.

The others followed him and they gathered around him when he stopped just inside the trees.

"From here on, we need to be careful," Bryan said. "When I was here last, he had security measures in place. Watch for trip wires and anything manmade that seems out of place."

"Are we talking about booby traps?" Mason asked before Blastmore could.

"No, nothing like that then. Just alarms and even some cameras," Bryan said. "But considering the circumstances, it is possible that has changed."

Blastmore looked around them. There was just pristine forest and no sign of technology.

"If he has cameras, are they battery operated?" she asked. "And what about his monitoring equipment?'

"I don't know. But when I was here last, he had an electric heater in that cabin," Bryan said. "I didn't ask him how it was powered."

"Maybe we need to call in more support before we move on the cabin," Blastmore said.

"We don't have the time," Bryan said. "Besides, you said the sheriff's department was ordered to stay out of this case. Who we gonna call, Ghostbusters?"

He pointed at Blastmore's bandaged arm.

"We've got an armed party not far behind us," he said. "I don't know exactly who they are or why they are here. But my guess is they're after Dad."

Blastmore nodded her agreement and they began walking around the lake just inside the trees.

Nathan and Deputy Barnes had not spoken a word in their trek. They had walked about 100 yards when she suddenly stopped and held out her hand signaling for him to halt. They both stood there silent for a few moments. Nathan could tell she was listening and he directed his own hearing outward.

He heard faint voices, seemingly coming from all around them. He focused his attention and within seconds he vectored in on the sounds as coming from the direction they had just come. Neither could make out the words clearly, but what they could make out convinced them the group, of unknown size and composition, was at the spot where she and Nathan left the stream.

They stood silently for a few minutes, then they heard a single voice that seemed a bit closer because they could make out what was being said.

"Send two men upstream to join the others and the rest follow these tracks until you find me," the male voice said.

Barnes pulled the hand-held radio from her utility belt and brought it to her mouth. She clicked the transmit button and there was a split second of static.

"Split," is all she said in as low a whisper as she could. She then grabbed Nathan's arm and led him to their left as quietly as she could.

A few hundred yards away Bryan heard the word "split" come from the radio clipped to his belt. He instantly knew those following them had divided into two groups, one following Nathan and Barnes and the other continuing up the stream.

He cursed under his breath. He knew that was a possibility, but his wishful thinking was that the entire group would follow his brother and the deputy. He quickly briefed the others, and they quickened their pace while still keeping a watchful eye on their surroundings.

Bantum also heard the crackle of static that he knew was not native to the forest followed by a one-word loud whisper. Because it was spoken in such a low tone he could not make out the word itself. But he could tell the speaker was female.

"That's not an eleven-year-old girl, that's an adult," he thought. *"That means that is not the grandfather and granddaughter up ahead. We need to follow the other group."*

He turned back toward the stream and began jogging. He keyed his throat mic, not caring if the two he was following heard him.

"Turn back to the stream," he said. "We're all going to follow it. This is a decoy."

Nathan and Barnes heard Bantum speaking and came to a stop immediately to listen. They caught the last sentence.

"We need to warn Bryan," Barnes whispered while pulling the radio from her belt again. She keyed the transmit and the same split second of static indicated Bryan could hear her.

"You full target," she said in the same low whisper.

As he was jogging back to the stream, Bantum did not hear this transmission. But Bryan did. He pulled out his own radio.

"Lake west side," he said.

Barnes looked to Nathan. He had his index finger up and was pulling out a map from inside his jacket with the other hand. He flipped it open. On the topographical map of the area Bryan had marked three Xs on it. Nathan assumed the southernmost mark was the cabin and the second, next to a small stream, was the camp they had just left.

The third X was next to a large lake tucked in a horseshoe of mountains. He pointed to the third X.

"That is where Bryan is headed," he said. "We've got to get going."

Bantum gathered his men at the waterfall. The group they were trailing could not have gone up the falls, so the question was, which way did they go to bypass them. His men fanned out and looked for tracks or any other indication the group headed anywhere but up past the falls. There were no such signs.

Bantum decided to climb the rock face to the left of the falls. It was a fifty-fifty shot and without knowing it, he had chosen the very direction Bryan had taken. When they were at the top of the hill, a few yards' walk put them at the top of the embankment standing right where Bryan and the FBI agents stood.

Unlike the others, they spent no time admiring the majestic scenery. They had a job to complete if they expected to get the remainder of their payment.

The mercenaries found no signs of the others on the rocky embankment. But back in the trees there were very faint signs of boot prints on the ground that had sparce grass. Bantum sent two men to check for signs to their right that indicated the group went that way instead. They carefully walked as far as they could, to where the lake water emptied into the stream that a few yards away fell over the falls. There were no tracks in the sandy edges on either side of the stream, so they believed no one went that direction.

"Alright, we go around the lake that way and hope we pick up their trail," Bantum said pointing to the left.

He ordered two of his men to stay at the embankment and keep watch.

"Those two who were the decoys might come this way to join the others," he explained. "You men need to make sure they don't get by."

He then set off with the other seven men around the lake.

Bryan, Blastmore and the other two agents made good time. They had come across a couple of trip wires and carefully stepped over them. They were very well concealed and Bryan, on the point with the others in single file behind him, had an idea what to look for so saw them in plenty of time.

So far, they had not seen any electronic surveillance equipment. But if his father had deployed such, he knew his dad would be smart enough to camouflage it very carefully.

George did not own any property around the lake, and the cabin Bryan suspected he had gone to was an old ranger station, as the lake was within the national forest boundary. The structure was not used, except during big game hunting season, which was months away.

However, national forest officials would not be happy with anyone setting up trip wires and surveillance equipment on public land.

"We're about one hundred yards from the cabin," Bryan told the others in a low voice. "I think I should go up there alone and try to talk to Dad."

Blastmore vigorously shook her head.

"No, this is our case and we're at the point where civilians should not be involved," she said, a little louder than Bryan was comfortable with.

"Agent, please keep your voice down," he said. "He could hear you from this distance."

"Point taken," she whispered. "But you're not going up there. This is where we need to take the lead."

Bryan sighed heavily.

"I understand where you are coming from, but you need to understand something," he said, getting almost nose-to-nose with her. "The people in that cabin are family and they mean something to me, especially Stephanie. If you go in there showing your FBI vests and guns, he could panic and someone could get hurt – or worse."

"I fully understand that," she said, with a stern tone in her whisper. "But I cannot allow you to go into a potentially dangerous situation."

"My father won't hurt me," Bryan said. "I think I have the best opportunity to talk him down."

"You don't know that he won't hurt you. He's in a desperate situation. There's no telling what he will do," Blastmore said.

Bryan started to protest again, but she held up her hand, palm out, to stop him.

"You're not going alone," she said. "But I will go with you."

Bryan did not answer, but Blastmore did not wait for one. She turned to Mason and Vallow.

"You two stay here and watch our backs," she said, then turned to head for the cabin. Bryan gently took her arm.

"Walk behind me," he said. "I don't want him to see that." He pointed to her chest where there were three large yellow letters – FBI. Blastmore nodded and they began to walk toward the cabin.

They were about twenty yards from the cabin when they heard George's voice from inside.

"That's far enough," he said.

Bryan and Susan stopped dead in their tracks. The structure was smaller than the one down the mountain, about half the size. In addition to the door, which faced the lake, there was a small window on the side they had approached. Bryan could see the barrel of a rifle poking through the open window. He could not see his father.

"It's me, Dad," Bryan said. "We need to talk."

"I know who you are," George said. "You and your FBI buddy need to turn around and get your asses out of here."

So, they had missed a surveillance camera – or more – on their way in.

"We can't do that, Mr. Wallis," Blastmore said.

There was a long silence from inside the cabin before George spoke again.

"Come around to the front, but keep your distance," he finally said, and the rifle barrel disappeared from the window.

After they had relocated to the front of the cabin, about twenty feet away right at the edge of the lake, the door slowly opened and George stepped out, with the rifle aimed at them.

"What do you want?" George asked.

Bryan held up his hand in front of Blastmore to keep her from speaking over him.

"Is Stephanie alright?" he asked.

"She's fine," George answered.

Before Bryan could say anything else, there was a chime from inside the cabin and they heard an explosion to the south. George was momentarily startled, but quickly regained his wits.

"What the hell?" he said, then ducked back into the cabin. Bryan and Blastmore heard a dead bolt being slammed into place. At the same time, Bryan heard his radio crack two words.

"Hostiles south."

Chapter 21

Nathan and Dawn moved quickly through the dense trees, not giving much thought to being stealthy, until they could hear the sound of cascading water. They slowed their pace. Almost simultaneously they came to a halt as they saw sudden movement through the trees.

Two deer ambled slowly through the forest to their left and downhill about thirty yards. Further up the hill and almost straight ahead, Nathan caught another movement out of the corner of his eye. It was a man dressed in what looked like full military combat gear with an AR-15 raised to his shoulder in firing position.

Barnes followed Nathan's gaze and when she saw the same thing, she nudged Nathan gently and while the man's attention was on the deer, they moved slowly behind a large blackberry bush. Just as they got settled, the man pivoted and pointed the rifle in the direction they had been standing.

Through a tiny gap in the bush, Barnes watched the man swivel his rifle in a one hundred-eighty degree arc. After two such searches, he lowered his weapon and turned away.

Barnes motioned for Nathan to follow and, crouching as low as possible, she led him straight up the hill, being careful to make as little noise as possible. They came to a point where the hill leveled out and they stopped behind a group of several trees.

On their way up, the ground had been covered with grass, some wild flowers, pine needles and fallen tree limbs. But to their left they saw the ground gradually turned to more of a rocky texture until it was just a bare rock face about ninety degrees to the horizontal. Somewhere in that direction is where they heard the cascading water. The waterfall was loud enough that Barnes believed they could talk openly, but still quietly.

"They left a sentry behind to watch their six," she said. "I suspect there's at least one more somewhere."

Barnes looked around at their surroundings and saw through the trees the sun glistening off the ripples in the lake generated by the slight breeze. She moved to the edge of the trees, stood behind a large one and peeked around it. She took in the granite embankment rising five feet above the small sandy beach. She saw where the water from the lake formed the head of the stream and disappeared into the small channel.

Suddenly, on the other side of the channel, she saw a man emerge from the trees. He was dressed just like the man they saw below, but his build was different and this man had a full beard whereas the one they saw earlier appeared to be clean shaven, or at least with five o'clock shadow. The man stopped at the edge of the embankment and looked first to his left then to his right. Seeming satisfied, he turned and walked back into the trees.

Barnes motioned for Nathan to join her. He had just joined her when they heard what sounded like an explosion. They looked at each other in wonder and with concern. But it was something they had to deal with later. Right now, they needed to find a way past the sentries.

"There are two, I don't think there are more than that," she said. "But we need help."

"Use your radio to call the sheriff," Nathan said.

"I'm not sure what he can do, since the governor took him off this case," she said. "Besides, these hand-held radios aren't going to have the range to reach town."

But she did pull out her radio, key to transmit and said, "Hostiles south," into the mic then replaced it on her belt.

"We need to get something with more range," she said as she looked toward where the sentry had stood on the embankment.

Inside the shack by the lake, George went to a small desk in a corner and looked at a computer monitor. The screen was split into four images. In one corner the wide angle black and white image showed a high angle shot looking down into a thicket of trees. Against one of them was a man sitting with another man tending to his leg. Both men were dressed in military tactical combat gear. The image was not detailed enough to show the extent of the man's injury.

"What's happening?" he heard Stephanie's trembling voice behind him. He ignored her and continued to study the images. Another view showed three similarly dressed men advancing slowly. He switched to another set of four images and saw nothing but empty forest, except for a lone elk grazing.

His next set of images showed the view from four cameras mounted on each side of the cabin. In the image marked south, he saw someone with FBI on their back running away from the cabin. On the image labeled east, he saw Bryan moving toward the door.

"What's going on?" Stephanie asked again, with a little more control and urgency in her voice.

Her grandfather looked in her direction with his index finger to his lips as he got up from the chair at the desk and headed for the door. Just as he got there, he heard Bryan's voice from outside.

"Dad, you need to end this," he said.

"What's going on out there?" George demanded.

"You've got highly armed mercenaries coming," his son said. "This is not going to end well unless you let Stephanie go and surrender to the FBI."

George took a step back from the door. Law enforcement he expected, but mercenaries? That made no sense.

"Uncle Bryan?" Stephanie said from across the small room.

"Are you okay, Stephanie?" Bryan asked.

"Yeah, but I want to go home," she answered.

George's mind was racing. This was much more than he had bargained for. It had been spinning out of control ever since he struck the teacher and now he was feeling like he was in a bit over his head.

He reached out and unbolted the door. Before he could press the latch to open the door Bryan had already done so and pushed the door open and stepped in. Stephanie immediately ran forward and wrapped her arms around him. He hugged her for a few seconds, hearing his father shut and rebolt the door.

Blastmore reached her agents in less than one minute. She found them kneeling behind trees with their weapons drawn pointing south. She dropped to a knee beside Mason but kept her pistol holstered.

"What happened?" she asked.

"I don't know," Mason said. "We were waiting here and all of a sudden there was an explosion off to the right."

"Bryan said his father wouldn't have any deadly booby traps," Blastmore said.

"Actually, he said he didn't think so, but under the circumstances anything could be possible," Mason said, noticing the irritated look on his boss's face. "But this sounded more like a flash bang than a grenade or C-4."

Suddenly they heard the crack of a twig ahead of them. Blastmore drew her Sig Sauer from its holster and held it pointed straight in a two-handed shooting posture. She turned to Vallow then Mason and mouthed, *"Hold you fire,"* to both of them.

"This is the FBI, you need to stay where you are," Blastmore yelled.

A second went by and the crack of a high caliber rifle echoed through the forest. A split second later Blastmore and Mason were showered with bark splinters from the shell impact in the tree above their heads.

Vallow squeezed off one shot from his Glock nine-millimeter handgun. Blastmore gestured for both agents to hold fire.

"Fall back," she ordered in a loud whisper.

Almost in unison they turned and started jogging toward the cabin. They hadn't gone far when they heard two more rifle shots and almost simultaneously saw a round strike a tree in front of them. Blastmore glanced toward Vallow to her right and saw him careening forward then fall flat on his belly. She ran over to him and knelt at his side. Mason took a position between them and their pursuers with his weapon at the ready.

Blastmore saw an impression in Vallow's vest between the "B" and "I" with an expended round embedded in the Kevlar. Vallow was gasping for air.

"If you can hear me, move your fingers," she said. The fingers of his left hand twitched.

"Can you feel your legs?" she asked. He lifted his left foot slightly. She quickly flipped him onto his back. He was no longer gasping for air, but his breathing was labored.

So far, there had been no more shots from their pursuers. Blastmore moved to a position at Vallows head and shoulders. She hooked her arms under his armpits and began to drag him backward.

"Let's go," she said to Mason, who walked backward with his gun still pointed at the threat.

"Contact south. Shots fired," they heard someone say as they went.

Nathan was not entirely confident in Deputy Barnes' plan, but he trusted her as a law enforcement professional.

They walked down to the sandy beach and to where it turned into the rock face. They stayed as closed to the granite as they could, keeping a sharp eye on the embankment across the channel where the sentry had come out of the trees earlier. When they got to the channel they crossed the stream, making sure not to disturb the water so much it could be heard over the waterfall, then flattened themselves against the rock face on the other side facing the lake. Nathan had to crouch down low so his head did not appear over the top. Dawn only had to stoop a little.

She rounded back into the channel and found some good hand and foot holds in the rock to climb up. Nathan stayed on the lake side. After waiting a few seconds, he reached down and grabbed a large rock and tossed it over the bank like a basketball hook shot. He heard it thump against a tree.

Dawn heard footsteps run up to the edge of the bank and peeked her head up. Seeing the sentry peering over the edge she completed her climb as he spoke.

"Who the hell are you?" he asked, looking down on Nathan.

Just as the final word left his mouth, Barnes body blocked him right in the small of the back. Taken by surprise, the man fell forward and landed on the sandy beach on the crown of his head. Nathan heard a sickening crunch on impact and the man flopped the rest of the way to the ground.

Barnes jumped from the top of the embankment, drew her sidearm and pointed it at the man's face. There was no movement and she saw a grimace of pain frozen on his face. His neck was at an unnatural angle and it was already starting to swell up. She touched her index and middle finger to his neck and felt no pulse. She shook her head at Nathan.

They quickly turned him over and found what they were looking for – a military field radio. They took it off the body and set it aside. They then removed his tactical vest and Barnes handed it to Nathan. With the tactical Kevlar vest Blastmore had given him on his own body, Nathan did not need the protection it provided, but the supplies in it could come in handy. Barnes grabbed the dead merc's AR-15, took off his utility belt that included a holster and sidearm and gave that to Nathan as well. She picked up the radio and began jogging away from the channel through the sand with Nathan following. They went up into the trees once they got past the rock face on that side.

Under cover in the forest, they turned and looked back from where they had come. They saw the other sentry come out of the trees on the other side of the channel. When he saw his comrade on the beach, he jumped down and ran to him. After checking him, he looked down the beach and saw the tracks in the sand Barnes and Nathan had left. He got up and started to slowly follow them, rifle at the ready.

Barnes motioned for Nathan to take the equipment a little deeper into the trees and she got down on the ground in a prone firing position with the AR-15 at her shoulder. She silently watched the figure coming toward them. Looking through the high-power sniper scope, she put the crosshairs at center mass. She guessed the man was about forty yards away as the man's chest filled the scope.

"Police. Stop where you are and drop your weapon," she hollered. But he kept advancing.

Barnes hesitated only for a second. She took a big breath, held it, then squeezed off two rapid fire shots.

Barnes looked up from the scope and saw the man lying flat on his back, unmoving. Nathan came up to her side in a crouch, but straightened up when he saw the man lying there.

"Is he dead?" he whispered.

"Not likely," Barnes said as she got up. "But I'm sure he's trying to catch his breath and he might have a broken rib or two."

While she was doing her best to stay calm and as cool as a cucumber, Nathan could see her hands shaking slightly.

"First time you've ever fired at anyone?" Nathan asked. She nodded her head, but kept the unflappable stature. He could see her hands still trembled a little.

"Go down and get his vest and equipment," she ordered, and he complied immediately.

While he was gone, Barnes got the field radio and turned it on. She extended the twin antennas, tuned to the local sheriff's department frequency and held the headset to her ear with the mic boom near her mouth.

"This is an emergency call for Sheriff Dan Feller, please respond," she said into the mic. When there was no response, she repeated the call.

"Identify yourself," came a clear voice.

"I am Deputy Dawn Barnes. I am with FBI Agent Susan Blastmore and other agents on the mountain searching for George and Stephanie Wallis. We have an emergency situation," she said slowly and clearly.

"Stand by," came the voice.

Barnes waited almost a full minute.

"This is Sheriff Feller," came his familiar voice.

"This is Deputy Dawn Barnes. We have a situation on the mountain. We were pursued and fired upon by armed men transported here by helicopter," she said.

"I know about the mercenaries. What is your situation?" he asked.

She explained the group had split up, but Bryan was certain he knew where George was.

"Have you taken casualties?" the sheriff asked.

"Agent Blastmore was wounded in the arm," she said. "But we just heard an explosion near where we think they are."

She paused a moment, trying to find the right way to report what she must.

"We have one mercenary dead in a fall, he fell on his head and broke his neck," she said, omitting that he had been pushed. "I just shot another one, but he was wearing Kevlar so I'm sure he's still alive."

"Give me your location," the sheriff said. Barnes described her and Nathan's location and the probable location of the cabin.

"I was on the phone with the governor since you left and finally convinced him to have Nathan's in-laws call off the mercenaries, but they are refusing to do so," Feller said. "He allowed me to call in a National Guard unit. They left this morning and should be there any time."

Just as Feller finished, Barnes heard two shots in the direction of the cabin. One sounded like a high-powered rifle, like the AR-15 she had just fired, and the other was definitely an FBI sidearm. She waited for a minute, then heard two more AR-15 shots.

"We've got gunfire near the cabin," she yelled into the mic. Just at that moment Nathan returned dragging the sentry's equipment and weapons.

"Did you hear the shots?" he asked, but Barnes waved her hand dismissively.

"Hang tight where you are, deputy, the Guard is on the way," Feller said, then ended the transmission.

Chapter 22

Blastmore drug Vallow to the front of the cabin and propped him in a sitting position just to the left of the door. Mason kept his gun trained to the direction they had just come.

"Bryan, are you inside?" she yelled. "I've got a man down."

Vallow was still having trouble breathing. But he was conscious and coherent. Blastmore heard the dead bolt pulled back and the door opened. Bryan stepped out and got under one shoulder and Blastmore got under the other and took Vallow inside. They sat him on the floor and propped him against the north wall.

Stephanie gasped and went to her uncle's side.

"Will he die?" she asked.

"Not if I can help it," he answered. He then heard his father's angry voice.

"You brought feds up here!" he yelled.

"Dad, you need to give this up," Bryan said.

George moved to the desk and grabbed his pistol, whirled and pointed it at Blastmore. Stephanie screamed and retreated to the back wall of the shack.

"You need to leave," George said to Blastmore, disdain dripping from his words as he moved to the center of the room.

"Mr. Wallis, I'm not leaving without Stephanie, and you in handcuffs," the agent said.

"That's not going to happen," George said.

They all turned to Stephanie when they heard her speak.

"Grandpa, I want to go home to my parents," she screamed.

"You will go home to your dad," George said, keeping his eyes trained on Blastmore, centering his gun's sight on her face. "You're not going to be taken away from him again."

Bryan took a step toward his father and George redirected the gun to him. Bryan stopped his advance.

"That's something that will have to be decided once this is over, Dad," he said. "But you need to end this now. We have bigger things to worry about now."

As if on cue, they heard Mason's voice from outside.

"We have company coming," he hollered.

George went to the computer monitor. On the squares marked south, west and north, he saw men approaching – two each from the south and west and three from the north. Each group was about thirty yards out and moving in slowly.

Bryan turned to the door and slammed the dead bolt out of the slot.

"Bryan, no!" his father yelled, moving back to the room's center.

But Bryan threw open the door and stepped out. At that moment a shot from inside the enclosed cabin made Stephanie and the FBI agents cover their ears, Blastmore with just one hand and she quickly drew her sidearm with the free hand. She fired on instinct. George jerked backwards and fell to the floor. Stephanie screamed, but did not move.

They heard another shot from outside and turned to the door in time to see Bryan dive forward. In mid dive they saw the heel of his left boot explode in a cloud of dirt and black rubber. He crashed to the ground a few feet from the cabin's door.

Blastmore pointed to Stephanie and Vallow looked at the girl as she started toward the door. Still struggling for breath, he quickly stood and grabbed her and took her kicking and screaming to set her down in a corner of the room. Blastmore was at the door in a second cautiously peeking around the corner to the left.

There was no way Barnes was going to "hang tight" and wait for the National Guard to arrive. Who knew how long it would be before they made their way up the mountain. She and Nathan heard an explosion and shots in the direction the others had gone. She wasn't going to leave them on their own.

One look at Nathan told her he was even more anxious than she. Who could blame him? For all he knew, his daughter could be in the line of fire.

Barnes handed Nathan one of the AR-15s. Nathan was not a novice shooter, although he owned no weapons himself. He and Cynthia had gone to shooting ranges from time to time, and they had planned to take Stephanie once she was fourteen. But he had never fired an AR-15.

While some people use the term "assault rifle," thinking that's what the AR stands for, the AR-15 semi-automatic rifle was developed by Colt Firearms in the late 1950s for civilian use. Over the years a number of variations and modifications were made available. What these mercs were using were military versions that had three firing modes – semi-auto, select fire and a burst mode.

Barnes had made sure the rifle she gave to Nathan was set for semi-automatic. She did not tell him about the fire selector, but she did explain the safety and how to operate it, and the basics of firing the weapon.

"But since you're not used to this kind of weapon, don't fire unless you really have to, or unless I tell you to," Barnes told him.

Nathan nodded, then she gathered up the two utility belts with ten clip pockets each attached, with clips of AR-15 ammo inside. She handed one to Nathan and buckled the other on herself. When they were both ready, she pointed to the lake.

"We'll make better time if we stay out of the trees as long as we can," she said as they set out.

They pair jogged along the sandy beach as it curved gradually from south to west in an almost perfect quarter circle. When the beach was aligned directly north and south, the curving stopped and it stretched on for about fifty yards where the beach suddenly ended with an outcropping of granite.

Barnes detoured them up the rocky terrain. Over the hump they saw the lake shore take a jag to the west and then continue north again. But this time there was no sandy beach, just about five feet of open, grassy ground between the trees and an abrupt two-foot drop to the water.

They continued along the narrow open ground until Barnes suddenly stopped and knelt down and put the rifle to her shoulder, looking through the sniper scope. She saw a man, dressed in full combat gear, moving slowly north about twenty feet inside the tree line. She followed his movements and when he passed into a gap in the trees, she put the scope's crosshairs on his Kevlar vest squarely between the shoulder blades and squeezed off a single shot.

The man fell forward and lay motionless. Barnes did not waste any time watching the downed man and motioned Nathan, who had knelt down slightly behind her, to follow. She double-timed along the narrow space between the lake and trees with Nathan on her heels. But suddenly she threw up her hand and slowed, and Nathan followed suit. Before them the trees were less dense and they could see a small shack. Mason was outside facing south with his gun drawn, but as they stood there, they saw the door open.

Bryan appeared in the doorway and took a step out. They heard a shot from the north and saw Bryan dive forward and his left foot exploded.

Bantum divided his small force, leaving three near the lake and taking four others up the hill to the west then turning and advancing north. He had instructed the three left behind to hold their position until they received further instructions.

After Bantum and the others had moved about 100 yards they could see through the trees what appeared to be a structure down near the lake. He sent three of his charges further north and instructed them to take a position on the north side of the structure. When that group reported they were in position, Bantum prepared to give his instructions.

First, he tried to check in with the sentries near the waterfall. He was puzzled when he got no response. It gave him a bit of hesitation. What if his rear guard had encountered someone? But if so, why hadn't they checked in? He was still pondering the possibilities when he heard an explosion in the direction where he had left his south team.

"South team, report," he said into his throat mic.

"We encountered what appears to be a booby trap," a voice said in his earpiece. "We have one wounded."

"What happened?" Bantum asked.

"We were repositioning and Smithers tripped a wire and there was an explosion," the voice said. "Painter was standing near an explosive of some kind attached to the wire. A big piece of metal from the canister is embedded in his calf."

"Is he mobile?' Bantum asked.

"Negative," the voice answered.

Bantum took a few seconds to consider his next move. He had a wounded man and two others that could not be accounted for. That meant it was most likely that thirty percent of his force was out of action. He had no idea how many people were in the group he was tracking, but remembering the blood they found at the campsite one of them was also wounded.

"All units move forward and watch for trip wires," he said into the mic. "There is a structure ahead of you. We'll rendezvous there."

"What are your orders if we encounter anyone," a different voice asked.

"Unless it is the little girl you have freedom of action," Bantum said.

He and his partner had only walked a few steps when they heard gunfire close to the lake. They hesitated only briefly then continued on. They heard more shots and quickened their pace as best they could in the trees and downed trunks. While moving, Bantum heard in his receiver, "South contact, shots fired." After they had gone another twenty yards they heard a slightly muffled shot followed almost immediately by another. Then they heard the crack of an AR-15.

"Report," Bantum said.

"South team, we have a man down by gunfire," a voice said.

"North team, shots fired inside a small cabin. We hit someone coming out," another voice said.

Now Bantum's force was down by forty percent. But there was no intel that indicated exactly who was in the cabin. Was it the people they had been tracking? Was the little girl even with them? Was it random hikers or campers? He was starting to question whether he would be able to complete his mission. He was also starting to believe this expedition had gotten out of hand, and they may be putting the little girl's life in danger.

"All units hold position," he said.

Just as the words left his mouth, he heard a familiar sound coming from the south. It convinced him it was time to cut his losses.

"Check, check, check," he hollered into his neck mic. "Fall back. Rendezvous at the waterfall."

As Bryan hit the ground, Barnes saw Blastmore poke her head out of the cabin door. Without any further hesitation, she raised the rifle to her shoulder and looked through the scope. She adjusted it to pull back the magnification. Panning the forest from the northeast corner of the cabin outward, she caught sight of a figure kneeling in a shooting position.

The scope's field of vision showed the figure from the ground to the top of his cap. Barnes zeroed the center of the scope on the exposed part of the rifle between the figure's chest and the left hand steadying the rifle by the forward grip. She fired one shot then scanned the forest again, catching site of another figure.

Just then she heard a shot from a handgun from the direction of the cabin. She opened her left eye and saw Blastmore fire another two shots into the forest. She lowered the rifle slightly and saw Bryan lying on his belly, not moving, his face turned toward the direction she and Blastmore were shooting. Suddenly he rolled over onto his back, pulled his pistol from the holster at his hip and fired two shots.

Nathan had been kneeling slightly behind Barnes. When he saw Bryan fall to the ground, his first instinct was to run to his brother to give any aid needed. But he had just gotten to his feet when the shooting started. He quickly went back to one knee. Out of the corner of his eye he saw movement to his left. When he looked he saw Mason pointing his gun right at him. But he quickly pivoted and aimed his gun away from the cabin to the south.

When he turned his attention back to the cabin, he saw Bryan on his back pointing his weapon into the woods. It was then he heard a familiar thump thump thump in the air. But it was not quite the same as he had heard earlier in the day. This time the thumping was much faster, and there was a low growl combined with a whine.

Nathan noticed Blastmore and Barnes cock their heads slightly for a few seconds then return their gaze in the direction of their shots. They had heard the sound as well, and apparently recognized it.

"Fall back, rendezvous at the waterfall," they all heard coming from somewhere behind the cabin. Because they heard it over the fast-approaching sound, they assumed the speaker was right behind the cabin. But Barnes and Blastmore recognized something else in the voice, more like a yell, and there was a slight echo as if it were bouncing off the hillside.

"I've got men down," they heard coming from the north, this one sounding much closer and accompanied with no echo.

They heard no response, but then heard running footsteps through the forest. They could tell they were headed south and they passed closely behind the cabin.

Blastmore, still in the cabin doorway, held up her hand.

"Hold your fire," she hollered. She was not only speaking to her comrades, but she hoped the pursuers heard her and would comply. But they were in full retreat and now the only sound was the mechanical noise in the air.

Chapter 23

The merc Barnes shot in the chest on the beach near the waterfall opened his eyes at the sound of the rotors beating the air.

He had been in and out of consciousness two times, maybe three – he couldn't tell –since the AR-15 rounds thudded into the Kevlar covering his chest. His open eyes saw a sharp blue sky with a few whiffs of thin clouds. They actually looked like puffs of thin smoke.

The rotor noise came closer and he thought Bantum had found the girl and called the chopper for evac. He looked to his left and saw the trees several feet back from the sandy beach. Turning his head to the right he saw the lake water gently lapping in miniature breakers onto the sand about six feet away.

Suddenly the rotor noise was almost on top of him and he looked straight up to see the olive drab green belly of a helicopter. The rotor wash pounded down on him and stirred the sand around him. He closed his eyes until he heard the noise pass over him and continue on its way.

The man tried to sit up but a searing pain shot through his chest and he flopped back down. He rotated his head until his chin touched the top of his sternum. In that position he could see the helicopter hovering just above the sandy beach about fifty yards away. He recognized it as not the Huey they had arrived in, but a UH-60 Black Hawk.

He watched as a rope dropped down from the chopper and a fully combat geared man slid down to the beach. Using both hands, the merc felt the ground on either side of him trying to find his rifle, with no success. He then went to his hip and found nothing where his holstered pistol was supposed to be. Feeling around his waist, there was no utility belt there.

The man who dropped from the helicopter was jogging toward him with his rifle at the ready. The merc began to feel a little dizzy and his vision became fuzzy. His head dropped to the sand again and the sky went from sharp blue to dark blue to black.

Nathan looked to Barnes, who was still looking toward the woods past the cabin. After a few seconds she lifted her left hand and waved him forward. Nathan ran to his brother's side.

"Are you hit?' he asked.

Bryan was now lying on his side, but at the sound of his brother's voice he rolled over on his back.

"I think I might have taken a round in my left foot," he answered.

Nathan looked down at his foot but saw no blood. In fact, he saw Bryan's tactical boot perfectly intact and tightly laced. He moved to where he could see the entire foot. In the area where the heel should have been there was a twisted, mangled mess. He could see about a dime-sized portion of the gray wool sock underneath.

"Can you move it?" Nathan asked.

He watched as his brother slowly moved the foot from side to side. He then looked at the grimace on his brother's face.

"Well, you're going to need some new boots, but I think you'll live," he said. "There's no blood down here, so it must have just torn your heel off and the impact might have strained your ankle."

"So, you're a doctor now?" Bryan said with a smirk on his face.

Nathan raised his hand as if he was going to slug his brother's injured foot, but when Bryan tensed he lowered it slowly.

"Help me up," Bryan said.

Nathan took his right arm and pulled him to a sitting position and Bryan bent his right leg to get his foot under him. Nathan pulled him up onto that one leg. Bryan gingerly put some weight on the left foot and felt a sharp shooting pain and pulled it up.

"I agree with your diagnosis, doctor," Bryan said.

Nathan wrapped his brother's left arm around his shoulder and helped him hobble to the cabin door where Blastmore was still standing. She looked inside then turned to the brothers.

"You two need to come in here," she said.

When Nathan ran past her, Barnes looked to the south. She could hear the noise, which she assumed was the same helicopter that had dropped off the mercs, coming from behind an outcropping into the lake with tress blocking her view. The aircraft seemed stationary. But within seconds she heard the engine rev up and then it suddenly appeared from around the trees and headed her way. She saw ropes dangling from both open cabin doors.

This helicopter looked and sounded much different than the other. She had seen Black Hawks before and this one looked like the ones she had seen. It flew to a point directly in front of her about twenty yards from the shore and the same distance from the water and hovered in profile. The rotor wash stirred the water below and creating waves that slammed into the shore in front of her.

She could see a man in the cabin pulling up and securing the ropes. Just in front of the open mid-cabin doors was an opening with a manned machine gun pointed at her.

Barnes quickly dropped the AR-15 and pointed to the word "Sheriff" on the front of her Kevlar vest. She pointed to her ear and held her other hand in front of her mouth. She hoped they would understand she was requesting communications. Her hopes were answered when the pilot flashed his fingers to indicate a frequency.

Barnes pulled the portable radio from her belt and adjusted the dial. She keyed the mic and identified herself.

"I am with three FBI agents and two civilians," she said. "We were searching for Stephanie Wallis. The civilians are her father and uncle."

"Stand by," the pilot said.

He spoke into his headset, but Barnes heard nothing from her radio. She assumed he was checking in with headquarters on a different frequency.

"Give me a sit rep," the pilot said a few minutes later.

"We were attacked by an unknown force," she said.

"Any casualties?" the pilot asked.

"We have at least one in our party. I think there are four from the attackers," she said.

"We found two back there," the pilot said, thumbing over his shoulder. "How bad are the other wounded?"

"Unknown at this time," she answered.

"Do a recon and give me a full report," the pilot said.

More interested in checking on the people she knew, Barnes went into the cabin. She had heard the shots emanating from there earlier and was concerned who might be wounded – or worse.

When she stepped through the doorway the first thing she saw straight ahead of her was George lying flat on his back with his sons on either side of him. They were applying pressure on his right shoulder. Blood stained his sweatshirt and she could see a slowly growing pool of it on the wooden floor below his shoulder.

She turned to the right and saw Vallow seated on the floor in the front corner of the room. Blastmore was kneeling beside him. He was still struggling to breath. Blastmore began to unfasten the Velcro straps to take off his Kevlar vest, but as she did, he grimaced in pain and gasped for air. She quickly put the Velcro back in place and his breathing returned to its previous ragged rhythm.

"What's wrong?" Barnes asked as she knelt beside the FBI agents.

"I think there's a broken rib or two," Blastmore said. "Not sure why releasing the pressure makes it worse."

Blastmore glanced over her shoulder at the Wallises in the middle of the room, then shot a questioning look at Barnes.

"Shoulder wound, looks pretty serious," the deputy said.

Her gaze then went to the back corner of the room where Stephanie stood against the wall, a terrified look on her face. Barnes walked slowly toward her. Stephanie never took her eyes off her grandfather, father and uncle. Barnes placed herself between the girl and the three men on the floor. She stood about a foot away from Stephanie. The girl slowly met the deputy's eyes.

217

"Are they going to be alright?" she asked.

Barnes could see the girl might be in shock, or headed there very quickly. The deputy struggled with how to answer her question. She wanted to put her at ease by telling her the FBI agent and her grandfather would be okay. But she also did not want to lie to her, or give her false hope. She opted for the truth and hoped for the best.

"I don't know," she said.

Stephanie's look did not change one iota.

"Please come with me," Barnes said extending her hand. "I need your help."

The deputy knew it was risky to take the child outside where there could still be armed men advancing on their position. But she believed the risk was minimal. The Black Hawk that continued to hover just off the lake shore surely would give pause to any group, other than fanatical militants, which she doubted they were dealing with here. The bigger risk was what the already traumatized girl might see out there.

Stephanie slowly raised her hand and placed it in Barnes'. When she closed her finger around the deputy's, Barnes was surprised at the strength of the grip. She could feel the small hand trembling despite the hold she had on her hand.

They walked to the door, with Barnes strategically placed between the girl and the Wallis men. But it really didn't matter, Stephanie kept her head turned straight ahead and did not glance to either side with her eyes. While it had been a steady thrum in everyone else's ears since it arrived, Stephanie's first conscious awareness of the Black Hawk's roar was only when they stepped through the doorway. She hesitated, but only for a second.

"Check to the south and see if there's anyone out there, then circle back and meet me behind the cabin and we'll scout to the north," Barnes told Mason, still standing, pistol at the ready, near the corner of the cabin. Though Barnes was not his superior, not even another FBI agent, Mason did not hesitate to contemplate her authority. He nodded and began to move slowly into the trees.

Barnes, with Stephanie's steely grip still on her hand, turned to her left and began walking parallel to the cabin's east wall, her eyes scanning from left to right. Because she did not want to alarm Stephanie, she had kept her sidearm in the holster on her right hip. But when she saw something in the trees about forty-five degrees to her left, she unfastened the safety strap and put her hand on the grip.

She veered toward what she had seen, maneuvering Stephanie behind her. But the girl worked her way back to her side. As they approached, Barnes saw it was a man lying face down on the forest floor. She could see a large bright red stain on the green wild grass. It reminded her of Christmas, but the potential deadliness of the scene jolted her back to the moment.

She advanced cautiously, but the man never moved. Kneeling next to the body, she first felt the side of his neck but got no pulse. She then examined the man's left leg just below the knee above the red stain on the grass. There was a neat hole on one side of the leg about mid-calf and another on the other side. The pant leg was a darkened version of the green-gray-black camouflage pattern where the blood had soaked into the fabric.

Stephanie had followed Barnes' gaze and took it all in silently.

Barnes knew she had aimed at the man's Kevlar vest when she fired at him from the edge of the lake shore.

"He must have dived for cover just as I fired," she muttered. She felt a surge of remorse, and some bile rising in her throat. About an hour earlier she had shot at her first human target. Now she had killed her second human being. But she swallowed the bile back into her stomach, and the remorse with it. Both deaths had not been her intention. Besides, those men put themselves in harm's way, not her.

After ordering his men to fall back, Bantum and the man with him waited five minutes, hoping the north team would join them. When he heard their running footsteps coming near, he keyed his throat mic.

"North team, friendly right," he said.

Within seconds, two men joined them, one with his right arm dangling at his side, blood dripping from the mangled trigger finger.

"We have a man down," one of the men said.

The implied request was clear – they should go back and get him.

"Negative, we have to move," Bantum said. "There's a Black Hawk in the area, that means armed troops."

Reluctantly, the men agreed and the four turned south and began to move through the trees as fast as they could. Bantum hoped his men to the south knew to stay in the cover of the trees. If there were armed troops sweeping the area, the trees would allow a measure of protection – if only a small measure.

Bantum's original two-man team had been high on the hillside before they started advancing on the cabin. When they halted the advance, they were still high enough to stay in the trees. But as the four men's retreat took them closer to the south end of the lake, the tree line descended the hill gradually. When they came to where the trees thinned out, Bantum could see two soldiers walking up the hill just outside the trees.

He gestured to his men to take cover. They stood next to standing trees or squatted behind fallen trunks, keeping those between them and the two soldiers as they walked past. Their heads were on swivels, scanning up the hillside and into the trees. But they went by without hesitation.

When he judged the soldiers were far enough away, he motioned for his men to follow and they continued down the hill, staying inside the tree line.

Barnes, with Stephanie still clutching her hand, made a quick sweep of the area in a thirty-foot radius of where they found the soldier's body. Finding no one else, she led the girl to the back of the cabin. They were there only a short time when Mason showed up.

"What did you find?" she asked, having to raise her voice to be heard over the still hovering Black Hawk.

"There was a guy out there who took a round to the back in his vest," Mason answered. "He was just catching his breath. I took his vest off to make it easier for him and sat him up against a tree."

He then held up an AR-15 and a handgun in one hand and a utility belt, including grenades and a knife, in the other.

"I disarmed him and told him to stay put," he continued.

"Do you think he will?" Barnes asked, reaching for the hand-held radio in her belt.

"Who knows, but at least he's not armed," Mason said.

Barnes keyed the radio's transmit button and reported to the helo pilot.

"We have two friendlies wounded in the cabin, one hostile wounded in the woods to the south and one hostile fatality to the north," she said.

"There's another wounded man to the south," Mason said, and Barnes relayed that to the pilot.

"How serious are the wounded?" the pilot asked.

"One in the cabin seriously with a GSW in the shoulder, the others not so much," she said, looking to Mason for confirmation on the other wounded man to the south. He nodded his head in affirmation.

"Can you move the seriously wounded to the beach to the south ASAP?" the pilot asked.

"We can manage it," Barnes said.

The pilot did not respond, but the chopper's engine pitched up and they could hear it bank away and head for the beach. That was response enough. The trio went around the cabin and entered. Nathan was continuing to tend to his father. Bryan was looking over the equipment George had arranged on the desk against the south wall.

The monitors were connected to a single laptop computer. Under the desk were five heavy duty truck batteries. One had cables connected to the posts and the other end to a large black box. That unit had several USB cables connected to the laptop and monitors.

Barnes and Stephanie walked over beside him.

"Can you believe that? He was using truck batteries for power," Bryan said when he noticed Dawn and his niece there.

"We've got to get your father down to the beach," she said.

Bryan snapped out of his fascination with his father's setup and looked around the room. There was an Army cot next to the desk and he pointed to that.

"We can use that for a stretcher," he said.

Barnes was able to dislodge Stephanie's hand from hers and helped Bryan, limping heavily, move the cot next to George. His eyes looked glassy and his breathing was shallow. Following Barnes' instructions, Nathan and Bryan lifted George to a sitting position. She told Stephanie to get her some cloth and the girl quickly brought five T-shirts from George's pack. She was surprisingly calm. Barnes roughly folded two of the shirts and placed them over an exit wound on George's back. Nathan held it in place while she repeated the procedure on the entry wound and Bryan held it while she used duct tape Stephanie had brought to her from the desk to hold the make shift bandages in place.

They folded the legs of the cot upward and lay it on the floor. Gently they and Nathan lifted George and put him on it. Bryan went to one end and Nathan, facing away from the patient. to the other and lifted it. They walked out of the cabin and turned to the right and started off with Mason following, carrying the weapons and equipment he had taken from the man in the woods.

Barnes went to where Vallow and Blastmore remained on the floor. Stephanie walked over there as well.

"Can you walk?" Barnes asked Vallow.

"Not without some help," he wheezed.

Barnes and Blastmore took each of his hands and brought him to a stand, then draped his arms across their shoulders. Their height difference between Blastmore and Barnes made it lopsided and increased Vallow's pain and difficulty breathing.

"I can help," Stephanie said, and stepped in to take Blastmore's place.

This was a better match and they headed for the door, with Blastmore following closely behind in case she was needed.

Chapter 24

The Black Hawk hovered a few feet off the ground, the right wheel over the water and the left over the sand. The rotor wash sent a wall of mist toward the center of the lake and sand swirled on the other side. Four National Guardsmen, with goggles affixed to ward off the sand, carried the cot with George aboard, face covered against the rotor wash, to the door and placed it inside.

The same four boosted Vallow into the helo's cabin, then a merc with a badly mangled foot, the man Mason had found, and the two men Barnes shot in the vest. There was already another dead body inside the chopper, the man Barnes pushed off the embankment.

The National Guardsmen came across the remaining member of the merc south team and took him into custody, relieving him of his weapons and equipment. He was escorted to the beach by one soldier. They found the man with the wounded leg and two soldiers took him back to the beach.

The next passengers into the Black Hawk were the remaining unarmed mercenaries.

Once everyone was aboard and secured, the Black Hawk swooped upward, banked to the right and zoomed over the tall trees. Because of the rush to get George to a hospital, the Guard commander decided to go back the following day for the dead man near the shack by the lake.

Nathan and Bryan sat with Barnes and the FBI agents on the ground just off the sandy beach watching the aircraft depart. They were all silent as the National Guard squad commander approached them. He knelt on one knee and they all turned to look at him.

"The man with the shoulder wound is in pretty serious condition," he said, glancing at Nathan and Bryan, who were seated next to each other. "Our medic said he's lost a lot of blood and is in shock."

Blastmore lowered her head, feeling a little guilty. Mason looked her way. He had gotten only the barest information about what happened in the cabin. He wondered what the details were. But he knew Blastmore was a by-the-book agent, so whatever happened she must have followed procedure.

Nathan and Bryan stared at the Guard lieutenant, showing no emotion at all.

"Is he going to make it?" Bryan finally asked.

"We're not sure," he answered. "But our medic said if you hadn't slowed the bleeding, he would have bled out where he laid on that floor."

The brothers had no response. Instead, they looked to the west side of the lake where the sun was approaching the top of the mountain. Once it dipped behind it, darkness and the cooler temperatures at this altitude would not be very far behind. Bryan estimated they had an hour, maybe ninety minutes before the sun was completely behind the mountain. They would have another half hour of twilight after that.

"My unit and I are going down to a clearing not too far from here where we'll evac out," the lieutenant explained. "You can come along with us. We can take you down the mountain. With three of my unit in the Black Hawk now, there will be room for you all."

No one spoke for a moment. Then Blastmore raised her head, a serious business look on her face.

"We'll go as far as the clearing with you, but we have vehicles further down the mountain we need to retrieve," she said.

"Alright," the lieutenant said, standing up. "We'll move out in ten minutes."

They remained seated for a few seconds, no one looking at anyone else. Then they stood, almost in unison, and joined the Guardsmen, who were gathering up weapons and equipment, their own and the mercs', preparing for the march down the mountain.

Nathan turned and took a last, long look at the lake and its surroundings. It was such a beautiful and peaceful scene. No one could tell there had been a battle there. But as magnificent as it was now, he never wanted to return to this place, or anywhere like it. But time was a great healer, and that emotional decision would eventually change.

The walk down the mountain was made in silence. Nathan and the others in his party replayed in their minds the last couple of hours before they started the march.

In debriefing Nathan and his group as the helo was being loaded, the squad commander said he learned the merc with the wounded leg had been standing within inches of a flash bang when his comrade touched the trip wire that controlled it and set it off. Normally, these devices are used to cause confusion or even frighten people in raid or breech situations.

But if someone is in close proximately to one when it goes off, they can be injured. In this case, the concussion broke the man's ankle and a six-inch piece of shrapnel punctured his tactical boot and sunk two inches into his skin just above the ankle.

The remaining members of that Guard group found the merc that Mason disarmed still sitting by the tree where he was told to stay. Another solder took him to the beach and the last soldier continued north. Shortly thereafter he came across Nathan and Bryan carrying George on the cot.

"We are with Deputy Barnes," Nathan said. "We need to get this man to the beach fast."

"The rest of our party is right behind us," Bryan told him.

The soldier waved them on and stood waiting. When Barnes and the others arrived, the deputy explained there was a dead hostile just to the north of the cabin. She agreed to go back with him to show him exactly where the body was.

The soldier examined the man carefully.

"Looks like he got hit in an artery and bled out quickly," he said.

The Guardsman radioed his commander for instructions and was told to put the body in the shack and shut the door to protect it from wildlife. They would have to come back for it the following day.

About the same time that the search team found the first merc, two other soldiers patrolling just outside the tree line walked past Bantum and his three comrades. Bantum was sure they had passed by without seeing them. He was wrong.

They radioed ahead to the squad commander and reported what they had observed. He sent two others up the hill, one outside and the other inside the tree line. The reporting soldiers reversed their field and took position behind the mercs.

Bantum and his comrades were grouped closely together, trying to make the quickest escape they could. Suddenly they spotted a Guardsman ahead of them on one knee in a firing position and Bantum raised his sidearm. He saw the muzzle flash from the soldier's rifle and almost simultaneously heard the man to his right fall.

Bantum dropped his pistol to the forest grass and raised his arms. The rest of his men followed suit.

The merc beside Bantum took the round on the left side of the neck, gouging a trench through the skin, but missing the carotid artery. Two Guardsmen marched the three unwounded mercs to the beach while the other two dressed the other man's wound. They then took him to the beach as well.

With all the mercs captured, wounded or dead, the Guard squad commander questioned them thoroughly. He learned who had hired them and what their objective had been. He was also told the exact instructions Jennifer McAdams had given them about how to achieve the goal.

As the lead law enforcement agent in the group, Blastmore was involved in the questioning. But she simply listened and took detailed notes. She knew Nathan and Bryan would want this information, but she did not believe this was the best time to share it. She asked the Guard lieutenant to also keep the details to himself until they got back to town and could take official statements from all concerned. He agreed.

The Guardsmen and others double timed it down the mountain, taking only 30 minutes to reach George's camp by the clearing. The sun had dipped below the western mountains and twilight was settling in by the time they got there.

Gathered in front of the lean-to, they heard the beating rotors of another Black Hawk approaching. The squad commander sent four men into the clearing to mark a landing zone with their flashlights.

"Are you sure you don't want to hitch a ride with us?" the lieutenant asked. "It's going to be pitch black very soon."

Blastmore looked up into the grayish blue sky, then at Bryan. He silently shook his head.

"We've got vehicles to retrieve," she said.

The squad leader looked out into the meadow as the helicopter came over the treetops and settled over the four flashlights positioned as corners of a large box in the clearing.

"You can always come back in the morning," the commander said, raising his voice over the roar.

"No, we've got to get them now," the lead FBI agent said. "They are rentals."

"Suit yourself," the lieutenant said, motioning his remaining men to get aboard the chopper that had settled onto the soft ground. He then turned and headed for it himself.

Bryan motioned for his brother, Stephanie, Barnes and the FBI agents to follow him. He skirted the tree line, heading for the other side of the clearing. About halfway there the chopper lifted slowly off the ground. Once it cleared the trees, it pivoted a quarter turn, lowered the nose and headed back to the airport.

As it passed over the trees, Bryan diverted into the trees and the others followed. Once inside the trees they were bathed in near total darkness and all five took out their flashlights and turned them on. Even with the illumination, their progress was slower than it was from the lake to the camp. Because of the darkness beyond the radius of the four flashlights, they had to be careful of wildlife that might come charging out of the blackness toward them.

It was a good precaution, as when they approached the cave they caught a buck deer on the fringe of the light from their flashlights. It was standing staring at them, much like if it was facing a car racing at it and was hypnotized by the headlights. As they got closer, they saw it was a large, four-pointer. The deer did not even flinch as the five humans walked past it about ten yards away. Then they heard it bound away as soon as they had their backs to it.

About two hours after they left the camp, they were at the cabin. Not a word was spoken, but they all gathered up the small amount of items they had left behind and packed them into the Suburbans. Bryan put his belongings in his father's Jeep.

"I'll take Dad's Jeep back," he told Nathan. "I got his keys before they loaded him on the helicopter."

Mason climbed in one of the Suburbans and Barnes joined him. While Sheriff Martin had told her not to let Nathan out of her site, she was confident he was not going to go anywhere other than back to town. Stephanie climbed in the backseat of the Suburban with Barnes and Mason. Nathan looked hurt.

"Don't you want to ride with your dad?" Barnes asked her.

"I want to stay with you," she said.

Barnes didn't try to talk her out of it.

"This has been a traumatic experience for her, she needs to process it in her own way," she thought. The deputy did not pursue the matter any further and gestured for Mason to get moving.

Blastmore and Nathan piled into the other Suburban and the small convoy started down the road.

They hadn't gone far when Blastmore, driving the last vehicle in the line, spoke for the first time since the camp.

"I'm sorry about your father," she said, keeping her eyes on the road, but stealing a quick glance of Nathan out of the corner of her right eye.

"It's okay, you did what you thought you had to do," Nathan said.

The agent replayed the incident inside the cabin by the lake in her mind. When George fired his pistol, she had reacted on instinct. She pulled her weapon and aimed dead center on his chest. But in the instant as she was pulling the trigger, she saw Stephanie cowering against the cabin's back wall just behind George's left shoulder. Afraid she might hit her with a through and through or ricochet shot, she started to raise the pistol up and to her left. But she had already put enough pressure on the trigger of her Sig Sauer that it fired and hit George in the right shoulder.

"But I nearly killed him," she said finally.

"He might make it, it was a pretty bad wound, but the medic said if they got him a transfusion quickly enough he might pull through," Nathan said.

"You don't understand. I had a center mass shot from just a few feet away," Blastmore said, then explained in detail how it had gone down.

Nathan's expression did not change.

"Still, you did what you thought you had to do," he said after a moment.

They were silent again for a while. When they broke out of the tree line, Nathan broke the silence.

"What did the National Guard guy learn from questioning those guys?" he asked.

Blastmore, though she knew he eventually would learn the details, hoped she would not have to answer that question, or the rest he would ask on the subject.

"They were mercenaries," she answered.

"I guessed that, and I'm sure they were there trying to get Stephanie," Nathan said calmly. "But why were they there? Who sent them?

Blastmore took the official line, hoping Nathan would accept that.

"This is an ongoing investigation and I can't really discuss details of an ongoing investigation," she said.

Nathan didn't care about that.

"Was my wife involved in sending them?" he asked.

"I don't know what her involvement was, if she was involved at all," she said, not really breaking the rules about ongoing investigations.

"What about my in-laws?" he asked.

"I don't know," she lied.

Nathan turned to face her for the first time. She took a quick look at him then focused back on the dark road as they approached the highway.

"You're not going to tell me anything, are you?" he asked.

"We need to take statements from everyone involved, Nathan, and I don't want anything I might say to you to influence what you will say," she said firmly.

It made sense to Nathan, but it did not dampen his desire to know who had sent the mercenaries after his daughter. He had a pretty good idea who it was, but he wanted confirmation.

But he knew he would have to wait. He hoped his patience would hold out.

The three-vehicle convoy pulled up to the sheriff's substation and everyone went inside. They found Sheriff Feller at his desk, but no one else was there, it being quite late.

Nathan had expected to find his wife and her parents, at least, in the holding cells. He also thought he would find the unwounded mercenaries locked up. His disappointment was devastating, and for a few minutes he was speechless. When he finally found his voice, his anger flowed out with his words.

"Why the hell isn't anyone in your cells?" he raved. "My wife and her parents hired a bunch of mercenaries to go out and kill people to get my daughter so they could take her away from me. What kind of Mickey Mouse operation is this?"

Feller put up his hand to stop him, but he was unsuccessful.

"I'm going to get a great lawyer and sue the pants off you and this department," he said.

Nathan paused to let that sink in and hopefully give Feller a chance to start issuing arrest warrants. He was disappointed again.

"In the first place," the sheriff said calmly, pointing to Blastmore standing to Nathan's right. "The FBI is the lead agency in this investigation."

Nathan slowly looked toward Susan. In the time they had spent together in the last days, he had gathered a great deal of respect for her. He felt a pang of regret – although a small pang – for his outburst. Blastmore did not look his way, but the corners of her mouth were turned up in a slight smile.

"Technically, Bantum's group is not mercenary, it is a private military contractor," Feller said. "They are legal to operate in countries where PMCs are allowed. Whether that applies here or not, because they were not hired by a law enforcement agency, is still being researched."

Nathan was trying to process that information when the sheriff, still speaking calmly, went on.

"As far as your wife and in-laws are concerned, their accountability regarding hiring this group depends on what we find about their legality," he said. "But there is the issue of interfering with an ongoing law enforcement investigation."

Nathan's face brightened a little, but Feller did not want him to get his hopes up.

"That's no slam dunk," he said quickly. "We were aware they were getting involved because your in-laws came in and informed us they hired their own 'security firm,'" he made quote marks in the air when he said the last two words. "But no one from the PMC came to us directly, and they did not share their plan with us."

"How did they know where we even were? Or where Stephanie and my dad were?" Nathan asked.

"Because your in-laws pulled some political influence and the governor ordered the sheriff to hand over copies of all we had discovered," Blastmore explained.

"And believe me, that is going to backfire on our governor, and probably the one in your state as well," Feller said, a little more firmness in his voice.

"So that's why no one's in jail?" Nathan asked, his anger tempered down several notches now.

"Mostly," Feller said. "The other reason is you all have no motels and you need somewhere to get some sleep."

"Mason and I will be at the airport at our jet," Blastmore said. "We need to return the rental vehicles."

"Whatever works for you," Feller said, then escorted Nathan out of his office where he joined Barnes and Stephanie. They all headed down the hall to the empty holding cells.

Spending a night in jail was not an experience Nathan wanted for himself or his daughter, but at least it wasn't because they were under arrest, and they could come and go as they pleased. But not this night. They each went to a cell, dropped onto the sparse bed and were asleep within seconds.

Chapter 25

Nathan emerged from the interview room exhausted. He had hardly slept during the night in the jail cell. It wasn't that he felt enclosed, because the cell door remained wide open, the same as Blastmore's and Barnes'. It was the trauma of the previous day.

But there was another factor that robbed him of sleep. Stephanie had refused to spend the night in the cell with him. Instead, she insisted on staying with Barnes. He did not fully understand it, but he could clearly read that she was afraid of him.

Why would a daughter be so afraid of her own father? Especially a daughter who had been so close to her father before this ordeal began with her mother whisking her away.

Trying to reason it out had blasted him awake every time he felt his eyelids closing during the night. It also played havoc with his concentration during the past two hours as he was being questioned for his statement detailing the last few days. The deputy directing the questions had to repeat his queries several times, and had to prod Nathan to continue when he answered but suddenly drifted off in thought.

But finally, he got to the point at which they arrived at the sheriff's substation the night before. As he exited the interview room, Sheriff Feller motioned him to enter his office. Nathan sat in one of the chairs opposite the sheriff's desk. Feller wasted no time getting to the point. There was a lot to be done and this was just one item to check off his list.

"We've set up open-ended motel rooms for you and Deputy Barnes," Feller said. "We're going to need you to stick around a bit until we make sure we have all we need to continue this investigation."

Nathan nodded his head, indicating he understood. But he said nothing.

"This should only take a couple of days," the sheriff said.

Again, a nod was the only response.

"Do you have any questions?" Feller asked.

Nathan thought for a moment. The burning question in his mind he was sure the sheriff could not answer. So, he asked another one.

"Is my father going to live?"

"Because of his loss of blood he is still unconscious," he explained. "They are listing him in critical condition and he is in ICU. Whether he makes it or not is still up in the air."

Nathan nodded again.

"See Deputy Drummette and he'll get you, Barnes and your daughter squared away at the motel," the Sheriff said. "If you need anything, call him and he'll take care of it."

Nathan gave his usual response as he stood up and turned to leave. Feller motioned to someone outside his office and Blastmore came through the door as Nathan was exiting. She put her hand on his shoulder and he looked at her with blank eyes.

"Hang in there. We'll talk later," she said.

Nathan just nodded absently. He glanced at his watch. It was just before ten in the morning. His stomach growled like a dog trying to ward off an intruder. He suddenly realized he had not eaten in more than twenty-four hours.

Feller and Blastmore knocked on the door of the motel room registered in Kenneth and Jennifer McAdams' names. Their main mission was to get their statements, as with all the others involved in the incidents of the past few days. They knew, from Feller's own experience with the McAdamses, this may not be an easy goal to achieve.

After their third knock, the door was jerked open by Jennifer. Remembering their last encounter, Feller steeled himself for another confrontation. She did not give him any reason to doubt that assessment.

"Where is my granddaughter?" she asked, her voice dripping with loathing like drool from a bulldog's mouth.

"She is safe and under our care," Blastmore said, taking the heat off Feller, at least for the moment.

"So why the hell isn't she here?" Jennifer spat.

Blastmore ignored the question.

"We need to have you, your daughter and husband come down to the sheriff's substation so we can take your statements," she said.

"And why on earth would we agree to that?" Jennifer said. "We are waiting for you to hand over our granddaughter so we can take her home."

The sheriff and agent heard muffled voices inside the room, but could not make out the words. Jennifer turned her head toward someone with a look on her face that could have curdled fresh milk in an instant.

"You will provide your statements voluntarily or after we arrest you," Blastmore said, starting to lose he patience. Sheriff Feller unfastened the clasp on his handcuff holster and brought the metal bracelets up so Jennifer could see them.

"You have nothing to arrest us for," Jennifer said, her defiant attitude intact.

"Oh, I think we do," Blastmore said.

"And what would that be?" Jennifer asked.

"Obstruction of justice," she answered.

"And just how did we obstruct justice?" Jennifer asked.

"For one, your refusal to give us your statements," Blastmore said. "But most importantly, your hiring of 54 Squad to retrieve Stephanie Wallis."

Jennifer's face went pale and the two law enforcement officers saw the unmistakable act of swallowing.

"Hiring them is not illegal, I checked," she said, a little less confident than she had been up to that moment.

"You may have been misinformed," Feller finally spoke. "And we've taken Joe Bantum's statement, and the instructions you gave him, quite frankly, are going to lead to other charges for him – and you. So, you come with us now voluntarily or in handcuffs." He held the cuffs up again for emphasis.

Jennifer's face took on a lighter shade of pale.

"Let me make a call first," she said, and started to close the door. But Blastmore used her foot to keep it open.

"Right here," she ordered. The agent knew exactly who the recipient of the call would be.

Jennifer dialed and, when there was an answer, announced who she was and demanded to speak to the governor. Almost immediately, the look on her face told the law enforcement officers she wasn't getting the answer she wanted. Then she held the phone in front of her face and scowled.

"One more call," she said, and started punching in the number before Blastmore or Feller could protest.

They heard enough of her side of the conversation to know she was calling her attorney. They were also able to determine that the attorney could not be there immediately and would arrange for a local lawyer to do the job until the McAdams' legal team could arrive.

"Alright, we will go with you," Jennifer said, with a tone of renewed confidence. "But we won't say anything until we have a lawyer present."

"Fair enough," Blastmore said.

Nathan had hoped once they had a chance to eat and settled into their motel rooms, Stephanie would open up to him. He was wrong.

At the restaurant a short walk from the motel, he sat alone on one side of the booth and Stephanie sat so close to Barnes on the other side it was like she was inside the deputy's pocket. She only spoke to give her order to the waitress. Throughout the time at the restaurant Stephanie averted her father's eyes.

Nathan wanted so much to engage his daughter in conversation, but for one thing he wasn't sure what to say to her without bringing up the traumatic events they had both endured, and for another he wasn't sure how he might react if she refused to talk to him.

When the meal was completed, the trio walked back to the motel. Unlocking the door to his room, Nathan opened the door, stood back and motioned for Stephanie to go inside. Instead, she hugged Barnes tightly and pulled her toward the adjoining room's door.

Nathan felt like a stake had been driven deep into his chest. Barnes gave him an apologetic look and took Stephanie into the room.

Fighting to keep the tears from coming before he could get inside his own room, Nathan gently shut the door and flopped onto the closest of the two beds and let racking sobs flow freely.

Cynthia sat trembling at the bare table in the interview room, an attorney by her side, at the sheriff's substation. Sheriff Feller sat across from her and a deputy stood near the door. She felt like a trapped animal.

"When can I see my daughter?" she asked meekly.

Feller, who had been questioning her for nearly an hour and getting only gibberish and non-answers, was feeling the frustration and knew his patience was nearing its end. But he had to hold it together. Her question about Stephanie had been asked and ignored several times during the time they had been in the room, but this time Feller decided to use it as leverage.

"That will depend a great deal on you," he said.

"What do you mean?" she asked.

"When you start answering my questions, we'll see what we can do about letting you see Stephanie," he answered.

Cynthia did not respond with words, but the look of hope on her face told the sheriff his tactic might now generate results. Jennifer McAdams' attitude, Kenneth's limited cooperation and Bantum's description of his dealings with Jennifer and her husband provided all the information he needed to understand what transpired between them. But now he wanted to know the extent of Cynthia's involvement.

The attorney whispered in Cynthia's ear, and Stephanie's mother shook her head vigorously. The attorney whispered something else and Cynthia sat silently staring straight ahead.

Kenneth confirmed he and Jennifer hired Bantum and his troop to retrieve Stephanie. But he insisted they instructed the 54 Squad owner and leader to cooperate with law enforcement and take no action without local law enforcement direction. But Bantum countered that by sharing the conversation he had with Jennifer in the field outside of town before the unit headed up the mountain.

In his description of his dealings with the McAdamses, Bantum said he had seen Cynthia only the first two times he met the family. He described her as being in the background. He had no knowledge of how much she was involved in the decision to hire his unit.

"So, tell me whose idea it was to hire the private military company to go find and bring back your daughter?" the sheriff asked Cynthia.

She looked to the lawyer, who nodded.

"My parents and I thought that would help us get Stephanie back," she answered.

"But tell me who thought of it first," he said, leaning forward over the table, trying to give as menacing a look as he could.

"My mom knows a lot of people and she talked about doing that," Cynthia said. But she realized her mistake as soon as the words were out of her mouth.

"But I didn't think she took that very seriously," she added.

"What do you think about it now?" Feller asked, peppering in a little sarcastic tone.

Cynthia sat silent for a moment.

"It probably wasn't the best idea," she muttered.

"When your mother brought it up, did you argue against it?" Feller asked.

"I wanted my daughter back safely," Cynthia blurted out, before the lawyer could stop her.

"And what about the safety of your father-in-law, your husband, the law enforcement officers on that mountain?" the sheriff asked.

Cynthia's trembling suddenly stopped and she took on a different tone. Feller watched as it went from genuinely frightened to something darker. Just like the trembling coming to a halt, her face took on a look of anger – maybe even hate.

"They were not my first concern," she said in a voice that made Feller shiver a little. "My daughter's safe return was all that mattered to me."

Feller looked toward the deputy, at the lawyer then back to Cynthia.

"So then hiring 54 Squad was really your idea," the sheriff said, not meaning it to be a question.

"Think what you want," Cynthia said. "My daughter is out of that madman's hands and that's all that matters to me."

Feller nodded and stood up.

"So, when do I get my daughter back?" Cynthia asked.

"I'll get back to you on that," Feller said as he left the room, leaving the deputy inside with Cynthia and the lawyer.

Bryan stood in the doorway of the cabin by the lake with Stephanie at his side. They stepped out, followed by Blastmore and Vallow and Mason. From his vantage point at the edge of the lake shore, Nathan watched as they turned to the right and began walking away from the structure. He went to follow them, but for some reason his feet would not move. He looked down and saw his boots ankle deep in mud. Each time he tried to lift a foot it was sucked right back into the muck.

He turned in the direction his brother and the others had gone, calling for them to help him. He watched as they continued ahead, not even looking around at his calls for help. Just as they disappeared past a particularly dense group of trees, he heard four quick bangs coming from an area ahead of where he saw the quartet going. He recognized them as reports from a high-powered rifle. He screamed his daughter's name, but what he heard come out of his mouth sounded as if he was yelling through a washcloth shoved in his mouth.

He then heard three more bangs. But this time he was not at the lake, he was laying on the forest floor, the left side of his head resting on a pile of leaves. He blinked his eyes, trying to clear his blurry vision. Through his clearing eyesight he saw he was not in the forest, rather he was lying on his belly on a bed, his head on a pillow.

Three more bangs brought him fully awake and he recognized the motel room.

Nathan scrambled to his feet and went to the door. When he pulled it open, Barnes stood just outside.

"Are you okay?" she asked.

"Yeah, I must have been asleep," he answered. "Was having some weird dreams."

He motioned for Barnes to come in and as she passed by him, he poked his head out the door, thinking he might see Stephanie there as well.

"She is asleep," Barnes said.

Nathan pulled his head back into the room and shut the door.

"Is she okay?" Nathan asked.

"Physically, yes," Barnes said.

"But....?"

Barnes sat down in one of the chairs at a small, round table at the window. Nathan sat in the other chair, his attention razor focused on the deputy.

"She has been through a lot, especially for someone her age. She'll need some help getting through it," she said.

"I'm sure it's not easy to see someone shot right in front of you, or to be kidnapped," Nathan said. "But I'll do whatever it takes or costs to make sure she gets the help she needs to get past it."

Barnes sighed deeply. Nathan thought it was an expression of fatigue, since they had all been through plenty of trauma. But when her face took on a more serious look, he tensed, expecting something worse.

"It's more than the kidnapping and shooting," she said. "Because it was your father who took her, there are some trust issues."

Barnes explained that Stephanie had talked with her extensively in whispers during the night in the jail cell. She revealed that she was afraid that if her grandfather could do the things he did, her father might be just as capable of the same.

"But I would never do anything like that," Nathan said.

"To her, especially after all she's gone through, it is a real concern," Barnes said. "And there's more that feeds that fear."

She paused for a moment, considering whether she should tell him the rest of what Stephanie had talked to her about.

"What is that?" he asked.

Barnes continued to stay silent. Nathan stood and turned toward the door.

"I want to talk to her myself," he said.

Barnes got up quickly, ran around him and barred his way.

"That wouldn't be a good idea right now," Barnes said. "Sit down and I'll tell you. But first you have to promise me you won't pressure her to talk to you about it."

He sat back down and nodded. She returned to her seat and looked across at him. This was not going to be easy for him to hear, but she decided it was something he should know now rather than finding it out later.

"Your wife and her parents fed her fears before your dad even took her," she said tentatively.

"What do you mean?" he asked.

"Your wife told her parents some very disturbing things about you to justify why she was leaving you," Barnes said. "She spoke openly in front of Stephanie about them."

"What kind of things?" Nathan asked, not sure he wanted to know the answer, but being devoured by curiosity.

Barnes swallowed. This was not going to be easy. Her only knowledge of Nathan had been as a possible suspect in his daughter's abduction. But in the time she had been with him, she observed that he was a loving, sensitive father who loved and cared very much for his daughter. She did not believe he was capable of what his wife had accused him of.

"She said you were unfaithful to her, including with a man; that you dealt drugs; and that you even killed some people," Barnes said.

Nathan felt his mouth fall open. Afraid his jaw had hit the table top, he put his hand to his face to make sure it was still in place. Kenneth had told him about those allegations Cynthia had made. But he had doubted she would say such things. Now hearing that Stephanie had confirmed them all was another one of those sledgehammer blows to the head.

"Your in-laws did not try to mitigate the accusations," she said. "In fact, your mother-in-law whole-heartedly agreed and kept hammering at it."

Nathan remained speechless. Barnes did not know where to take the conversation from there. It was going to take time for the implications of it to sink in for Nathan.

Chapter 26

They were all gathered inside the passenger cabin of the chartered FBI jet. Nathan and Bryan sat side by side in seats facing the rear of the cabin. Across the aisle were Barnes and Stephanie. Agent Susan Blastmore sat in a swivel seat turned to face Nathan and Bryan. Mason and Vallow, his breathing still a little labored, sat across the aisle.

The bullet strike to his Kevlar vest broke a rib and it nearly punctured his right lung. He was breathing deeply, using the exercises doctors had given him. They had wanted to keep him in the hospital one more day, but he discharged himself so he could be part of the debriefing.

Sheriff Feller sat in a swivel seat behind Mason and Vallow. He shared with the others what his office had uncovered, which was nothing more than they knew the day before.

"More might come out as we dig deeper," he said. "But at this point you can all go home." He indicated Nathan, Bryan, Barnes and Stephanie. "We'll contact you if we need anything more, which I doubt. But I will keep you posted on our progress."

Blastmore made the same report, adding that interviews with the McAdamses, Cynthia, Bantum and his surviving men were continuing.

"We have a pretty good idea where this is going to go from the FBI's perspective, but we have some T's to cross and I's to dot," she said. "Obstruction of justice charges will eventually be filed. We're just determining who all will be charged and the level of the charges."

"What about our father?" Bryan asked.

George was still unconscious in the hospital, his condition remained critical.

"If he survives, he will be charged with kidnapping and the murder of the teacher," Blastmore said, shooting a glance at Stephanie who sat emotionless next to Deputy Barnes.

Everyone was silent for a moment.

"That's all we have to share with you officially," Blastmore said. "But personally, I want to say that I wish we had all met under different circumstances."

"Me too," Bryan said, cheerful for the first time since the battle for Stephanie at the lake. He looked at Blastmore then at Barnes. They both knew what was going through his mind, and they both blushed ever so slightly, but enough that he noticed, giving him some satisfaction.

Blastmore stood and motioned for Nathan to come with her to the back of the cabin. They sat in seats with the aisle between them.

"I noticed your daughter is keeping her distance from you. What's going on there?" she asked. She was certain the trauma she had experienced was part of it, but was sure there was something else.

"She confided in Deputy Barnes that her mother made some ridiculous accusations about me and her grandparents played into them," Nathan said, a little reluctantly. But he listed them off to her.

"I get it," she said. "Now she's not sure about you."

She leaned across the aisle and put her hand on his forearm.

"I can't picture you doing any of those things," she said. "I'll have a talk with Sheriff Martin and see if he will investigate each of these. Once he has a written report, if he finds no merit to the accusations, we can get you a copy of that report to share with your daughter. Maybe that will help."

Nathan nodded, and thanked her. He wasn't sure he liked the idea of being investigated for such vile crimes. But he could see the logic in her reasoning.

They joined the others at the front of the plane.

"A little secret rendezvous, eh?' Bryan joked.

"Worked for me," Nathan said. They all, except Stephanie, were surprised at Nathan's levity. It was the first he had shown in days. Stephanie remained emotionless.

"Well, time to say good bye," Bryan said, moving toward Barnes with his arms extended for a hug. But she grasped his right hand in hers and shook it.

"It's been interesting," she said.

Then Bryan turned to Blastmore, again expecting a hug. She put up her hands, palm out. She didn't shake his hand or say anything.

"Well, damn, shot down in flames twice within seconds," Bryan said. "That's a first."

He flashed a charming smile at the two women, shook the hands of Mason, Vallow and Feller, then turned and exited the aircraft. Nathan, Barnes and Stephanie followed without a word of parting. They all had a plane to catch that would take them home.

Two months went by since the parting on the chartered jet before Nathan heard from anyone in law enforcement.

In the meantime, when he returned to his sister's home, he found that all the jobs he had applied for were no longer available. The business owners apologized profusely, but said Nathan's abrupt departure, despite the circumstances, put them in a position where they had to fill the open positions. So, Nathan was back in job hunting mode.

It was a major disappointment. Without a job, he had no source of income. He had hoped to find a place of his own to live so he could make a home where Stephanie could join him. He had already decided there was no more room in his life for Cynthia. He couldn't shake the feeling that she had been all in on her mother's desire for her to end the marriage and get full custody of their daughter.

Without an income, though, that was a goal that was unreachable.

But then he got a visit from Bryan.

"I want you to manage my business," he told Nathan after the greetings and catching up ended.

Nathan was surprised, as his brother had done a good job in that role since he started his outfitting and guide business. But as Bryan explained, he had done such a good job he had more bookings than he could handle while also serving as manager of the company. He had started the business to operate during hunting seasons only. But as his reputation grew, he got more requests for trips into the mountains out of season by tourists who wanted to see the high country, not just in Colorado but also up into Wyoming. He needed to take on more people to help.

"When I do that, I need to spend more time on that part of the business. I won't have time, unless I work twenty-four/seven, to do the financial and marketing part of it," Bryan said. "Besides, that's not my forte anyway."

They discussed it for a while to work out exactly what Nathan's role would be. Even Carolyn and Tessa, who had come for a visit, thought the arrangement would be a winner when Bryan ran it by them before talking to Nathan. Bryan shared that with his brother. Finally, they had worked out all the details. Bryan was generous, giving his brother a slightly larger salary than he would have made at any of the jobs he had applied for and a chance to earn up to forty-nine percent of the business ownership. That also came with a profit-sharing plan based on his percentage of ownership.

Nathan initially rejected the ownership option, believing his brother offered it because he felt sorry for him.

"Bullshit. I was going to do this anyway and would have offered the same thing to anyone I hired," Bryan said. "This isn't a charity deal. You'll have to earn everything you get."

Nathan eventually agreed. He began work immediately, found a nice house to rent not far from Carolyn's home. Because he was not involved in the actual guide and outfitter part of the business, he worked from his rental in Illinois. By the end of two months had earned ten percent ownership.

One day he got a call from Sheriff Martin, asking that he come to the substation the next day. When he walked into the sheriff's office, he spotted Susan Blastmore sitting in one of the chairs. Nathan sat next to her in the other one.

They all exchanged pleasantries, then Martin got down to the business at hand.

"Agent Blastmore shared the accusations made against you by your wife," he said. "We thoroughly investigated them all and found absolutely no evidence to support any of them."

He then handed Nathan a thick folder with copies of the report.

"Thank you," he said with satisfaction.

"And I'm here to update you on the investigation," Blastmore said.

She first reminded him that his father had died of his wound less than two weeks after being taken off the mountain. He had gotten word about that within days of the death. Blastmore again apologized for shooting him, and Nathan dismissed it. He had long ago decided his father got his just desserts, not only for what he put them all through but for all those years he wasn't much of a father to his own children.

Blastmore then revealed that before he died, George regained consciousness long enough to give a full statement, which absolved Nathan for any involvement in what he had done.

She then told him Kenneth and Bantum pled guilty to obstruction of justice charges. But Jennifer and Cynthia pled not guilty to that charge of reckless endangerment. Kenneth and Bantum agreed to testify against them when it went to trial in a few months. Kenneth and Bantum were each sentenced to five years in jail, suspended, and a fine of five thousand dollars each.

"They will most likely want you to testify in your wife's and mother-in-law's trial, but I was able to convince them it would do more harm than good to have Stephanie testify," Blastmore said. "I don't think it would be good for her to have to relive that."

"I agree, and I appreciate you doing that," Nathan said.

"How is she doing, by the way?" Blastmore asked.

Nathan took a breath before answering. Blastmore read the anguish all over his face and in his body language.

"We still haven't spoken. There are trust issues there because of all that happened and what her mother said about me," he finally answered. "She's been staying with Deputy Barnes, with my permission, since she seemed to become attached to her."

Nathan paused to wipe away a stray tear that rolled out of his eye.

"She's getting some counseling, and I'm hopeful things will turn around," he said.

"Well, I hope so," Blastmore said, handing Nathan one of her business cards. "If there's anything I can do for her or for you, don't hesitate to call."

"That goes for me, too," Martin said, standing up and offering his hand. Nathan stood and shook it. He then turned and extended his hand to Blastmore. Instead of taking it, she stood up and moved toward him and gave him a long, warm hug.

In the following month, Nathan threw himself into his new job. In addition to the home office, he also set up the second bedroom for Stephanie for when she came to live with him. He was sure that would happen eventually.

One of the reasons for his certainty is that he filed divorce papers with the court and asked for full custody. With Cynthia facing felony charges, with a maximum sentence of twenty years in federal prison, he was sure the decree and custody would be granted.

But it wasn't that easy.

Cynthia refused to sign the paperwork and wanted it to go to court. Nathan was convinced Jennifer was behind that decision. Jennifer was so possessive of her granddaughter that Nathan doubted she would ever give up trying to have her at hand constantly. That controlling attitude blinded her to the fact that she would never achieve that goal from a federal prison. And even if she was found not guilty of the charges, which Nathan doubted, just having been charged would make her having any contact with Stephanie a near impossibility.

But after some pressure from the judge overseeing the divorce and custody case, Cynthia finally signed and the deal was done.

While Nathan had not heard officially from law enforcement in the first two months after Stephanie was rescued, Dawn Barnes had checked in with him periodically to keep him up to date on

Stephanie's progress. With each call, the news was increasingly optimistic.

Barnes had suggested, and Nathan agreed, that he not meet with Stephanie's counselor. She believed that would create a situation in which there could be some influence on Stephanie's treatment. She asked if Nathan was comfortable with her speaking for him if the counselor wanted information. He readily agreed.

With Nathan's written letter of permission, Barnes enrolled Stephanie into summer school so she could make up for the time she had missed after her grandfather had taken her from the school property. It was through a different school district, of course, but the story of what happened in the town just thirty miles away had made its way to her summer classroom.

Because of that, Stephanie's first week was difficult as the other students pestered her for details. She gave up very little, and eventually they left her alone about it. She started to make friends and that helped her focus on her class work. Barnes said she was near the top of the class in grades. She was also looking forward to starting school in the fall.

Things were looking up and Nathan was enjoying his new job. One day his cell phone range and the ID caller showed it was Barnes. For Nathan, it was a mixture of excitement and dread when he swiped to answer the call.

"Hello."

"Hello, Nathan. I'd like to see if I can come over and talk to you."

Nathan's heart went to his throat. So far, her updates had all been by phone. If she wanted to see him in person, this was something important. Only negative scenarios were going through Nathan's mind. Things had been going so well for Stephanie, according to Barnes, that he was afraid the other shoe would drop.

"Sure. When do you want to do this?" he asked.

"How about now?" she asked.

"I'll be here all day," he said.

"See you in a bit," Barnes said, then ended the call.

Nathan had no sooner set the phone down when the doorbell rang. It startled him, as he had no idea who would be at his door. When he opened it, Barnes stood there in the small vestibule.

"Wow. I wasn't expecting you to have called on my doorstep," he said.

"Well, this is something I wanted to get said as soon as possible," she said. "Someone would like to speak with you."

Nathan's heart skipped a beat. He was finally going to meet and speak to the counselor. He only hoped she had some good news. Barnes stepped back and motioned for someone to come to the door.

Nathan's knees went rubbery when Stephanie slowly rounded the corner from the driveway. Her hair was longer and she was more filled out than he remembered.

He did not know how to react. He wanted to grab his daughter and hug her tightly. But he was afraid she would reject him. Stephanie, too, stood still next to Barnes, unsure of how her father would receive her. But Barnes looked over at her and gave her a gentle nudge forward. She took two steps forward, then threw herself into her father, wrapping her arms around him and squeezing tightly.

"I love you, Dad," she said through tears. "Can I come home?"

Nathan was overcome and began crying himself. Father and daughter stood there bear hugging each other and crying for several minutes. Finally, they released each other and locked eyes.

"I have your room ready for you," he said.

She suddenly turned and went back to the driveway, returning quickly with two duffel bags. Nathan motioned for Barnes to enter the house and he showed Stephanie where her room was, then returned to the living room where Barnes stood waiting.

"She's ready," is all she said.

"Thank you for everything," was his short answer, at a loss for words.

Later that evening, Nathan listened as Stephanie told him all about her counseling and summer school. She talked non-stop and Nathan just soaked it all in. When she finally took a break, he decided it was time to tell her something he had put off since she arrived at the house.

"Your mom and I are divorced," he blurted out. .

"I figured that was going to happen," she said.

"How do you feel about that?" he asked uneasily.

She was silent for a moment, which only increased his unease.

"I understand why, and I don't blame you, Dad," she said.

His heart filled with relief.

"I still love Mom, but with everything that happened, I know why you don't want to be with her," Stephanie said. "I'm not sure I would want to, either."

"I don't ever want you to stop loving your mom," Nathan said.

They sat in silence for a while.

"So, what will you do now?" she asked.

"Well, I'm working for your uncle and really liking it, and....." he began.

"No, Dad, I mean about dating," she said.

"Oh, I think it's a little early for that," he said.

"What about Deputy Barnes, will you still talk to her?" Stephanie asked.

"I suppose, if there's anything to talk about," he said.

"Well, I think you should see her from time to time," his daughter said, with an impish twinkle in her eye.

It took Nathan a moment to get her meaning. He blushed a little, and she noticed and smiled.

"She's a bit young for me, don't you think?" he said.

"Age doesn't matter when two people love each other," she said with the same impish twinkle.

Nathan was at a loss for words for a moment. He had spent a lot of time with Dawn Barnes, but in that time romance was never in his mind. He was so focused on getting Stephanie back safely. He assumed the same was true with her. But Stephanie had spent a lot more time with her in the last three months and they had developed a relationship close enough that his daughter felt comfortable opening up to her. Did that go both ways? And did Barnes say something to Stephanie to indicate she had feelings for him?

Nathan thought about asking his daughter those very questions. But it seemed so high school to him.

"I agree," he finally said. "But people need time to get to know each other before they decide they are in love."

Stephanie just sat looking at her father, the look and smile on her face was of someone who thinks they have a juicy secret and is itching to share it.

"I suppose anything's possible," he said. "But we'll just have to see how things go."

Stephanie threw her arms around him and gave him a hug so tight he thought she would never let go.